ROOSEVELT'S BEAST

ROOSEVELT'S
BEAST A NOVEL

LOUIS BAYARD

HENRY HOLT AND COMPANY · NEW YORK

Henry Holt and Company, LLC
Publishers since 1866
175 Fifth Avenue
New York, New York 10010
www.henryholt.com

Henry Holt® and 🏛® are registered trademarks of
Henry Holt and Company, LLC.

Library of Congress Cataloging-in-Publication Data

Bayard, Louis.
   Roosevelt's Beast : a novel / Louis Bayard.—First Edition.
      pages   cm
   ISBN 978-0-8050-9070-3 (hard cover)—ISBN 978-1-4299-4686-5 (electronic
book) 1. Roosevelt-Rondon Scientific Expedition (1913–1914)—Fiction.
2. Roosevelt, Theodore, 1858–1919—Fiction. 3. Brazil—History—1889–1930—
Fiction. 4. Adventure fiction. 5. Historical fiction. I. Title.
PS3552.A85864R66 2014
813'.54—dc23   2013028721

Henry Holt books are available for special promotions and premiums.
For details contact: Director, Special Markets.

First Edition 2014

Designed by Meryl Sussman Levavi
Map and family tree by Laura Hartman Maestro

Printed in the United States of America

10 9 8 7 6 5 4 3 2 1

To Jill Hilliard, who thought I might make a go of this

"Battle not with monsters, lest ye become a monster, and if you gaze into the abyss, the abyss gazes also into you."

—FRIEDRICH NIETZSCHE, *Beyond Good and Evil*

Roosevelt's Journey

Caribbean Sea

Panama

Venezuela

Colombia

Orinoco

British Guiana (Guyana)
Dutch Guiana (Surinam)
French Guiana

Atlantic

Ecuador

Amazon

Manáos (Manáus)

Amazon

B r a z i l

Madeira

★ River of Doubt (Rio Roosevelt)

Rio Kermit

José Bonifacio

Vilhena

Peru

São João

Arinos

Juruena

Utiariti (Utiariti)

Tapirapoan (Tapirapua)

São Luis de Cáceres (Cáceres)

Corumbá

Bolivia

Paraguay

Asunción

São Paulo

Rio de Janeiro

Bahia (Salvador)

Ocean

Tucumán

Uruguay

Pacific Ocean

Santiago

Mendoza

Buenos Aires

Montevideo

Valdivia

C h i l e

A r g e n t i n a

N

KEY

··············· T.R.'s South American tour
October 18, 1913 – December 12, 1913

·············· To the River of Doubt
December 12, 1913 – February 25, 1914

★

━━━ Descent of the River of Doubt
February 27, 1914 – April 26, 1914

0 Miles 400 800
0 Kilometers 800

map by Laura Hartman Maestro ©2013

ROOSEVELT'S BEAST

June 3, 1943
Anchorage, Alaska

AFTER ALL THESE YEARS, HIS BEST FRIEND IS MALARIA.

Even on the brink of an Alaska summer, it comes calling: a bone-deep chill one night, a ministry of sweat the next. Calling him back to old battles. That afternoon he spent shivering in the Baghdad desert, say, while hundreds of Turkish camels and men rotted around him. Or those mornings on the Rio da Dúvida when old Dr. Cajazeira, like a miser with a golden hoard, would reach into his jaguar-skin pouch and dole out his drabs of quinine. Jesuit's powder, they used to call it, and in memory it does sit like a Communion wafer on each man's tongue. Never enough to keep the sickness at bay, but enough to keep it within bounds.

Vile stuff. The British had the right idea, stirring it into sugar water. In the old days, whenever Belle raised an eyebrow at one of his gin and tonics, Kermit would murmur, "Prophylaxis, sweetheart."

Gin is lost to him now. Whiskey, too. Scotch and soda. His stomach sends it all back. Wine is the one drink he can hang on to: a glass upon rising, two more before lunch, and then punctually through the rest of the day and evening.

There are days he thinks he should give up even that. The problem, as always, is finding a replacement. Tobacco has lost its savor; sex is a memory. A year ago, there was some small hope of mortal peril. The Japanese still held a pair of Aleutian Islands, and any minute a fleet of Lilys and Bettys might come roaring out of the clouds, raining down fire.

But the skies have stayed silent, and the Japs have been blasted out of Attu, and word is they'll soon be evacuating Kiska. The danger has passed, and Major Kermit Roosevelt—recipient of the Military Cross, veteran of campaigns in France and Norway and North Africa and Mesopotamia—is a toy soldier.

No one expects him to show up for reveille, drills, parades. His presence is no longer requested at officers' mess. His pilot friends have long since shipped out. "We're going where the action is," they said.

Left to his own devices, he reads, a little. Plays poker if he can find anyone to play. Contract bridge, if he can snap his mind around it. When that fails, he strolls into town, although even this is not without its risks. He loses breath without warning and stumbles. He's been known to tip over in the street. There are moments when he catches sight of himself in a shop window (tottering along like an ancient sexton, fleshy, freely sweating) or, worse still, finds a knot of young recruits studying him from a half-respectful distance. He shuts his eyes, but he can always hear someone whispering his name. And someone whispering back: *"Him?"*

It takes work, he wants to tell them. To look like this.

HE IS FIFTY-THREE. FATHER was roughly the same age when he took a bullet to the chest. Scorned the doctors and strode straight to the lectern of Milwaukee Auditorium. Flung open his coat to reveal the blood blossoming across his white vest. "It takes more than that to kill a bull moose!" he cried.

The doctors never did get the bullet out. He carried it, nestled against his rib cage, for the rest of his mortal coil.

Well, that's how he was. Snubbed Death at every turn, wouldn't give it the time of day. Kermit, being more hospitable, makes a point of greeting it each morning in the washstand mirror. Noting how much thinner the arms have grown since yesterday and, by contrast, how much more pronounced the bloat of his face and belly. Inch by inch, the finish line approaches, and all he can think is: *Get on with it.*

No, that's not quite true. Sometimes he thinks: *I have never looked more like Father.*

ANCHORAGE SHOULD HAVE BEEN just the tonic for him. Wilderness on every side. Black and brown bear, moose, Dall sheep. Salmon and trout and grayling practically climbing up your fishing line. Unholy numbers of stars.

Father would have loved the place. At least until evening, when Anchorage casts off its virgin's weeds, and the soldiers swarm into the bars and canteens and USO clubs, seeking liquor and women, both of which come easily but never cheaply.

Even tonight—nine p.m. on a Thursday—the town is bursting at every seam. Fights are breaking out, only half in earnest, and privates are howling to a moon that is still hours away from appearing. The air is thick with beer and vomit and rotting sheepskin.

No, the Colonel would not have approved of Anchorage at night, but for someone with no stake in things, the town has its uses. Not a soul stops him as he traces his usual path past the Anchorage Hotel and the Arctic Commercial Store. He follows the ruts in the streets, stepping over discarded gas masks and bomber boots and coming at last to an old passenger car, formerly affiliated with the Alaska Railroad and now refitted as Nellie's Diner. His second home.

Leaning his bulk against the door, he catches the familiar sting of grease smoke billowing from the kitchen stoves, the scents of bourbon and beef juice. His eyes, ranging through the half-light, pick out an empty stool at the end of the counter. Then he hears a voice calling after him.

"Major!"

In the newly built dining room, a man rises from one of the booths. Jug ears and a sun-fissured face and a nonregulation musk-rat coat. Major Marvin Marston.

"Come join me," says Marston.

Kermit is conscious now of his own panting. He takes a dodgy step forward. Pauses, then finishes the rest of the distance at his own pace.

"Nice surprise," he says, easing himself onto the leather banquette. "Running into you here."

"No surprise at all," says Marston with his grim smile. "I was hoping to find you."

"Well. I am found. If you like, you can make the rounds with me tonight. I'm supposed to enforce the blackout."

"It would be my pleasure."

A blur of movement at their flanks. Nellie herself: moonfaced, barely as tall as the table.

"Hiya, boys! Lemme guess: Dry muscat for Major Roosevelt. Shot of Johnnie Walker Swing for the other major."

"Make it a double," says Marston.

"Special tonight is calves' liver and bacon."

Kermit's stomach performs a slow revolution.

"Just the cold ham sandwich, Nellie."

"Toast is five cents extra."

"So be it."

"Sirloin," says Marston. As Nellie strides back to the counter, he calls after her, "Keep it bloody, huh?" With a dreamlike slowness, he folds and refolds the napkin in his lap. "Say now," he says. "This is some Army we got ourselves mixed up in."

"General Buckner, is it?"

"Naw, it's everyone underneath. Toadies, desk jockeys. A fella comes along with an idea—an honest-to-God idea—they want to drown it in paper."

Kermit is familiar with Major Marston's idea: the Tundra Army. A guerrilla force to be composed entirely of Eskimos and Indians, patrolling the Alaskan coastline for enemy incursions. The first and last word in homeland defense.

"I don't understand," says Kermit. "The Army's given you rifles, haven't they?"

"Springfields and Enfields. Older than my granny. Even that was a struggle. *What if they turn around and use 'em on us?* Morons. Not one of our bright shining military lights has a clue what these people are like."

Two glasses come sliding across the table. Marston seizes his and drains it.

"I'm telling you, Major, my boys need a champion."

"A champion."

"Someone way over Buckner's head. Someone who can rally public sentiment."

Smiling softly, Kermit begins the slow decanting of wine into throat. Feels the old flush of warmth in his sternum. The warning shot from his belly.

"I can't be sure," he says. "To which of my cousins are you referring?"

"With all due respect, the First Lady'd be just the ticket. Give me two days with Mrs. Roosevelt, my little army would never want for anything again."

The food saves Kermit from replying. Very studiously, he prizes the slab of ham from his sandwich. Pushes it around the plate with his fork and then, on further consideration, leaves it alone.

"Well, you see . . ." He gnaws off a corner of bread. "My standing, you see, within the larger family . . . I mean, the only reason I'm even here, the reason I'm able to share this delightful meal with you, is that neither the president nor the First Lady particularly wants me to come knocking. Any more than my brothers do." He stares at the bun and returns it to its plate. "Now, the U.S. Army may be every bit as incompetent as you say, but they *have* found the one stage in the entire theater of war where I can't embarrass anyone. All of this by way of explaining—I'm not sure I'm the man to woo Cousin Eleanor for you. As happy as I would be to . . ."

His voice is already flagging. With a grunt of despair, he adds, "How about that governor of yours? Gruening. He's a presidential appointee, isn't he? Just the man to make your case in Washington."

"You're probably right."

Marston has few social graces, but he never sulks. Blocked in one direction, he simply fixes his sights on another. *Over, under, through,* thinks Kermit, recalling Father's old directive. *But never around.*

Kermit waits quietly for Marston to finish his steak. Then he tosses down a ten-dollar bill and, steadying himself against the table, rises from the banquette.

"Let's take a stroll, shall we?"

TEN O'CLOCK, AND THE sun has only begun to sink. It will be nearly midnight before it disappears altogether, and five hours later it will pop up again, taking with it the last promise of sleep. What a terror summer can be.

They walk past Providence Hospital, Marston's loping stride held in check by Kermit's shambling. The streets are thinning out, but at the boarded-up entrance to the Federal Building, they come across a young seaman earnestly negotiating with a woman. The sailor's like something from a Maxfield Parrish print—ginger-bearded, with a gold earring—but it's the woman who catches Kermit's eyes. Anywhere from ten to twenty years older than her client. Rawboned, in a green silk dress, her face carved by cosmetics into a mask of scorn.

But that same mask, as Kermit passes, dissolves in the lamplight, and a new face flashes out at him. Dusky skin. Hair parted down the middle. Flecked hazel eyes. He stops.

"All right?" asks Marston.

"Yes . . ."

The woman and her suitor are squinting at him now.

"Nothing here for you, sir," says the sailor.

"Apologies."

Kermit staggers away. Marston follows close behind.

"Friend of yours?" he asks.

"Just a—"

Just an old relation, he wants to say. *Someone I see now and again.*

THE LAST TIME WAS in a hospital room in Vancouver. He'd been peeing blood, and a Canadian doctor, not knowing what else to do, had kept him on a soft tide of morphine. It rolled him in and out of consciousness and then woke him for good late in the evening. She was there, standing in the room's shadows.

I want you to take him with you. . . .

And then the room reconfigured itself, and it was Belle standing there. Belle. The mother of his children. Looking tinier than ever in an ermine coat he was fairly certain he'd never bought for her. He almost called her by name, but she put a finger to her lips. A minute later, she was gone.

Such a long way to come, he'd thought, for such a brief audience. He can only believe that, before severing the last cord, she had needed to see him in that bare unaccommodated state, without the distractions of the other women—the other *Roosevelts,* all those voices telling her what to do. *(Think of yourself, the children, your reputation.)* Here she could look at the man who was her husband, at this lowest of ebbs, could stare into his damp, bleary, blood-drained face and realize there was no reclaiming him. That to be unreclaimed was, in fact, his fondest wish.

She came, she saw, she left without a word. And now she is gone—gone for good. And he is here.

Here. Where is *here*?

In this exact moment, as he walks with Marston through the streets of Anchorage, nothing seems real. The fat cadences of "Cow Cow Boogie" on an out-of-tune piano. A pickup truck parked halfway up the curb. A hardware-store owner rolling down his blackout screen. ("Many thanks," calls Kermit.)

Or this: The sign posted at the turn for Fort Richardson. A bucktoothed, bespectacled Jap with talons for fingers. *He likes your snapshots*, the sign warns. *Think before you snap.* Kermit has seen it any number of times, but tonight those talons are actually rising from the signboard, promoting themselves to the third dimension.

"Ha," says Marston, scowling at the sign. "That's the closest *we'll* ever get to the enemy."

"Well, war is a . . . it's . . ."

And now even Marston is changing. That pencil mustache, sidewinding like an eel.

Kermit jerks his head away. "War is a young man's game. . . ."

"Are you sure you're all right, Major?"

"I'm quite well, thank you." He nods, several times in succession. "Another drink, that might be just the ticket."

"Lights out for me, I'm afraid."

"I'm happy to treat," says Kermit, cringing at the hysteria in his voice. "I know how the local merchants gouge."

"It's very decent of you, Major, but I'm off to Seward tomorrow, 0600. Another time."

Kermit gazes out at the jagged silhouette of the Chugach Mountains, marbling in the evening sun but holding their shape, too; that's a relief. Maybe if he stands here long enough . . .

"I might write a letter or two," he says. "If you think it would help. Naturally, I can't promise anything."

He hears Marston's tiny grunt of satisfaction.

"You won't regret it, Major. They're good people, these Eski-mos. Most self-reliant folks I've ever met. Loyal, dependable. Not an ounce of malice to 'em."

Kermit grabs hold of the signpost, and it's already too late. In the next instant, he's borne away on a writhing, foaming river, black as tea. He stares at his feet, half expecting them to be submerged, but the river is inside him. And, somewhere in the canopy above, Marston is talking.

"The point is, these Eskimos are ready to serve Uncle Sam, and I mean to let 'em. Why, if you could have been with me last week in Ketchikan . . ."

Every joint, every fiber in Kermit's body is blazing with ice.

"And do you know," says Marston, "when I asked the local chief if he wanted to be compensated, he actually got steamed at me. 'You give no money,' he said. 'We no want money.'"

A man doesn't recoil from his friends. That's what Father would say. *He looks them dead in the eye.*

And so, by agonizing degrees, Kermit turns toward the sound of Marston's voice. Knowing what he will find there. Feeling once more the old tremble as he watches the skin and tissue peel in long serrated strips from Marston's face.

And there stands the face's owner, blathering in the twilight. His own skull grinning out of the depths.

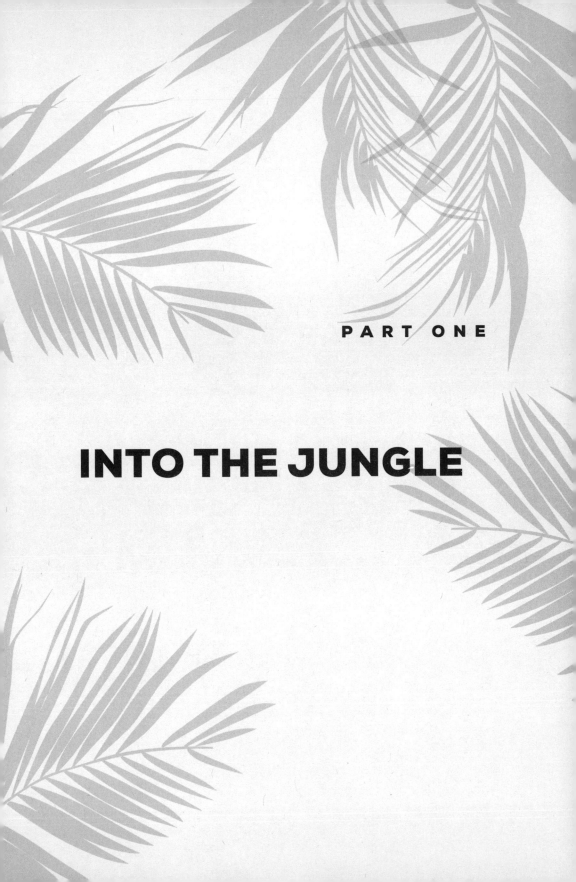

PART ONE

INTO THE JUNGLE

1

He slept to it, and then he woke to it. Rain.

Steaming down the balloon-silk fly tent. Gushing through the trees. Pounding the river.

None of the fat greasy drops of last night but a hissing cataract of water, monotonous and unceasing. And then, from the buzz, a single silvery note emerged, followed by another, then another. And from Kermit's brain, the first bubble of consciousness rose up.

Christ.

The bugle's notes fell away, and he would have followed them back into sleep if the tent hadn't shaken. His eyelids squeezed apart. In the granular light of dawn, a heavily muscled black man was crawling toward him, smiling as he came.

"Bom dia."

It was Juan. Somehow managing to contain in one hand three aluminum cups and the handle of a steaming pot. He began to pour, and as the smell of the coffee came coiling through the damp air, Kermit felt reality settling in its hooks. He was here. The coffee was pouring. Juan was smiling his soft, abashed smile.

"Obrigado," Kermit muttered.

"De nada."

The *camarada* crawled back out. For another minute or two, Kermit lay in his cot—already half sopping, for the morning breezes were blowing the rain straight in. With his fingers, he interrogated the sores on each of his legs: all the garden-variety bruises that, through infection, had acquired ideas above their station. Then he mapped the scorch marks of last night's mosquitoes—a cluster on the elbow, another on the ankle, a necklace around the collarbone. There was one particularly prominent ridge above his right eyebrow, as if a whole regiment of mosquitoes had stayed through the night, feasting.

I should have offered them brandy, he thought dazedly.

"Is that coffee, Roosevelt?"

As usual, Dr. Cherrie had woken without a fuss, his eyes—dry and calm—swinging open to the light, his hands lacing together under his head. He lay in the next cot, gazing up at the bulge of water in the tent's roof.

"It *looks* very like coffee," said Kermit, handing Cherrie his cup.

"Well, that's something."

The two men were silent for a time, listening to the rain.

"Good weather for ducks," said Kermit.

"And who knows what else?"

This was not idle bravado. Cherrie was the in-house naturalist and was always on the lookout for new species to catalog. With a light groan now, he swung his legs toward the ground. "Shall we wake him?"

"I suppose."

"Seems a shame," said Cherrie, studying the humped snoring figure in the third cot. "He needs his sleep."

"We all do."

"But when I think how he used to be when we started. Every morning, up before dawn."

"I know."

"Used to wake up the bugler."

"It's true."

Kermit knelt by the sleeping figure. Touched the forehead and felt the current of heat rising through his fingertips.

"Still running high?" Cherrie asked.

"A bit."

Kermit leaned in to the sleeping man's ear. Made at first to whisper and then simply spoke.

"Father."

Gasping, clutching his blanket, Colonel Roosevelt wrenched toward the sound. His white lips slackened. His naked, mole-like eyes twitched in the dimness.

"It's all right, Father. It's Kermit."

Several seconds passed before the intelligence seemed to break through.

"Of course you are," said the old man. He raised himself onto his elbows. "You must . . . give me some time to . . . shake the cobwebs out."

"Reveille has sounded."

"Has it, now?"

"Your coffee's here."

"I'm glad to hear it." With a coo of something like pleasure, he folded his hands around the cup. "Still hot. God bless you, Juan."

He took two short sips, then another. Then, as he studied his two companions, the first smile of the day crawled through the brush of his mustache.

"Raining, is it? Well, never mind."

Waving away his son's proffered hand, the Colonel tipped himself out of the cot and spilled toward the ground like a pile of luggage, wincing a bit when his left leg landed. He reached into the damp sock he had wrapped around the tent pole and pulled out his spectacles. Wiped them on the sleeve of his pajamas and then, with great and painstaking care, slid the glasses up the bridge of his nose, waiting for the world's edges to rush in.

"March," he declared. "The fifteenth."

"Yes, Father."

"Year of Our Lord nineteen hundred and fourteen."

"Indeed."

"Third Sunday in Lent."

"Yes."

"I officially declare it: As good a day as any!"

He said the same thing, of course, every morning. And every morning Kermit silently composed the same reply. *Another day in hell*.

He used to reproach himself for his irreverence. But now it had become a form of survival. And a sign, too, a welcome sign that some aspect of him still remained apart.

The old man took a few more sips of coffee, waiting for the blossom of heat and acid. Then he raised his eyes toward the sky.

"I like a bit of rain first thing. Cools things off."

"Certainly," said Cherrie.

"And cooler oarsmen are happier oarsmen, are they not? Therefore more productive. I shouldn't be surprised if we made twenty-five kilometers by day's end."

"Could be," said Kermit.

"Thirty!" said the old man, rising to it. "Mark my words!"

Kermit and Cherrie made no reply. After all these weeks in the South American wilderness, they were able to indulge the Colonel so far and no further.

"Here," said Kermit, reaching under the old man's cot. "Your spare drawers, Father. And you might as well use this handkerchief; it looks a bit fresher than the others. . . ."

"I'm certainly capable of dressing myself. You needn't—I'm not a—damn me, where have I put my specs?"

"On your face."

"Ah!" He giggled. "So they are! Never mind, let's be dressed and be off. Stiffen up the sinews, ha! Summon up the blood!"

THEY ATE IN A full downpour. It was almost a blessing that breakfast was so sparse. A handful of rice, a handful of beans. Biscuits hard as gneiss.

To think—try as he might, Kermit couldn't help it—to think how much food they had brought with them! Fresh ox meat and sliced bacon and sardines and chicken and pancake flour and potatoes and malted milk. An entire case just for spices and condiments. In the early days, if a curious native had happened to wander out of the forest with a request for olive zest or grapefruit marmalade, the members of the Roosevelt-Rondon Expedition would have been happy to oblige.

But after they passed Tapirapuã, the midday meal was excised from their schedule. Breakfast and dinner shrank down to rations. "All this life," Cherrie said. "And nothing to live on."

Even so experienced a hand as he had expected to find a horn of plenty waiting in the jungle. Fruit and nuts for every meal. Pigs and deer. Dolphins and otters and boatloads of fish. A groaning table, night after night. Instead, they had . . . moss and bromeliads and epiphytes and tree roots. Insects.

And this strange lightness that followed them wherever they went. As though their bones were being hollowed into bamboo.

Kermit peeled away the fringe of mold from his biscuit. Began to toss it away, then caught his hand in the act of throwing and shoveled the whole thing into his mouth. He chewed and gummed it down until it was just a dry paste, then let it slide down his throat and drop, plashing, into his stomach.

Through the falling rain, he heard Colonel Rondon's cry:

"Iniciar as Ordens do Dia!"

The Orders of the Day. No different, Kermit knew, from the Orders of the Day Before. Row until something stops you. (Something will.)

Even as the *camaradas* rose from their Japanese-wrestler crouches and stood in respectful silence, Kermit yawned and turned toward the jungle. The morning fog was melting from below, and the dark base of the forest came blurring out of the vapor like a section of old oil painting bleeding through the new.

"It's time," said Cherrie.

Kermit nodded, and together the two men helped the *camaradas* drag the canoes toward the water. Cursing, as they did every morning, the sheer crazy heft of the things, each weighing more than a ton, and first thing in the morning or last at night, it felt like two.

It would have been easier to bear if the beasts were seaworthy, but they sank nearly to the waterline. They were impossible to steer. They leaked water. The seats were hard and rough and wet. The more Kermit reflected on these massive hollowed-out tree trunks, the more they seemed to epitomize the whole misbegotten adventure.

The sand slipped beneath him, and as he struggled to keep his balance, the dugout crashed into him, touching off a prairie fire of pain that blazed up and down his shin. Biting down on his own cry, he soldiered on—and became, for the first time, aware of the two figures standing by the river's edge.

The Colonel and Colonel Rondon, gesticulating in the falling rain—their private conference made public by the Colonel's high squeaking roar.

"Plus vite! Plus vite! We must go *plus vite!"*

Even if the Colonel's voice hadn't carried, his French would have. A bizarre non-Aryan sort of French, no tense or gender. But it was the one tongue he shared with Rondon, and when an expedition has two leaders, they must find common ground somewhere.

The Colonel's tone at once grew more civil but no less urgent. *"Je m'incline, il faut dire, à votre connaissance supérieur, mais les observations. Peut-être ils prennent trop de temps?"*

"Ah, oui," replied Rondon, more quietly but every bit as distinctly. *"On doit examiner la question. . . ."*

We must consider the question. Which, as the Colonel well knew, was Rondon's way of discarding the question. Rondon would no more dispense with his hourly sightings than with the daily ritual of hammering a painted hardwood signpost into the forest floor. He may have stood only five feet and three, but to his men—in his own mind—he was geological and eternal, and the main reason he and the Colonel remained cordial after all these weeks was simply this: The Colonel still considered himself Rondon's guest.

"Merci pour votre considération," said the Colonel. He nodded pleasantly and squared his shoulders and made as if to walk away but stopped and lowered himself, by stages, toward the earth, where even now a felled section of couratari tree was rising to greet him.

"Father?" called Kermit.

The Colonel was already waving him away.

"Not to worry! Doing a spot of surveying!"

So he sat there. Sat for long minutes, studying the river. The river that was killing them.

THE RAIN HAD STOPPED by the time they got on the water, and as soon as the *camaradas* drove their oars in, the first shard of sunlight broke through the clouds. A small swell of laughter and applause rose up from the men—until Colonel Rondon frowned them into silence.

As usual, Kermit took the head canoe. Right behind him, Colonel Rondon and Lieutenant Lyra. Then the two baggage balsas and, bringing up the rear, Colonel Roosevelt, Dr. Cherrie, and the expedition's physician, Dr. Cajazeira.

In the early-morning hours, the sun didn't have the brassy glare

of midday but a softer, silvering touch. It drove the chill from Kermit's skin, steamed his clothes to something approaching dryness,
and when he looked at the jungle front, the gloom and opacity
seemed to boil off. He saw rolling clouds of leaves, and palm trees
flinging out their plumes, and vines hooped like ship's rigging from
one mast to the next, and even a dome of lilac near the jungle's
crown. So rare to see any blossoms in this sheer, shadowless front,
and yet there they were, stained-glass pebbles of light in a silent
ocean of green.

Maybe Father's right, he thought. *Maybe we'll make thirty kilometers today.*

Normally he would never have dared such a hope, but the
current was strong beneath them, and his oarsmen, João and Simplício, were rowing freely and sweetly. Trigueiro, Kermit's yellow
mongrel, was crouched alongside him in the front of the canoe.
The river breeze was blowing the dog's mouth open, and the saliva
that dripped from its black gums registered as the perfect antidote
to despair.

A further blessing: Rondon stopped only twice that morning
for sextant sightings. The work was quickly done—horizon captured
in one glass, sun in the other, latitude and longitude jotted down
in Rondon's journal—and they were back in their boats, and the
breeze came full behind him, and the river, for once, forbore to
wind. Slowly, the forest drew back as if to consider them, and the
land on either side erupted into bouldered hills and hissing green
mountains.

Kermit felt his eyes traveling up the battlement of cliffs and trees,
resting at last on a high promontory—halfway to the sun, or so it
appeared. Fastening his eyes there, he wondered—idly at first and
then with a mounting intensity—if someone at this very moment
was looking down, watching him pass. Watching the whole expedition. What a strange sight they must have been! A small band of
bedraggled white men, outnumbered by both their porters and

their trunks, hustling northward down a twisting ribbon of black water, with an air of deep intention. *Looking* for something, but what?

Even if Kermit could have communed with that distant observer, how could he have begun to explain? They weren't looking for anything or anyone in particular. They were merely attempting to see where this river would take them.

On each side, the canyon walls continued to surge up, and for a minute or two Kermit had the impression that the river was decanting in response, that they were traveling down a chute, not a river, and it would speed them farther along than they could ever have imagined. Twenty-five kilometers, just as the Colonel had said. Thirty.

He did then what he always did when hopeful. He pressed the packet of letters against his sternum. He closed his eyes and thought of Belle. "Not long," he whispered.

And then, from a hundred yards off, came the old roar.

In later life, he would find it impossible to explain just how dismal that sound was. How it shrank the soul. It was only water, after all. Water rushing down a terrace of rocks. But to the men of the Roosevelt-Rondon Expedition, that sound was the death of all hope, because it meant rapids.

Rapids that were, ninety times out of a hundred, too steep—too treacherous, too violent—for their unwieldy dugouts. Rapids that would force them to put down their paddles and haul all the canoes to shore.

Then the *real* work would begin.

Fourteen men would ply themselves against the jungle's densest thickets, using their machetes to hack out a primitive road along the riverbank. They would corrugate it with a couple of hundred logs. They would twine rope around their waists. Then, with the aid of a block and tackle, they would portage every last one of those 2,500-pound canoes around the rapids and then winch them back down, inch by inch, to the water.

In theory, it was an irritation, an obstacle. In practice, it was spine-cracking, muscle-rending, life-draining work, conducted under the probing stinger of every insect in the Amazonian jungle.

The dangers were great. One misstep, and a man could crush a toe or a hand or tumble into the river—or disturb a coral snake from its slumbers. Beneath their feet, the makeshift paths wore down into ledges of sandstone that gouged wood from the canoes' keels, and if the lesions grew deep enough, they would have to set the boats down and caulk the cracks and let them dry and then hoist them up once more. This was not a labor of minutes. It was a labor of hours—of hours upon hours. It could take them three days just to travel seven hundred fifty yards.

And so this sound—the mere sound of rushing water—was more than Kermit could bear on this particular March morning. He closed his eyes. He waited for Colonel Rondon's stentorian cry.

"Barcos para a beira mar!"

Boats to shore.

Not even staying to see if his command was followed, the little autocrat had already leaped onto the first square of dry land, and he was striding down the shoreline, looking to see exactly how steep the rapids were and how far they stretched. But as far as Kermit was concerned, this was a mere formality. He knew what Rondon would conclude: The canoes couldn't be risked. The nightmare would begin again.

From behind, Kermit could hear the Colonel calling after him.

"Didn't you hear? Come to shore."

He looked at João and Simplício. They had lifted their paddles from the water; they were just awaiting the word. As Kermit listened to the roar of the water and the roar of the Colonel, another sound rose up inside him. A pair of words.

I . . . won't. . . .

He wouldn't lose the rest of the day to portaging. He wouldn't go to sleep tonight knowing they were no closer to their final destination. Knowing that Belle and the rest of the world were as far away as ever.

With a violent twitch, he cast his eyes toward the fall line. He peered through the shroud of mist, seeking . . . a harbor . . . a counterargument—something to prove Rondon wrong.

The seconds ticked away, the water began to slap and churn against the canoe's keel, the *camaradas* shifted uneasily on their benches, and Kermit was on the very verge of giving up, when something hard and fixed and tangible rose from the mist. He blinked, refocused. Land. A tiny island, surging up from the teeming water. Splitting the river in half.

The calculations sped through his brain. What if this island gave them a vantage point for riding the rapids? What if it actually diverted the falls to one side and left an easier passage on the other? Wasn't it worth at least exploring?

But he knew what Rondon would say. And he knew what his father would say. And he heard *himself* say:

"Nós não vamos a beira mar."

We're not going to shore.

"Senhor?"

Simplício was staring at him with a mask of bafflement, and in his brown eyes was an expression so thick and bovine and unyielding that it became in that instant a symbol of everything Kermit was contending against. With a flash of teeth, Kermit pointed to the island that was now rushing toward them. He shouted, *"Lá! Vá lá!"*

The paddlers gave each other the briefest of looks. Kermit knew what they were thinking. The island was at the very brink of the falls. If they missed it, the whole canoe would go right over. But when Kermit repeated the order, they dropped their heads and dug in their oars and steered as straight a course as they could, and such was their skill that, within seconds, the boat was lodged on the island's southernmost margin.

"Ha!" cried Kermit.

He left Trigueiro in the boat and clambered over the side, grinning at the feeling of sand and wet rock beneath his boots. He crept forward, waiting at every moment for his instincts to be confirmed.

And then he stopped.

He was staring down a fifteen-foot drop. Below him lay only howling water and bubbling heaves of foam.

His error was now blindingly apparent. The rapids would be no easier to breach here. The island hadn't altered the river's direction or force at all, just bisected it. On either side of him, the falls raged with equal ferocity.

"Damn," he muttered. "Utter damnation."

It wasn't just the shame of guessing wrong, of having to weather Rondon's frown. It was something worse. He had, to all intents and purposes, stranded his boat. There was no way forward, no way back. Their only hope was to guide the canoe back to shore and hope they weren't swept over the edge.

This was the hope he clung to now as he darted back to the canoe and leaped in. *"Lá!"* he shouted, pointing to the margin of sand where the Colonel and the rest of the expedition were even now standing, gazing at the boat's plight in a helpless spectatorial thrall.

"Um," called Kermit. *"Dois . . . três . . ."*

Their doom was sure from the moment they pushed off. João and Simplício plunged in their paddles and beat as hard as they could against the current, but before they had made it halfway to shore, the boat began to whirl like the hands of a clock. Then, with a shudder, it jerked back into axis and headed straight for the falls.

In the midst of the spray and roar, Kermit dimly perceived that João was no longer rowing. He was hurling himself into the teeming water. Only now did his purpose become clear. He had grabbed the hawser rope and was trying to drag the boat to shore. But the riverbed was too slippery beneath his bare feet. Struggle as he might, he couldn't keep his balance, and the current tore the rope from his bleeding hands, and the dugout, relieved of any further obligation, streaked downstream.

Trigueiro barked. Kermit and Simplício exchanged the briefest of looks. Then the river took them all.

Never in Kermit's memory had water been such a punishment. It slammed his sun helmet over his face. It grabbed him by his jacket and dragged him to the river's bottom and, every time he found a crevice of light, it snuffed the light out.

His eyes swelled against their sockets, and the cold crawled into his bones as the black water swept him downstream, as easily as if he were a bird's nest.

He could actually taste the bubbles of his own breath. Somewhere, though, in his extinguishing brain, he sensed that the river was growing calmer, that the eddies and whirlpools were giving way once more to a single straight current. This current was now, in a spirit of chivalry, bearing him up—so that, with just a slight effort, he could lift his head above the river's surface.

And with that single motion, all the agony of his still-living body flooded in. The spikes in his lungs, the vise around his head. The torment of these eyes, opening once more to the sun—and discovering a single stark outline.

A branch.

Afterward, he would be unable to recall the moment of grasping. He remembered only the effort it took to haul himself free. To pull himself up, inch by inch, with all his senses blazing—and then canceling one another out. So that he slipped straight from agony to unconsciousness.

WHEN HE AWOKE, THE sun was frowning from the end of a long tunnel. He felt sand in his fingers . . . water at his ankles. Something else—neither sand nor water—baptizing his face.

Trigueiro.

Half-gargling, half-sobbing, he pulled the dog's head toward him. Then from out of the woods came a measured tread. A pair of boots, unnaturally burnished. Rondon.

"*Bem,*" he said at last. "*Você já teve um esplêndido banho, hein?*"

You have had a splendid bath.

Kermit's first instinct was to laugh it off—or brazen it out—as if he'd been caught with a pack of cigarettes by a Groton prefect. Then he remembered who he was. Not his brother Ted. Not his brother Archie. He was Kermit Roosevelt: a young man incapable of charming his way out of any situation.

As this realization leached through his oxygen-depleted brain, other things winked into clarity. His gear was gone. His beloved Winchester .405 was gone. The canoe! Dear God, the canoe was almost certainly destroyed. It would cost the expedition days to make a new one. The conclusion was obvious. Thanks to Kermit's rashness—a young man's rashness—a detour of three hours had stretched into a sojourn of several days.

By now Trigueiro's tongue had become a kind of torment against his skin, and yet he hadn't the strength to push the dog away. He could only lie there, waiting for the reproach that was his due.

But the only thing Rondon said was:

"*Aonde está o Simplício?*"

Kermit blinked. He propped himself up on his elbows, gazed upshore and downshore. Simplício was nowhere to be seen.

"He was . . ." With a great expense of energy, Kermit raised himself to his feet. "He was right next to me. . . ."

Rondon's stare was as baleful as Kermit had ever seen it. What a relief to look over the colonel's shoulder and see João—sopping from his own bath—galloping toward them. João would know. He'd seen them go over the falls. He'd followed them the whole way. *Tell them*, thought Kermit, squeezing his eyes shut. *Tell them.*

But the words that came out of the *camarada*'s mouth were identical to Rondon's.

"*Simplício? Aonde está o Simplício?*"

* * *

FOR THE REST OF the afternoon they searched. They thrashed the river with their paddles. They traveled downstream as far as a mile, canvassing both shores. They hacked notches out of the jungle front just in case Simplício had been thrown clear.

By day's end, the search parties had netted only a single paddle, chipped but still intact, and a box of rations. Their calls had long since given way to whispers: *"Ele está perdido."* He is lost.

But around the campfire that night, they whispered something else.

Assassino.

And lest there be any doubt about the assassin's identity, they would lift their heads from time to time and cast dark looks in Kermit's direction—looks that stopped just short of insurrection. The whispers built into murmurs, until Colonel Rondon himself rose and silenced then with one peremptory motion of his forearm.

That night, in his journal, Kermit wrote: *Simplício was drowned.* Such a bare sentence. His pencil hovered over the page, touched down again and again. No more words came.

He closed the book and lay on his cot, listening to the frogs and watching the mosquitoes land, one by one, on his exposed arm. Silently cataloging them: *anopheline . . . culex.*

"You mustn't blame yourself," said the Colonel. He was sitting up in his own cot, smearing his face and neck with fly dope. *"He* doesn't blame you."

Kermit closed his eyes. "Rondon, you mean?"

"Naturally."

"For a second, I thought you meant God."

The Colonel huddled around that and then, with a chuckle, said, "Do you suppose there's a difference?"

Kermit said nothing.

"The point is," the old man continued, "I've spoken with our great leader, and there was no sense of—no need to *advocate* on your behalf; he considers you entirely exonerated. He understands, Kermit. You were trying to do the right thing by all of us. It's obvious, it's self-evident. . . ."

Kermit was quite sure that, in Rondon's mind, in Rondon's heart, he was not exonerated. But the Brazilian was a pragmatic man, disinclined to jeopardize the long-term success of his expedition by alienating its illustrious co-leader. It was for Father's sake—for Father's sake alone—that Kermit would escape punishment.

"I don't care," he said at last. "I don't care if Rondon blames me. *I* blame me."

"Now, see here. I won't have any of this morbid self-pity, do you hear? We all embarked on this expedition—every single one of us—knowing we might not come back. That is the first proviso in the explorer's code."

"So it is."

"And may God strike me down, but . . ." He paused. "If I'd had to choose between you and Simplício, you know which way I should have gone. The point is, it wasn't my choice. *Or* yours. It was Destiny."

Destiny, thought Kermit. *What is that?*

It was a question he had yet to surmount. Or maybe it had just shrunk to a smaller question: Why had he reached for that branch?

Even now, looking back, he was amazed at how calm he'd been in the face of death. Not in the manner of a soldier, as his family might have preferred, but in the manner of a monk resigning himself to the Maker's plan. All fears, all regrets washed away. He was *ready*. Yet when the branch presented itself, he had grasped it without another thought.

Only now, hours later, could he discern what had risen up in that moment: The image of Father. Father standing over his son's drowned carcass. Father telegraphing the news to Mother. Father, in his sable suit, hoisting up one corner of the coffin . . .

That was all it took. Kermit reached for that branch. Now the

Colonel could carry on, as great men must. And Kermit could go on being a great man's reflection. For a second, he had a vivid, almost erotic image of that branch pulling away at the last second. Of his own water-swollen body borne along to its destined end.

"Enough chatter," said the Colonel. "A few hours' sleep always does wonders, I've found. You'll have a whole new perspective on things come morning. Good night, my boy. Twenty-five kilometers tomorrow! Mark my words."

THEY HADN'T THE TIME or energy to build a new canoe, so the next morning Colonel Rondon politely asked Kermit to join him in his. Stepping toward his new seat, Kermit heard Rondon speak, for the first time, in English. Two words.

"After you."

THE NEXT DAY—AT the point where latitude $-11°57'$ met longitude $-60°20'$—the Rio da Dúvida suddenly widened, and the boats began to swirl atop an unguessed current. On their port side, the dark solemn forest broke open. A blanket of espresso-colored water, white-capped by wind, came rolling toward them.

"*Novo rio,*" murmured João.

It was indeed a new river—a tributary, materializing from something like nothing—and, at seventy feet in width, easily the largest tributary they'd come across. Rondon celebrated the moment in his usual way: by dragging out the sextant and taking a sighting. They set up camp at the confluence point of the two rivers. The next morning, Colonel Rondon used the Orders of the Day to make a signal announcement. The mysterious waterway along which they now stood would henceforth be known as the Rio Kermit.

There followed an interval of stunned silence. Then, grinning like summer, the Colonel slapped his son on the shoulder. "You've arrived, my boy! Into the gazetteer with you. With both of us, I should say!" For Rondon had already christened the Rio da Dúvida the Rio Roosevelt.

After breakfast, Kermit walked very deliberately to the shore of his new river. The rains had swollen it to such a level that most of the boulders and fallen trees and branches were submerged. All that was left was a silvery skin and the wrinkled reflection of the lightening sky.

He thought then of the signpost they had left behind to commemorate Simplício—the signpost that the jungle would tear down in a matter of weeks. The only consolation Kermit could find in that moment was imagining the dead man still alive . . . still traveling . . . beneath the surface of the Rio Kermit.

Simplício returned that very night, in Kermit's dreams, his arm outstretched, his skin glittering with terror, his mouth opening as if to scream—but nothing came out except bubbles of blood, and each bubble carried the same word.

Socorro . . . socorro . . .

Help . . . help . . .

2

KERMIT WASN'T SUPPOSED TO BE HERE.

His father wasn't supposed to be here.

The only reason Theodore Roosevelt had come to South America in 1913 was to speak (a thing he did well). He was to deliver three lectures to grateful Argentinians and take back with him the sum of thirteen thousand dollars. It would all make for a grand holiday— the Colonel was even bringing his wife—and if the occasion gave him the chance to mold an embryonic democracy and reassert America's rights of intervention under the Monroe Doctrine, so much the better. And if by chance he stopped off in Brazil along the way to visit his son Kermit, who was making such a promising career for himself, better still!

Oh, there'd been talk of the old man making some sort of river jaunt. Up the Rio Negro, perhaps, or down the Orinoco—well-traveled waterways that would offer Amazonian flavor without much danger. But all that changed in October when, during a ceremonial visit, the Brazilian minister of affairs ("Such a cultivated man, Kermit. Reminds me very much of Hay") broached a new idea. Might

Colonel Roosevelt prefer a more challenging mission? Might he even be interested in leading a scientific expedition down an uncharted river?

Rio da Dúvida, the Portuguese called it. The River of Doubt. For good reason: It refused to be known. The jungle explorer Cândido Rondon had discovered its headwaters in the course of laying telegraph lines, but no man—no white man, anyway—knew where it led. Indeed, what set it apart from other rivers was its maddening elusiveness. It twisted wildly, curving toward every point of the compass, doubling back on itself, sometimes even plunging beneath the earth. It seethed with rapids, falls, whirlpools. It harbored caimans and anacondas and catfish that feasted on monkeys and lived on blood. Only a fool—or a great man—would have pitted himself against such a river.

Was not Theodore Roosevelt such a man? Was he not on record as despising the "ordinary travelers" who hewed to the beaten path and let others do all the work and embrace all the risk? Such lollygags were no better than valises, carried from point to point, accomplishing nothing. But here was a chance to do something else entirely. To ride and master a previously unknown river that stretched quite possibly a thousand miles—as long as the Ohio or the Rhine—and swarmed with creatures never before cataloged. A great blank space on the earth's canvas, waiting for somebody—*some*body—to slap his name on it.

In so doing, that man would secure himself a permanent part of recorded history, to be spoken of in the same breath as Speke and Burton, Scott and Amundsen, Peary and Shackleton. The *true* immortals. Presidents—ha!—they came and went, but rivers went on forever, just as the poet suggested, and if Theodore Roosevelt were to map *this* river, then he would be renowned for all time, his name on every map and atlas, in every heart and mind.

Dear Lord, how could he possibly have said no?

It was true, the crew he had brought to South America was not the most inspiring: two naturalists, a failed North Pole explorer, and a social-climbing priest named Father Zahm. But the Colonel would have a formidable ally on his journey: the legendary Rondon, who, as the leader of the Strategic Telegraph Commission, had already traveled through more than fourteen thousand miles of Brazilian wilderness. Many a man had lost his life under Rondon's command, but none had rebelled. He was hard as obsidian, unconquerable, brooked no dissent, and countenanced no obstacle—a savage's temperament, it was said, wedded to a saint's self-discipline. With Rondon in the mix, the expedition's success was virtually guaranteed.

And to cap it off, the Colonel's own son, though recently engaged, had volunteered to come along!

Kermit had acquitted himself with great distinction in his father's African safari, and he had spent the last year building tracks and bridges for the Brazil Railway Company, where his bravery, diligence, and uncomplaining nature had won him plaudits on all sides. He was resilient, resourceful—and a gifted linguist, whose fluency in Portuguese would make him the ideal go-between for Rondon and the Colonel.

"You *know* what they say," the old man declared. "A good interpreter is worth his weight in gold. Now, don't you worry, Kermit, we'll have you back to your gainful employment in no time. Of course, Rondon's being cagey on the subject of *duration,* but I've consulted with some highly intelligent gentlemen who assure me we'll get to the thing's end in just a few short weeks. We'll be descending the whole time, of course, and these rivers don't waste time. They get where they're *going,* by God!"

But getting to the river—this would be an ordeal in itself. First a boat ride up the Paraguay River and then a grueling mule journey across four hundred miles of Brazilian Highlands: desert and jungle, scrub forest and open plains. The rain hammered; the sun seared. They slogged through vast wastes of mud. They quarreled among themselves. The Brazilian *camaradas* grumbled at the Americans' enormous freights of luggage, and the Americans wondered why the Brazilians couldn't keep order. "It's like starting over again every day," allowed the Colonel, in a rare moment of protest.

A week into the journey, Kermit's old malaria came back with a vengeance. He could barely keep in his saddle, and under the constant jostling of his mule, abscesses sprang up on his buttocks and the insides of his legs. Every bounce and jolt sent another blade of pain through his fevered brain, and the only way to distract himself was to repeat, again and again: "I'm to be married in June . . . married in June. . . ."

Malaria was digging in everywhere—not even the Colonel was immune. By the time they reached the river, they were so exhausted and their supplies so diminished that the leaders made the strategic decision to split the expedition in two. One party would be sent down the Gy-Paraná to the Madeira—a charted river and a less dangerous journey but a useful effluent for such irritants as Father Zahm, who had alienated everyone (the Colonel most of all) with his highfalutin airs and pettiness. The others—and they included Rondon, the two Roosevelts, and Cherrie, the naturalist—would take up the challenge of the Rio da Dúvida.

It was just a few minutes past noon on February 27 when they prepared to launch. Kermit climbed into the lead boat, already chafing at its narrowness. João and Simplício pushed off with their oars and, a second later, the current swept them up and bodied them forth. From somewhere far behind him, Kermit heard a single voice calling.

"Good luck!"

HERE WAS THE THING about traveling down an uncharted river: You could only say how long you'd been traveling; you could never say how long it would be. Here they were, five weeks later, winding down the same black river and stymied at every turn by rapids.

They could travel no more than a few miles before the next roar of water came echoing from around the bend. Never once had they made more than a mile and a quarter a day. Altogether, they had traveled less than several miles—and that through bitterest labor and with no small risk.

They had lost five canoes and, thanks to Kermit's rashness, one of their crew. They were wet. They were starving. They were ravaged by insects. They were riddled with disease and so tired they had forgotten what it was like to be anything else.

And the black river wound on.

I'm to be married in June. Married in June.

Late in the afternoon of April 2, a new set of rapids rose up. They found a level margin of sand and set up camp. Kermit and Lieutenant Lyra went ahead to scout and came back with news of what lay ahead. More rapids. Rapids running as far as the eye could see. Ready to smash any canoe that dared ride them.

The sun was sinking like a fist over the mountains on their left flank. Quiet had fallen over the camp, except for the sputtering of the sodden wood that Franca was coaxing into a fire.

Kermit sat on the foreshore, his sun helmet at his side, a wad of tobacco in his cheek. He was staring through the canyon to where the river was already churning out of sight, as black and opaque and unknowable as the day he first saw it. The thought caught him unawares.

What if it leads nowhere? Nowhere at all?

Blinking, he gazed about at his fellow travelers. There was Cherrie, shaking out his poncho in long slow arcs. And over there Dr. Cajazeira, gravely thin, parceling out his rations of fly dope. The *camaradas,* bowed and sore-pocked, were hauling up bags, tying hammocks, and swinging their machetes through thickets of vine. Kermit saw them now in the light of his own question, and the truth settled over him like a pall.

They were dying.

It was true. Everyone—and everything—stank of the tomb. The slabs of mountain on every side. The trees arching like the groins of a mausoleum. The lethal fecundity of all these trunks and leaves and vines, writhing and coiling and sometimes leaving the ground altogether and sprouting in midair, and every sprout sprouting anew, weaving round.

We should have found a better place, thought Kermit in a daze. *A better place to die.*

Kermit swiped his forearm across his face and closed his eyes. Sucking in the wall of his cheek, he drew down the last dregs of tobacco juice. A minute, two minutes passed, before his eyes were stung open by smoke. Franca's campfire, sending out fumes of coffee.

Coffee and . . . what? Kermit made a quick calculation. The two piranhas they'd caught last week had dwindled to nothing. The coconuts were gone. So were most of the Brazil nuts. There was some wild honey, a little palmito. Soda crackers.

By way of compensation, there would be much *talk* of food tonight. Cherrie would speak of pancakes with maple syrup. (He was from Vermont.) The Colonel would extol the mutton chop. "With a tail to it!" And Kermit would make the usual noises about straw-berries and cream, but, in his heart, he would be longing for bacon.

Not just any bacon, but the kind he and his brothers used to eat on camping trips. Three or four times a summer, they'd row with Father to the same secluded neck off Oyster Bay, and as the sun fell, they'd make a driftwood fire and fry up a rasher of bacon. And whether it was because of the romance of their situation or the exer-tion of rowing four miles, bacon had never tasted as good. Nor would again.

Bacon. A Cortland apple. Hamburger steak with onions.

A bubble of saliva welled up from the corner of Kermit's lip. Strange how alert he'd become to the nuances of dampness. The morning dampness of his socks, for instance, was altogether different from the smoky dampness of the day air and the sealskin dampness of the river. He felt a tiny fleck of drool—he cupped it now with his fingernail—pearly and self-contained.

Finally a more pressing dampness at his elbow. Trigueiro, worming his way through the gap beneath Kermit's arm and depositing his camel-colored snout on his master's lap.

"No luck?" asked Kermit. He scratched a semicircle around the dog's ear. "Not even a squirrel?"

Kermit canvassed his body's coordinates. His left buttock, where an abscess still throbbed. The running sores on his shin. His thigh, bruised last week by a paddle and no closer to healing.

The chest . . .

Already his fingers were stealing toward the oilskin envelope beneath his rag of a shirt. Belle's letters. Still there.

"Senhor." One of the *camaradas* was leaning toward him. *"Sua barraca está pronta."*

"Obrigado."

Preparing his tent was the one chore Kermit suffered the laborers to do for him. And only because he had come to require this particular space in the day. His eyes traveled down the shoreline to where the Colonel sat on a stump of tree, studying the river. He watched then as the old man rose to his feet and tottered back toward camp, dragging his left leg a little behind.

"Franca!" called the Colonel (to the cook who spoke no English). "I am expecting culinary wonders tonight." Then he disappeared into his tent.

Kermit pried Trigueiro's head off his thigh and lowered it, in slow increments, to the ground. With a soft groan, he raised himself to his feet and heard a gravely cheerful "Heigh-ho!"

It was Cherrie, coming to him with a gift: dark and hard and twisted. A *bird,* in fact. Ten inches long. Rich-brown feathers, a yellow rump and crest, and a red stripe on its cheek.

"Chestnut woodpecker," said Cherrie.

"Easy to bag?"

"Oh, no, he was dead when I found him. Not sure I've ever seen one this far south." A line of skepticism in the older man's lips. "Not much use to us, eh? Scrawny thing."

"Maybe he ate a termite or two," Kermit suggested, "on our behalf."

Nodding, Cherrie tucked the bird under his arm and gave it a proprietary pat. "Your father will be pleased," he said.

"I'm sure he will."

"I only wish I could have brought us something more—well, never mind. How about a nip, Roosevelt?"

They were on their last bottle of Scotch. The first two had gone quickly and, in order to make the third endure, they had resorted to marking off the allotted increments. It worked out to a couple of drams a night, but if you took them before dinner, it was almost as good as a jigger.

Just a few yards from Cherrie's hammock, they were stopped by a sound. *Sounds*—raucous and queerly throttled—from deep in the forest interior. Locusts, one might have thought, only the rhythm was more intellectual than zoological.

"Guess we should have expected them," said Cherrie.

"Who?"

"The *two*-legged fauna."

The men looked at each other.

"Are you sure?" asked Kermit.

"Sure enough."

As they stood listening in the fading light, the voices seemed to make strands around them, and Kermit had a curious impulse to thrash himself free. But the sounds vanished as quickly as they came, leaving the jungle that much quieter.

"Part of me wishes they'd show themselves," said Cherrie. "Part of me wishes they'd stay far away. God knows we'd be in no shape to hold them off."

"The Nhambiquara were friendly enough."

"Why, because they gave us canoes? I'd say we paid them well enough. The trick being we knew *how* to pay them. Because we were able to talk to them. Because we were able to see them in the first place."

It was true. During the last week, no face, no body had emerged from that impenetrable forest, only signs. A well-worn path. Footprints. Old fishing baskets. Trees methodically stripped of their bark. Somebody was out there.

With a small shock, Kermit registered the fact that Cherrie was laughing. Revealing, with that simple act, just how much of him had withered away. All you could see of him were his teeth, scandalously oversized, jabbering like a fun-house skeleton, and, beyond that, the chasm from which words were somehow emerging.

"I'd ask them for supper," said Cherrie, "if there were any to go around."

3

Dinner passed in a blink, and the expeditioners, lacking strength even for talk, retired to their tents and hammocks. Except the Colonel, who found a tiny clearing ten yards down the shore, seated himself in a camp chair, draped mosquito netting over his sun helmet, and swaddled his arms in fringed gauntlets, leaving only his hands free.

He looked, thought Kermit, like a dowager aunt on a transatlantic crossing, but Kermit knew the old man didn't care. He had work to do. He had contracted with Scribner's to keep a daily journal of his travels, and keep it he would, no matter how low the sun or how the insects chaffed. And he would give himself so thoroughly to this work that an hour might slip by without his missing it, and Kermit could stand there—as he was doing tonight—and be acknowledged no more than a moth. Only the sight of a cup waving back and forth before the old man's eyes broke his concentration.

"Coffee?" he gasped.

"The last of the last."

"Well, then," he said, unfurling his netting. "Don't mind if I do."

There was no other chair, so Kermit sat on the ground, watching the old man fold his mouth around the cup's rim.

"You're well?" the Colonel asked.

"Well enough."

"I was just setting down how . . . how very *optimistic* I'm feeling. About the day ahead."

"Yes?"

"The current is quite obviously picking up. As is the breeze. Once we're past those damned rapids, we should make at least ten kilos before sunset. Twelve, if the gods smile."

"You may be right."

"And in that event, we should reach the Aripuanã before another three weeks have passed. From there to the Amazon, and from there, home." He nodded for emphasis. "We'll get to the end of this."

Kermit's gaze settled on the river, simmering in the quarter-light.

"Of course, you must promise me," the Colonel added, "that when we reach civilization, you will take a razor to that growth of yours."

Smiling, Kermit ran his fingers through his beard. He had grown it in solidarity with the *camaradas,* and it stretched now to his clavicle.

"I can't shave it, Father. It's the record of our days. Here now . . ." At random, he plucked a mote from the brown shawl. "This was the stinging ant I was wrestling with just this morning. Touch and go, I tell you. And this little termite? Don't let his looks fool you. I caught him eating Colonel Rondon's hanky last night. Subjected him to the hideous Death by Follicle."

Strange. He was rarely funny with anyone else. But, then, there was no reward quite like the Colonel's laughter. You had the sensation of riding it.

"Oh, and this?" he went on. "Intestinal grub. Completely lost his way. I've persuaded him he's crawling through my colon, and he's invited all his pals to join in. Quite the merry clan, and more expected any minute. One way or another . . ." He began to wave his beard like bunting. "This thing will catalog more species than Linnaeus."

The Colonel dabbed his eyes. "In that case, we must ship you straight to the Natural History Museum. I fear you'll never again see the light of day."

"My gift to science. In return, I ask only . . ."

"Yes?"

"The privilege of examining your leg."

The Colonel's grin drooped into a scowl. "Why? Cajazeira's been fussing over it all day."

"Indulge me, please."

With a bearish rumble, the old man rolled up his left trouser leg. From the pallor of his shin, a hot red hard bruise snarled out.

"Larger than yesterday," said Kermit.

"I'd say not."

"And what of this?"

He fingered an abscess just above the Colonel's knee, looking up just in time to catch the old man's wince.

"I leave you *your* bruises, Kermit. You might do the same with mine."

"That's hardly a bruise."

"It's the price of my clumsiness. When a fellow goes and bangs himself against a rock for no good reason, he must pay the consequences."

"Has Cajazeira lanced it?"

"Just this morning."

"And your blood pressure?"

"A trifle low, I'm told."

"Temperature?"

"A trifle high. Kermit, I beg you to stop nagging. You sound like Old Mame," he said, rolling the trouser leg back down. "If you must know, a spot of fever has its benefits. It leaves a fellow less keen on supper—which, under the circumstances, is to be encouraged. Tomorrow night you may have my entire cracker, if you wish."

It was true the Colonel didn't yet have the gaunt, stropped look of Rondon or some of the *camaradas*. He had started the expedition at two hundred twenty pounds. But the loss of weight was, if anything, more noticeable in him, for it seemed to carry with it a measure of spirit.

"Kermit," he said. "Do stop worrying. I am as well as can be expected."

"If you say so."

"I dreamed of home last night."

"Yes?"

"The way it looks now, I mean. Early April. Almost shocking how clear everything was. The robins, the meadowlarks. Maple buds, red as I've ever seen them. And there was your mother, out in some meadow, not ours—*some*one's. She was gathering windflowers and bloodroot, and there were patches of snow all round her, but she wore no gloves. She had a . . . a very particular color to her cheeks." The old man paused. "She never saw me. Never even turned her head."

"Perhaps she didn't wish to intrude. It was *your* dream, after all."

"She's thoughtful that way. All the same, I wish we could send word of some kind. Tell her we're—well, you know . . ."

"She's a soldier," Kermit said.

"None braver."

"You've been parted from her before. We were gone half a year in Africa."

"Why does this feel longer, I wonder? And what of you and your Belle? Keeping a young man from his fiancée, that's peculiarly ungallant."

"Absence," said Kermit, casting his eyes to one side. "Heart. Fonder."

"We will presume that to be the case, but we will not press our luck. Look at me, Kermit. I want my faith to be yours. Before too very long, we will all be reunited with the ones dearest to us. And we will never again eat hearts of palm."

"Hear, hear."

With a grunt, the old man clapped his journal shut. "Scribner's subscribers will have to wait until tomorrow. I should warn you, Kermit, you are shaping up very much as the hero of the piece."

"Ah, fiction, then."

"On the contrary, I am informing my readers that the flesh of my flesh toils as hard as any man in this party. Harder than most, and sick half the time. Never a word of complaint. We'd be . . . we'd—"

Then the air cracked open.

It was one of the curious things about this forest that it could remain so austerely silent during the day and swell with noise the moment the sun began to sink. Behind those green walls lay an entire symphony orchestra. Clangs and crashes and rattles, punctuated by screeches and bellows. A thousand living things, freed by darkness.

But the sound that came for them now was different. A high oscillating whinny. Purposeful. *Present.*

"Did you hear that?" the Colonel whispered.

Kermit scanned the tree fronts. "Not a howler," he said.

"No, indeed. A spider."

They'd never actually seen a spider monkey, but Cherrie had always made a point of identifying its call whenever it came singing down from the canopy. This was the call that resonated now in their ears. A private summons from the jungle's largest primate.

The two men jumped to their feet. No more than twenty seconds passed before the sound came whirling back, even louder than before. Wheezing softly, the old man pointed to a high buriti palm surrounded by handlike fronds.

"Fetch the rifles, Kermit."

"Are you sure? There's not much light left."

"There's enough."

"The doctor says you must stay off your leg."

"What I *must* do is bag tomorrow night's supper. Now, if you'd care to accompany me . . ."

When the younger man still hesitated, the Colonel rounded on him and snapped, "What are we dallying for?"

How often he had heard that question as a child, and how great was its impact still. In the next instant, Kermit was dashing toward camp, snatching up Cherrie's .405 Winchester, and rummaging through his father's duffel bag and yanking out the Springfield and a pair of cartridge bags. Working so feverishly and in such haste that Cherrie raised his head from his hammock and drawled, "Something brewing?"

"Oh. Just humoring the old man. Back shortly."

"Well, for God's sake," Cherrie called after him, "take a torch with you."

Kermit found a milk-tree branch buried in the sand. It was just dry enough to take light after a minute in the campfire. Gnats and piums and eye-lickers pinwheeled around the torch's flame as he jogged back down the shore.

He knew, of course, their mission was doomed. The sun had sprinted from the sky, and if they proposed to pursue this monkey, they would have to penetrate the jungle at its densest part. Three *camaradas* might labor an hour with machetes just to hack through a few yards of vine and trunk and epiphyte. Imagine how little progress an old man would make, even with the help of his son.

But, to Kermit's surprise, the Colonel had found a small breach. Nothing like a true path, but an *opening*. With a few blows from their rifle butts, this opening, by some fluke, expanded. Enough, at least, to whet their appetites, so that before long they were *driving* into the forest. Kermit could hear the old man's asthmatic wheeze, he could feel his own sweat like rust against his skin, and, with a private shock, he realized he was happy, supremely happy.

Something else he realized: They were standing. Unobstructed. In a small clearing.

The sun had finally dropped from the sky, and the darkness of the jungle closed around them.

Expedition members were instructed to never stray too far from camp, but here they were, a hundred yards off, and it might as well have been a thousand miles. Later Kermit would think that this was the moment on which everything hinged. Because they might have found their way back. It would have taken them no more than a few minutes, and everything would have followed its usual course.

But, in that same moment, the spider monkey's whinny came funneling down to them. It vibrated along their spines. In the torchlight, Kermit could see his father wiping the fog from his spectacles. Motioning for silence. Raising his rifle higher . . . higher . . .

"Wait," whispered Kermit, putting his hand against the barrel. "We don't have a sight on him."

"He's up there."

"*Where?* You can't possibly land him."

"I don't mean to land him, I mean to roust him. Look, now, you wait till I fire. As soon as you hear the rustle, you follow it, and you fire right into it, do you hear me?"

He's mad, thought Kermit.

Yet he understood that the Colonel, being myopic, had always hunted through some triangulation of senses: sound and smell filling the gaps in vision. He gave the nod, and the old man once more lifted the barrel of his gun. A second . . . two seconds . . . and then the forest seemed to explode with the rifle's report. Only to contract in the very next instant.

Kermit tilted his ear up to the canopy. Waited for a cry or a rustle, but there was none.

Once more the Colonel fired, and once more the forest caught the sound and held it. Everything else shrank into silence, and the Colonel was raising his rifle for the third shot when they heard a faint whistle and, from the blackness above, something began working its way toward them.

Kermit nearly laughed. *A Brazil nut.*

But no Brazil nut, no coconut in his experience had ever made such a commotion on its way to earth. This was a thing of weight, of moment, and it was coming to them tier by tier, and the breath froze in Kermit's chest as he waited. . . .

Just when he had resigned himself to waiting forever, a great black bundle dropped from the canopy and pooled on the forest floor.

Kermit's torchlight was already picking out the splay of black limbs. The surreally long tail. A spider monkey, as sure as night, prostrate at their feet.

Even so, Kermit held back. It was the Colonel who stood over the carcass and, in a voice of unmistakable satisfaction, said:

"We shall have a grand feast with this one."

Kermit knelt now before the carcass. Studied the eyes, which had passed beyond cloudiness into white agates. Something was wrong.

There was no blood.

No blood on the head. On the feet. In the abdomen.

He pushed the monkey onto its back—and was astonished to see it split open. *Wide* open.

A monkey rug, he thought wildly. But something had to have climbed that tree. Made that sound . . .

Then a new sound broke on his ears: a tremulous, high-pitched bark. Trigueiro, galloping toward them. The mutt had followed their scent, and his fawn-colored flanks were pumping, and he was longing with every particle of his soul to be where they were.

Only he never made it.

A stifled yelp. A hiss. Then silence.

Trigueiro's front paws were sprawled before him. Projecting from his back was a single arrow, so freakishly long it might have been one of Jove's thunderbolts, pinning him to the forest floor.

"Trigueiro . . ."

Then the tree shivered open once more, and a black shape dropped from the branches—straight for the Colonel.

The old man flailed for his gun, but it was kicked away. He raised his fists like a pugilist, but the thing wrapped round him and squeezed. It was like watching a man wrestle with his own shadow—and lose.

With a shout, Kermit sprang at the shape, but he was already too late, he knew that. Knew it even before he felt the blow on his own shoulder and saw his torch flying into the dark.

The second blow caught him on the chest. He reeled . . . and then sank, with supreme awkwardness, to the forest floor. He watched his own torch descending on him—a blaze of heat and weight.

"Father," he cried. And fell out of the light.

4

"YOU'RE AWFULLY SHY."

He was dreaming of Belle. Belle, as he'd first seen her two years ago.

"Shy for a *Roosevelt*, I mean."

If any other woman had said that, he would have stammered . . . well, something about never speaking too quickly for fear of speaking amiss, this being the course approved by Lord Acton and . . . and Dryden . . . oh, on and *on*, defending himself, and it would have been worse than saying nothing. He didn't even have the courage of his own quiet.

But beneath the glitter of Belle's cornflower-blue eyes, there lay a kind of watchful patience. She would wait for him. It would be worth the wait. And, with that, he realized the words were already there.

"They also serve who only stand and grunt."

In the next instant, he had his reward. She laughed. A gleaming plenitude of teeth.

"Well, now," she said, stretching her vowels as far as they could go. "Do you also *walk* and grunt?" She curled her white hand around his elbow. "At least as far as the punch bowl?"

When he hesitated, she added, "You may ask anyone who knows me, Mr. Roosevelt. I don't bite."

"Nor do I, Miss Willard. I assure you."

"Then we may proceed in safety."

HIS SISTER ETHEL WAS the one who'd invited her to Sagamore. "Now, you *will* be sociable, won't you, Kermit? She's a Democrat, of course, so we can't talk too much in *that* line, and you must forgive the fact that she comes from scads of money, because she's really tremendous fun. Her father owns a chain of hotels, so hospitality runs in her veins. Oh, don't smile like that, you know what I mean."

He'd had little occasion to speak with Ethel's friend on the first two days, but he did notice how well she took to a horse. She was a little thing, but her carriage was erect and springy—*charged*—as though any second she might leap off and chase the quarry on foot. She was a sure shot, too, knew her way around Winchesters, even helped to dress the deer she shot. She propelled a skiff like a champion crewman. Beneath that nest of blond ringlets, he suspected, lay a barely rehabilitated tomboy—the kind he might have seen playing hockey, in winters past, on Duck Pond.

But it was summer now, and as the days and nights passed in hikes and rowing and lunches among the wild plum bushes and afternoon teas on the veranda and parlor games and midnight bonfires, he could see how far she had left the pond (and him) behind. Through training, through inclination, she had become everything he was not: facile, vivacious, nakedly curious, a talker, a laugher, a dancer. When she laughed, she had a way of tilting her head back as if she were imbibing the joke from a great stein. Her hands tilted up, and her long white neck glowed like coral.

"It's easy for her, isn't it?"

"What is?" Ethel asked.

Living, he wanted to say. There wasn't a slough of despond that Belle Wyatt Willard couldn't skate right over—with a sly backward wink as if to say, *That wasn't so hard, was it?*

But it is hard. It's supposed to be hard.

That's what he had always told himself—although if he were to look at his father, springing out of bed every morning and flinging himself at the waiting day, he could see how very easy it was for an elect few. To their company must now be admitted this young woman, who handled every second of her allotted time as a gift. Treated even him as a gift.

ON THE NIGHT BEFORE Belle left Sagamore, they stood alone on the piazza overlooking the Sound, watching the lights of the Fall River steamers, listening to the green warblers and the purple finches and the bobolinks. From the beach came a pipe scent of rosemary.

"I'm going to South America," he said.

He had taken a job with the Brazil Railway Company. He was going to carve railroads and bridges out of the Brazilian jungle. The pay would be minimal at first, and the danger considerable. More than one of the company engineers had been killed by Indian arrows; many more had died of malaria. Yet it was the closest thing to a calling he could discern: to be so far from civilization's grasp. He still savored the memory of the year he had spent with Father in the wilds of Africa, and in South America he would find a place even more remote, more mysterious, a continent with a great black hole at its heart, waiting to be filled with light—not the light of salvation but the light of *knowledge,* yes, of human understanding.

He spoke in a great hurry, his eyes cast down. He understood now that this moment was a test and that, so long as he avoided her eyes, the test need neither be passed nor failed but held in a permanent suspension.

"But that's on my list," she said.

He raised his eyes. "Sorry?"

"My list of adventures. Sailing down the Amazon comes in right at number four, directly after visiting the Pyramids. Oh, but I would happily bump it to the top!"

By the time they had parted, she was already laying her plans. "Father will jump at the chance to join me. Why, it's South America, after all; who could say no? And I *know* I can persuade Ethel to go, too. Don't you think it would be good for her? You just leave it all to me." On impulse—or was it the result of long premeditation?—she pressed his long bony fingers lightly between hers. "You'll write, won't you, Kermit? I should be so pleased."

ON BOARD THE *OLYMPIC,* he dashed off a pair of letters and mailed them as soon as he landed in Bahia (along with the two volumes of Edwin Arlington Robinson he'd brought with him).

Her reply came a few weeks later, postmarked from Hot Springs. *It has been too lonely here this past week,* she said. *Of course, I won't let the family forget about South America and am now trying to persuade them that the trip will be most beneficial to Elizabeth* [this was Belle's sister]—*I'm sure Mother won't go without her. I have thought of two other things I want to do. Wolf hunting in Russia . . . and tiger shooting from elephants' backs in India!*

He could only smile at her handwriting: a wide indolent childish sprawl that consumed reams of hotel stationery—so different from his own sparrow tracks. She wrote with the confidence that fresh paper would always be found.

It's too wonderful, she wrote him in December. *Apparently we are sailing for S.A. on Jan. 25. I can hardly believe it true, and of course many things may happen between now and then.*

Something did happen. Belle's father was called up by President Wilson to serve as ambassador to Spain. The plans for South America were quietly scrapped, but Belle's letters carried on: from Paris, from London and finally Madrid. The flutterings and flickerings of a social butterfly, borne aloft from dress fittings to dinners to weddings to balls. *We have had so many many things to do that after each more & more hectic day I go to bed more & more exhausted & wake up equally so.*

Yet she had time to ask after his health (*What are you doing with fever so constantly?*) and to tuck in news clippings, postcards, a photograph of a Brancusi sculpture from the Armory Show. And names—these she was sure to drop in. *Mr. Percy MacKaye was here yesterday. . . . I gleaned quite a lot of information from a Mr. Nodge, who was here to dinner last night. . . . Mr. Page's secretary is an attractive boy named Harrold Fowler—I wonder if you have ever heard of him? He has hunted a lot in China, India, East Africa etc and found some new specimen of sheep which are in the Smithsonian.*

Kermit had never heard of Harrold Fowler and could only hope he would be stampeded by his own sheep. It was presumptuous, he knew, to be jealous. He and Belle had plighted no troth. They had never trembled in each other's company. They had merely . . . got along. But surely it was Belle's intention to give him these glimpses of *other* suitors, *other* paths she might follow. With a sinking feeling, he realized that his own paths were converging down to one—one woman, one heart.

THE WORK OF BUILDING bridges through the wilderness was hard, hot, exhausting: eleven hours a day, seven days a week. (He had counted on having Sundays off.) At night, he went to sleep with French poetry: Villon's ballads, Ronsard's sonnets. He was adopted by a dog that he found one evening sleeping in his open suitcase; he named the mongrel Trigueiro.

In August, he was riding a heavy steel joist to the top of a new bridge when the derrick that held the joist broke. There was no time to jump to safety—only time to drop. He fell a good thirty or thirty-five feet, by his own calm reckoning, and as he tumbled down the ravine, bouncing from rock to rock, he was amazed by how quiet he was in mind even as his body registered each new insult. At last, when he could fall no farther, he rolled onto his back and saw the steel joist coming straight for him. He closed his eyes and waited to die.

Against all expectations, the ballast of steel caromed off an outcropping and sailed right over him. As they hauled him out of the ravine, his first thought was: *Wait till she hears of this.*

Writing to her from the Hospital Samaritano in São Paulo, he was careful to play down his injuries: two broken ribs, some water on the knee. A great deal of scarring on the head and hands, *which looks bad and means nothing.* He was really lucky to get out at all, but he was hopeful (and here is where truth gave way to bluff) that, in a few days, he might be able to join a hunting party at one of the local *faziendas.*

Her reply came a month later on Hotel Astoria stationery and carried just the note of gentle chiding he had hoped for. *I had visions of you spending long weeks of suffering flat on your back,* she wrote, *instead of which you've apparently been having glorious sport, hunting & riding, etc. So much sympathy wasted!*

There followed some softening. *I wish you could be here to browse in old book stores with me. I can't go without a maid, and they are such a nuisance. Besides I don't know what is good and what's trash—I've begun Spanish but haven't gotten that far. Some of the old bindings are musty and I long to know what's inside.*

Then the old twist of the knife: *I have gleaned so much interesting information about Spain from a wonderful man Archer Huntington. . . .*

IN THE MIDST OF his recovery, one bright light remained on his horizon: Mother and Father were coming.

They had embarked, improbably enough, on a goodwill tour of South America, and who better to shepherd them through Brazil than their son, with his hard-won knowledge of the native terrain? By the time he boarded the SS *Voltaire* for Bahia, Kermit was walking without a limp. Only his heart was hobbled. He stayed on deck for most of the voyage, watching the foam furrowing out from the steamer's prow, and his thoughts flew to the other side of the Atlantic. To Belle, glittering like a plumed bird in the Spanish sun, smiling at princes and embassy secretaries and penniless Madrid poets. Waiting for them to stake their claims.

The test, he realized, had just begun on the piazza at Sagamore. The critical moment was now.

He went down to his cabin. Lit the lantern and read her letter once more. Then he carefully refolded it and set it on the nightstand. He blew out the lantern and sat for some time in the darkness. He could no longer consent to imagine the Archer Huntingtons of the world. To imagine Belle as their wife.

And yet how could she possibly choose him over them? What did he have to offer beyond a name?

The long days of tropical labor had given him, it was true, a casing of sinew and muscle, but nothing had changed the fact that he was a quiet, moody cuss, given to gray spells and black silence. "Byronic brooding," his sister had once teased him, "without the poetry." He shrank from the public eye; he tossed his hat in no ring. He was, in everything that mattered, a second son.

He thought of his brother Ted, living a squire's life in Manhattan with his wife and daughter and pipe, selling bonds on Wall Street, playing squash with his old Porcellian Club pals. Was that the only life that counted? Kermit could just as soon make a wage and raise a family in São Paulo or Buenos Aires as New York. And when South America paled—when too many of the blank spaces had been filled in—he would find somewhere even more remote. He would live a life of the body and a life of the mind, too, mastering new languages, corresponding with literary lights, holding forth at salons. He would be respected—lionized, even—by the small society that cohered around him. And standing at his side, bathing him in the effulgence of her devotion, would be a woman. One woman.

HE DINED THAT NIGHT at the captain's table but excused himself early and carried a cordial of cognac down to his cabin. He closed his eyes, rested his forehead on the trestle of his hands. Then he drew out a sheet of the ship's stationery and began to write.

Dear Belle, I've been thinking about this letter for a very long time. . . .

Right out of the gate, he felt it: the inadequacy of mere words. Where was Camões when he needed him? Where were all the Portuguese balladeers he'd been committing to heart? Here, at the brink of immolation, they abandoned him.

I couldn't go on writing you and not tell you for I do love you so very much, and tho' I know how very unworthy I am of you, I can't help writing you this. . . . I would do anything in the world for you Belle, leave anything, or go anywhere if I felt you wanted me to do that; for I must try to prove myself in some way worthy of you, no matter in how small a way. But oh Belle if we were . . .

Were what?

. . . we could go anywhere and succeed, I know that.

Only he didn't know it. He knew nothing. This letter, which was to be the purest expression of his love, was just the map of his chaos. With a keening groan, he rushed to his conclusion.

Please, please forgive me if this is all wrong to you, and I should never have spoken, but it was more than I could do not to write for I love you so, that all the time that you were so far away just seems so much time when I'm not living but perhaps might be. . . . I've wished and prayed so much that you might you love me, and perhaps you might . . .

And, once again, he backed away.

. . . tho' I can't seem to believe that you could.

A single gritty tear was scorching its way down his cheek.

Good night, Belle, and please forgive me if I'm doing wrongly.

It was the most equivocal proposal a man had ever written, but he hadn't the strength for a second draft. He mailed it as soon as the ship landed. It would take two weeks to get to Madrid, another two weeks to get her reply. A *month,* at minimum, before he would know.

He was fortunate that his father's presence was so coveted. Every day brought a whirligig of formal luncheons and dinners, men with gold teeth pumping the Colonel's hand and girls bringing sprays of corsage orchids and grandmamas offering him their cigars and German padres sounding out his theology and officers' wives pouring him cups of yerba maté.

Even though plans were afoot for some sort of jungle voyage, Kermit was only too happy to leave his father and his coconspirators to their plans and dig into the shelves of the English Library or catch the trolley to Corcovado. One morning, he took a hike from Tijuca. He followed the Jesuits' old moss-grown aqueduct and saw on one side the sea and on the other the rolling carpet of mountain shade. Was this on Belle's list, he wondered?

Coming back down the Rua Aqueduto, he was hailed by a messenger boy.

"*Uma carta,* Senhor."

A letter, addressed to him. He recognized the handwriting at once and stuffed the envelope into his pocket. For another day, it seemed to pulse there, breathing out its secret contents. All those fragments of regret—he could just imagine them. *You can't know how honored I am . . . I only wish . . . Hope you'll understand . . . Dear fellow . . .*

He was a coward not to open it. Why should the words of a young debutante hold such terror for a man of promise? The next afternoon, he strolled over to the Rotisserie Américain. He sat outside and ordered a tumbler of cachaça, and, by the daggerlike light of the Brazilian sun, he read:

Dear Kermit, I'm very glad you did send the letter, because
I do love you, and will marry you. I don't know how, or why
you should love me—perhaps because I too have prayed,—&
been unhappy—and now you love me and my heart is very
full—What have I done that God should choose me out of
all the world for you to love—but as He has done this, so
perhaps He will make me a little worthy of your love. May
He keep you safe for me! I love you, Kermit, I love you.

He left without paying for his drink. He found the old man in a
rattan chair in the hotel lobby, scissoring away at another speech.

"What's wrong?" the Colonel asked. But all he had to do was
look at the letter still clutched in Kermit's hand. "*Well,* now! I believe
congratulations are in order. Oh, but you've chosen wisely, Kermit.
She's a dear girl."

A dear girl, yes. He was going to marry the dearest girl in the
world. The girl who had read *War and Peace* just for his sake and
had "enjoyed it all thoroughly" (though she didn't "agree with Tol-
stoy's theories"), and had she really read it, and did it really matter?

"Of course, you'll have to tell Mother right away. You don't want
her reading it in the papers, for heaven's sake. Remember, please,
how women are when it comes to their sons' weddings. They *do* like
to stick their oars in, so be prepared. Just smile and nod and get the
hell out of the room, can you manage that?"

That's exactly what Kermit was prepared to do when he knocked
on his mother's door. Smile, nod, get out.

She was standing by the window, looking down at the Avenida
Beira Mar. She didn't turn when he walked in, but she must have
known who it was, because her very next words were:

"I need you to go with your father."

"Go with him?" Kermit closed the door behind him. "Where?"

"Into the jungle. The old fool is bound and determined to go,
and God help us all when he does."

The edge in her voice was enough to stop any reply in his throat. And then her blue-gray eyes found his.

"You *must* go with him, Kermit."

"Why?"

She took his hand between hers. "Father is not so young as he used to be, you know that. He needs someone to look out for him. You can be certain *he* won't."

"But my work . . ."

"Oh, you can ask for a leave of absence, can't you?"

"I already have. Just to come here. It's—it's not that simple, Mother; I'm an *employee* now."

"I think it *is* that simple," she answered with a placid smile. "You need only tell them who your traveling companions are. Rondon's name alone should suffice. And if you need further incentive, tell them about all the contacts you'll be making along the way. All the land you'll be surveying. Why, it's nothing more than a business trip."

She had thought it out, of course.

"Mother, you don't understand. I'm getting my leg up. I have *men* depending on me . . . a great deal of *work* to be done."

"It will still be there when you get back."

She spoke with an air of finality, as though she were shutting all his objections into a casket. But when he made no reply, the edge of asperity stole back into her voice.

"You went with him to Africa, you know. Without a second thought."

"That was different, Mother. That was *sport.*"

"And just think what sport you'll have in the jungle! You and Father will be hunting creatures nobody's ever seen before!"

"Mother, it's not—I can't—"

He pulled his hand free from hers. Jammed it into his pocket, felt the answering touch of Belle's letter. The silence piled on top of them.

"I'm to be married," he said at last.

There was the lightest of pauses.

"I supposed as much," she said.

A sag in her voice. The same sag in her mouth. There was no use being surprised; Mother had never really taken to Belle. "The Fair One with Golden Locks," she'd called her in an unguarded moment.

If Kermit hadn't felt so cornered, he might have found some way to explain to his mother why she was wrong—wrong! He had just persuaded the prettiest girl in the world to choose him as her husband. He would be a married man and, in due time, a father. Here at last, at the ripe age of twenty-four, his life was moving forward. In the same way that the Brazilian rail line was moving forward—against nature's own dictates, through sheer inhuman dogged persistence.

"We would like to be married in June," he said. "In Madrid."

"I see. June."

She folded her head down, then raised it again.

"Well, then. That still leaves you plenty of time for your trip."

"Mother, please. *You* should know better than anyone, there are . . . preparations—"

Though at this moment he was hard-pressed to say what they were. The ring, of course. Clothes—a great deal of clothes. Invitations—dear God, how many people would they have to invite? Should Cousin Philip be best man?

"Father needs you," she said.

"He doesn't."

"Kermit." Her voice began to shag over with weariness. "Don't you understand how this family works by now? *Father needs his scope.* And we are the ones who give it to him."

IN THAT MOMENT, KERMIT could only recall the message his brother had cabled him last year on election night. Ted had been stationed the whole evening at Progressive Party headquarters in New York, poring over returns. Alone among his father's advisers, he could see where the votes were heading—away from Roosevelt, away from Taft, straight to Wilson—and by evening's end there was only one question remaining in Ted's mind, and that was the question he fired off to Kermit in São Paulo.

WHAT WILL OLD LION DO?

Kermit had misinterpreted at first. Father would do what any gentleman does in such a situation. He would send a congratulatory note to Wilson. He would accept the results with good humor and contentment. He would call for a united front as America faced its foes and rallied its strength, et cetera, et cetera.

It was only later, under the glow of two caipirinhas, that Kermit grasped the real tenor of Ted's question. What would the old man do with the remainder of his days? How would he keep the adventure alive?

In the months that followed the election, the Colonel professed himself busy, content. He saw old friends, fraternized with Rough Riders. He planned lecture tours, a scholarly talk on History as Literature, a scientific study of African game animals. He had the queer notion of writing his autobiography. His letters to Kermit were full of the usual bluster and cheer.

But the letters from Mother spoke of how quiet it was at Sagamore. No telegraphers or typewriters. No delegations of potentates. No reporters clamoring for the great man's last word. No shouts ringing up and downstairs. None of that steady current of well-wishers at the front door, bringing their offerings—their pies, their knitted scarves and mittens, their babies waiting to be sanctified. A man may lose many things, but he may not lose a people's love without some cost.

What *was* the old man going to do?

This was not a disinterested inquiry, as Kermit grasped even then. Whatever course the Colonel decided on, the family would have to close ranks around it. It was what they had always done; it was what they were put on earth to do. To give an old man his proper scope.

And what of my *scope?* thought Kermit. *Am I to be nothing more than a satellite for the rest of my life?*

It was an irony that had long vexed him, more for never having uttered it out loud—that in becoming more of a man, he must be less of a Roosevelt, and in becoming more of a Roosevelt, he must be less of a man.

And what of Belle? How much further her pale specter receded from him with each passing second. Oh, Mother was really asking too much of him! Damn it, she was! To sacrifice not just himself but the woman he loved. The thought of it was like oil of vitriol leaking through every pore, and what made it even more scalding was the realization that he was already losing—giving way, as he always had, before a superior will.

"Very well," he said, in a small dead voice.

Smiling, his mother took him once more by the hand.

"I knew I could count on you. . . ."

THAT VERY AFTERNOON, HE sent a cable to Brazil Railway. And another to Belle. DON'T WORRY. WEDDING STILL ON.

He was now officially a member of the Roosevelt-Rondon Expedition, and no one seemed more surprised than the old man himself.

"See here, my boy, are you quite sure? I'd feel rotten taking you from your work. You've only just got on your feet."

Ah, yes, thought Kermit. *But you need your scope, don't you?*

"It won't be too long," he heard himself say.

I'M TO BE MARRIED in June . . . married in June . . .

KERMIT AWOKE TO BLACKNESS.

Utter blackness, swallowing his hand the moment he tried to penetrate it.

Carefully, he canvassed his other senses. Touch: He could feel his own leg, yes. Smell: His nostrils picked out must and earth and something like straw. Hearing: He could hear his own breath, in ragged pulses. Taste: Yes. He could taste the bitterness rising up inside him—coming out of his mouth in a hot heavy gruel. As he wiped his mouth clean, a single outline startled from the darkness. And then another and another. All vanishing as quickly as they appeared.

Then, from the nothingness, a petal of light budded forth. It swelled and, to Kermit's astonishment, began to divide. Into an arm. A shoulder. The curve of a jaw.

Someone's there.

5

It was a woman. A young woman.

Not Belle; no, that would have been too much to hope for. This was a woman he had never seen before. She was holding the lit branch of a tree. (*My torch,* he remembered, with a rush of sadness.) The light whittled her into such a confusion of shadow and non-shadow that it took him some time to grasp that her bare arm led to a bare shoulder, and this shoulder sloped to a bare breast. . . .

For a moment he thought he had slipped back in time—just a little—back to his days in the Xingu Valley. Naked women had been something of a staple. Who could blame a fellow, after a long week of laying railway ties and raising up bridges, if he wanted a few minutes in a darkened room? The girl didn't even have to be smiling. (She almost never was.) She had only to stand there, in a state of complicity. Saying . . .

Como vai você? How are you?

The same question this young woman was asking him now.

"Como vai você?"

"Bem," he managed to mutter. *"Obrigado."*

(Even under duress, the old courtesies.)

"Pardon," he went on in Portuguese. "What day is it?"

"I could not tell you."

"What time is it?"

"It is night."

"Where are we?"

"Here."

Here.

"No," he protested. "I was . . . Where are my comrades? *Meus amigos?*"

"Oh, your friends. They are far away now."

How far away? A mile? Two? Ten? There was no way of knowing.

"You are here with us," she added encouragingly. *"Na nossa aldeia."*

In our village.

He raised himself up on his elbows, felt another wave of nausea. Squinting into the emptiness, he began to dredge up the last fragments of memory.

The jungle at twilight. That strange whinny. The monkey that wasn't a monkey. Those shapes dropping from the canopy.

Father.

With a rumbling groan, he rolled to his knees and swept his hands across the ground. Amazed to find the darkness springing away at his touch—until he realized the woman was standing over him, following him with her torch.

The Colonel lay no more than five feet away. Heavy and crumpled. White as cream.

"Father . . ."

The old man's spectacles, still intact, dangled from his left ear. His mouth had swung ajar, and his hand had curled into a half talon. But the only thing Kermit could see in that moment was the cockroach that had climbed onto the old man's face. Four inches long, translucently pale, with softly thrumming wings. Crawling through the gray underbrush of the old man's mustache.

Shuddering, Kermit knocked the insect away. He lowered his ear to the old man's lips, then to his chest, then back to his lips. Waited, in a madness of suspense, for a sign of life. And heard at last the stream of breath, rasping but steady.

Tears stabbed his eyes. He heard the woman say:

"He will be well."

"No," he answered, smearing a forearm across his face. "He will not be well."

"I am speaking truly. The . . . the *physician*—" She was stopped by the squelch of her own laughter. "You will forgive me. You must forgive me. I haven't spoken Portuguese in so long. It sounds funny now. What I would like to say is, the physician has looked at him."

"Physician," Kermit repeated. "You mean some . . . some *feiti-ceiro* with feathers and beads shook a rattle over him and declared him well. Is that what you mean?"

She said nothing.

"My father is not well. He has not been well for some time. He will need a great deal more than rattles."

And what wouldn't he have given, in that moment, to be proven wrong? To see the Colonel come roaring to his feet. Filling the air with words. *Rot! Bunk! Flubdub!*

Kermit staggered to his own feet—and felt his head slam against a thick, rough thatching.

"You are very tall," said the young woman.

"Yes," he said, clutching his skull.

"What is your name?"

He looked at her for a long minute.

"Kermit," he said.

"Kurr . . . meet."

"I am this man's son. I have . . . I have enjoyed very friendly relations with the Indians of Brazil."

Wincing at his own phrase: *friendly relations.*

"Indians," she said.

"Yes, like . . ."

Like you, he wanted to propose. Only he was beginning to see she was a bit of an anomaly, too. Yes, her dark hair was parted down the middle in the native fashion, but her nose was long and full, her eyes—for these he could see clearly—a lightly flecked hazel. For the first time, he began to feel a trickle of hope.

"Well, now," he said. "You have the advantage of me, Senhorita. You know my name, and I don't yet know yours."

"My *name.*" For some time, she was silent. "Luz. Except that nobody calls me this anymore."

"That's a very pretty name. May I ask you something, Luz? Do you think you might help us?"

"I don't see how." Her brows crowded down. "Oh, wait! I can help you talk to them. How do you say that? The person who does such a thing."

"*Intérprete.*"

"*In-tér-prete.*"

"Luz, I don't mean helping us that way. I mean: Can you help us leave this place?"

"Oh, decidedly not."

Such a prissy formulation that, in different circumstances, he might have laughed.

"You speak our language," he pressed on. "One of our languages. You understand better than anyone that a great crime has occurred. My father and I, we have been kidnapped. Taken against our will."

She nodded absently.

"And where there is crime," he went on, "there must be punishment, is that not so? Any minute, I assure you, our comrades will come for us. There will be much bloodshed, do you understand that? For your people. I would not want this fate to fall on you. I can . . . I can give you my word as a gentleman that if you take us back to our friends—back to the river—you might—"

"I am not so sure your friends will be able to find you."

She spoke without a trace of triumph. If anything, she was pitying him.

"This man . . ." He jabbed his finger at the Colonel's unconscious form. "He is a figure of great renown. The leader of a great nation. He has met *kings*—and . . . and . . ."

Here was the trouble: Kermit had never had to apotheosize the old man before. The world had always done that.

"He is a great warrior. He has won wars and fought injustice. He has . . . *built canals*."

"Canals," she echoed. "What is he called?"

But the name produced only a faint sadness.

"I don't know it," she said.

"Many people know it. They will pay large sums, great treasures for his return. Gold and silver."

"Oh, gold," she said.

How strange her Portuguese was. Stiff and brittle, as though every word were tottering on stilts.

A fine mist of sweat had formed along Kermit's temples.

"Luz, listen to me. I think you are made of finer stuff than the men who took us. I think . . . I think there is great kindness in you."

"Do you have a wife?"

For several seconds, he was incapable of answering.

"I am engaged. To be married."

"You are marrying someone."

"Yes."

"What is her name?"

"Her name is Belle."

Once more, his hand, without any prompting from him, flew to his chest. The packet of letters, still pressed against his sternum.

May He keep you safe for me! . . . I love you, Kermit, I love you.

In a flash, it was Belle standing in this dark enclosure. Belle's naked shoulders, burning in the darkness. Belle's breasts . . .

He clenched his eyes shut.

"I spoke something wrong," said Luz.

"No, it's . . . Being a gentleman, I am not used to conversing—at length, I mean—with women in a . . . a state of undress."

"Undress." She stared down at herself, then crooked an arm loosely across her breasts. "Are you engaged to anyone else, Senhor Kermit?"

"No one else."

"Ah."

She turned away. In the flickering light, he could make out the braid of her spinal cord.

"You're not one of them," he said.

"I don't know what you mean."

"I believe you must have a home somewhere else. Somewhere you'd like to return to. We might find it for you, we might take you back there."

She said nothing.

"The men in our party," he went on. "Our friends, they come from all over. From Brazil, from *America*."

"America."

The lightest glimmer to her voice.

"Would you like to go there?" he asked. "We can arrange that. We can arrange anything. All we ask is that you lead us back to the river. And then we will *all* be free, do you see? In America, every-one is free."

"Free," she echoed. With such a dying fall that it laid waste to his hope.

All this time he had wasted on rhetoric, on persuasion. When what was truly needed—he could hear the Colonel barking it—was *action*. They weren't bound, for God's sake; they weren't manacled.

They could easily overpower this young woman. They could leave whenever they wished.

But already he grasped the limits of this freedom. For even if he managed to drag the old man to his feet and get him walking again on that rummy leg, how would they find their way back—in the very blackest night? They were every bit as helpless as if they had been bound.

"We are forbearing men," he heard himself say. "We wish ill on no one. We came here only to map a river."

"Map?"

"Yes, to . . . to make a map. Latitude and longitude."

She gazed at him in mild astonishment. "Why ever should you do that?"

"So that others might know. So that . . ."

So that they might come.

The first note of protest crept into her voice. "What if we don't wish to be known?"

"You can only remain hidden for so long. Civilization will find you."

"Oh," she said, shrugging. "Civilization."

His head was an agony, his eyes like stones. But he forced himself to move in slow, ever-broadening circles.

"Very well, Senhorita. Since you refuse to be our guide, I would ask you to be our messenger. Tell the men who brought us here that we wish to speak with them."

"They will," she answered. "They will speak with you."

His hand brushed against more thatching. They were indoors.

"How many are there?" he asked, slowly sketching out the space.

"Oh, a few, I suppose."

His hand found a corner. Then a new wall, sprouting at a loose angle to the last.

It's a hut of some kind. Which means there must be a way out. A door, an opening.

He kept moving, and in the very next second the wall fell away, and his hand met emptiness. He felt a lick of steam on his face. Heard a rustling.

"Senhor Kermit?" called Luz.

"Yes?"

"They are ready for you."

Given a few more minutes, he might have seen them for himself. But only now were his dark-adapting eyes able to pick out those *other* eyes, staring out from the blackness.

They've been there the whole time, he thought. *Waiting.*

They moved quickly, and with such a grace and common purpose that he had no thought of resistance. Even as their hands were fastening around him, he heard Luz murmur:

"You must not be afraid."

6

IN THE SPLASHES OF FIRELIGHT, HE SAW THEM FULLY.

Twelve men, all told. No taller than his clavicle, but mighty in sum—lean and smooth and sinewy, with armlets and hawk-feather headdresses and swaths of bark armor around their waists and long-bows that stood six feet high, and in each bow a fire-hardened bamboo arrow. Kermit had only to recall Trigueiro's final moments to grasp how much force it must have taken to draw back that rigid wooden frame and send the shaft flying.

One of the men now stepped forward—set slightly apart from his kinsmen by his air of barely contained ferocity and by the scar that took the place of his right eyebrow. Grunting softly, he jabbed the point of his bow into the ground. From the darkness beyond the circle came a woman, plumper and rounder than Luz, the beads around her wrists clicking as she set a bowl by Kermit's foot. Food fumes rose up in an unbroken stream.

"You are to eat," murmured Luz.

"I will not."

A gentleman never obliges his captors. That's what the first voice said. And the second voice said: *Don't be an idiot.*

It was the second voice that made his eyes sting and his stomach contract. He dropped to one knee. Gazed down at those grayish-brown morsels, still simmering from the fire.

It will make you stronger. You need your strength.

The smell had crawled inside him now.

With a groan, he snatched up the bowl.

He sawed the food into two portions. Scooped up his share and ate it right out of his cupped hands. And when his hands were empty, he sat back on his haunches (grimacing at the abscess on his left buttock) and began to lick his fingers. Sucked each one clean and then swept his forearm across his mouth and licked the forearm.

He looked down at that bowl, with its uneaten share.

He knew what Father would say. Oh, he knew well. *The theft of food comes next to murder as a crime and should by rights be punished as such.*

Strange how vivid the old man's voice sounded in his ears. Kermit could hear it even now, ringing the years away. . . .

"Did you eat the rest of the gooseberries, Kermit?"

"No, Father."

"We agreed to leave them for Ted, didn't we?"

"I know."

"Are you quite sure you didn't take them?"

"Yes, sir."

"Because if you *did*—well, now, to take something that wasn't yours from your own flesh and blood, that's not in the gentleman's code, is it, Kermit?"

"No, sir."

"You like to go exploring, don't you, Kermit?"

"Yes, sir."

"And you know that nearly the worst crime an explorer can commit against his fellow explorers is to take their food from them. Why, it's very nearly as bad as murder."

"Yes, sir."

"So I will ask you once again, and if you don't tell me the truth like a little gentleman, I believe I will be the saddest man on the face of this earth."

It was the worst threat he could have uttered. Making his father sad would have been like putting out the sun.

"I'm sorry. . . . I'm sorry. . . ."

"I'M SORRY," HE WHISPERED, as that other voice sang out from inside.

He'll never know it's gone. Who would tell him?

Plunging his hands into the earth, Kermit dragged up strands of mud and smeared them across his lips. But the taste, the *taste* of that meat stayed. And, once more, his gaze swerved back to that plain wooden bowl. . . .

In the end, he was stopped by the scent.

A *larger* scent. Ripe and delirious. He raised his face to it and saw, framed between two of the warriors, a great fire, hissing sparks.

There, at the fire's edge, flickering in and out of the light, a single human hand.

He threw up his dinner as quickly as he'd eaten it. Not a quiet disgorgement but a chain of convulsions, his body protesting the whole way: *No. No.* He had never been so at war with himself.

When he was done—his stomach even emptier inside him, his shirt rimed with vomit—they took hold of him once more. They dragged him away from the fire, and they laid him on the damp ground.

Still his stomach kept convulsing, so violently that his whole body began to buck. It was a measure of his disorientation that, when they began to put their fingers to him, applying the viscous smear to his face and chest and arms, he assumed they were curing him.

Sure enough, the bucking began to subside, and a calmness took hold of him. With each passing second, he felt less tethered to himself.

He gazed at his fingers. They were no longer his fingers. His legs weren't his legs. Even his head—bearer of all his terrors—grew lighter, and heavier, too. Try as he might, he couldn't lift it.

"Be brave," he heard Luz call. "Be brave, Senhor Kermit. . . ."

Move, he commanded himself.

But nothing obeyed. Only his eyes; only these were fully awake, registering the exact moment when they dragged out the Colonel and applied the same white unction to his face and neck and arms.

"Stop," whispered Kermit. "You . . ."

You can't.

Knowing how absurd it was as he thought it. They could. They *were.* It seemed to him that he could already see the paralysis stealing into his father's body, layer by layer.

The villagers worked in silence, and it was only when their project was done that they gave themselves over to sound. The very strangest of symphonies: a cacophony of animal sounds. Note-for-note imitations of macaws and jacus. Tapirs and capuchins and screamer storks. And spider monkeys, yes. All indistinguishable from the real thing. The sounds shrilled and thickened as the twelve warriors slowly converged on their two captives.

So this is how it will be, thought Kermit.

How many times had he died in his own fancy, but it had always been on a battlefield, surrounded by sighs and tears. Witnesses. There would be none of that here. Only these *sounds,* jangling and soaring.

When the sounds had reached their farthest extremity, they began unexpectedly to fall away. Voice by voice.

And when the last sound had died out, Kermit's eyes trembled open. Closed again. Opened again. The villagers were gone. He and Father were alive.

FOR SOME TIME HE lay there, numbed and prone, on the knotted ground, listening to the shallow timbre of his breath. The forest clattered with crickets. Beetles and millipedes rustled through the leaf rot.

He thought of Belle.

Belle, as she had described herself in her last letter. Sitting by her window, looking westward to the sea . . .

. . . and out across the world to you—and oh Kermit I want you so tonight—You don't know yet that I love you and won't for many many long days, and after that there will be more endless days and nights and weeks before I can have even one word from you Kermit—my Kermit—and you love me! The wonder of it all . . .

"Belle . . ."

And even the name wouldn't come out. Just a dry croak. He closed his eyes and drifted into a half sleep. And then woke with a start.

It was raining.

Hard straight lines, catching and pooling in the leaves and then charging for earth. For several minutes altogether, he could see nothing else. No sky, no trees. Just rain. Down and down it came, pummeling his half-dead skin, and when at last it was finished, he lay there, stunned and still, like chiseled marble.

His nerves were beginning to reawaken. From somewhere near his shoulder blade, he felt a faint liquid pressure. It scaled the column of his neck and pushed through the tangle of his beard and all the way to the outcropping of his nose.

He knew it, finally, by its mass. A river of army ants.

Hundreds of them in a blind, chattering phalanx, searching for prey, never guessing what a torture their passage was to him. Every foot, every antenna, every tarsal hook. They swarmed over him, *colonized* him pore by pore, and, paralyzed as he was, he could lift neither finger nor foot to stop them. On and on they came, and when the last ant had abandoned the last square of him, his throat pushed out a long gasp.

There was no time for relief, for new sounds were rolling out of the underbrush. One, in particular, that seemed to beat a space of silence around it. Kermit had only to hear it, and he was once more exhorting himself.

Move. Move.

But the only thing he could move was his head—and only an inch or two. Just enough to angle toward the sound and to find, staring out from the bushes, a pair of amber eyes, blinking.

He knew these eyes.

Just three months ago, he and the Colonel had been invited to Las Palmeiras, Senhor de Barras's ranch on the Rio Taquari. A special treat was in store for them. They were to be given the chance to hunt for jaguar, king of South American game. The old man was no longer so avid a hunter as he used to be, but, being a good guest, he announced himself agreeable. It took them a long day of slogging through the marshes on shabby little horses before they came on fresh tracks at the edge of the jungle. From there, it was short work. The Colonel shot a female jaguar perched among the forked limbs of a taruman tree; Kermit, for his part, shot a male out of a fig tree. Since then, he had given the two animals no more than a second of thought.

Until tonight.

For now the wheel—the "Wheel of Things," a Buddhist might have said—had spun the other direction, and a jaguar, perhaps some near relation of the dead cats on the Taquari, was coming for *them*. Wishing very much to return the favor.

Oh, it was true, jaguars rarely attacked humans. But how many humans were as helpless as Kermit and Theodore Roosevelt in this exact moment? The pickings could not have been much easier.

Kermit watched as the gem eyes advanced by inches. From behind him, he heard a strange straggling wheeze. It was the Colonel. Making a sound that could scarcely be decoded as a word.

"*Heee . . .*"

The sound tapered away but came back even stronger.

"He . . . shall . . . make no . . . meal of us. . . ."

"No," whispered Kermit.

And added to himself: *He'll make a meal of just* one *of us.*

With a terrifying swiftness, the prayer rose up.

Take Father.

AFTERWARD, KERMIT WOULD BE unable to find the demarcation line between the jaguar's approach—the presentiment, no, the certainty of doom—and what followed. Indeed, it was hard even to speak of something following, for that implied a progression from one thing to the next, and nothing about what happened was logical or sequential. It might have played out across two perpendicular axes, intersecting for no more than a few seconds.

All he could say finally was that, as he and the Colonel lay helpless in the night, something shifted. Everything shifted.

The stars sprang back, the trees shook, the ground bent. Kermit's own breath fled from him at sharp angles. In the next instant, the jaguar was changed to a creature of suffering.

"Rrowwww-*ohhhh . . .*"

Never had Kermit heard an animal attain such a refinement of agony and subjection. The wretched cat howled, *howled,* as if every last one of the world's torments had been concentrated into the purest possible solution and dropped into each pore. The jungle snatched the sound and doubled it, so that you might have thought there were two jaguars, or ten, or twenty, all trying to outdo one another for martyrdom.

It was a terrible sound, so terrible that Kermit was on the verge of screaming back, when the cry began unexpectedly to subside.

First into paroxysms, then shudders, then sighs, then a long sibilant rattle.

But as terrible as the cry had been, the quiet that followed was worse. Still worse was the low and steady lapping that now filled their ears. An oddly gentle sound, like a kitten slurping up milk. The jaguar's conqueror was now reaping its reward—drinking its fill.

And preparing to do the same to us, thought Kermit.

His numbed lips trembled into speech. "Our Father . . . who art in heaven . . ."

In the darkness, he heard his father's counterburden. No prayer at all but a snatch of old verse.

"Out of the night that covers me, Black as the pit from pole to pole . . ."

Still the lapping went on—unquenchable, implacable—reverberating in the air around them, caressing their necks, their flanks and groins.

"I thank whatever gods may be," croaked the Colonel. *"For my unconquerable soul."*

This time, Kermit's eyes were wide open. He was magically curious. He longed to look the thing in the eye.

But there was nothing to see. Only the sensation of absence—something *lately* there, its echo still lingering in every atom of air and soil. In Kermit's own grunts.

"Huhh . . . huhh . . ."

The ground righted itself. The sky tumbled back into place. One by one, the jungle's night sounds crept into hearing. Every creature celebrating its deliverance.

And Kermit, too exhausted to celebrate, watched himself vanish down a long inky river.

I'm to be . . . I'm to be married. . . .

HE SLEPT LIKE A dead man.

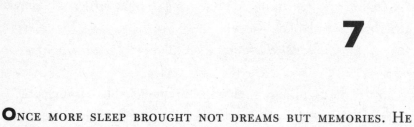

7

ONCE MORE SLEEP BROUGHT NOT DREAMS BUT MEMORIES. HE found himself tumbling out of the tropics . . . out of the twentieth century . . . landing finally on an August afternoon in Sagamore. Here was his sister Ethel, transformed back into a girl, all pins and hems, breaking into his reverie.

"Kermit! We're playing hide-and-go-seek in the barn!"

He was once again a boy—eyeing her like an old man. "Who else is playing?"

"Just Ted and me. It's silly to play without a third. You must come!"

She knew enough to know this was the one game he would consent to play with them—because (and this she didn't know) it was the one game that left him, for long intervals, as alone as he was the rest of the day.

"It's not the sardines kind of hide-and-seek?" (He had a disagreeable memory of being packed in a broom closet with four young relations, praying to be found.)

"No," said Ethel. "The regular kind."

"Oh, fine."

The reluctance was mostly a show, for in fact he had found the perfect hiding place. Not in the loft; that was too obvious. Nor in any of the tunnels the children had made in the hayricks—you could hide there for only so long before being found. In the course of his private explorations, Kermit had found beneath two loose floorboards a small earthen cavity, where, if a boy didn't mind field mice for company, he might lie concealed for quite a while. Even better: If the day was sunny, he would have enough light streaming through the crevices to read, uninterrupted, for hours.

Relishing that prospect, he strolled into the barn with a copy of *The Prince and the Pauper*. Ted began the count, and Kermit waited until his sister had ducked out of sight before easing himself into his burrow. He smiled as he heard Ethel scuttling . . . Ted thumping . . . the muffled shouts of discovery or near-discovery. A stray horsefly circled around his head. Kermit brushed it away, and as his hand settled back to earth, something answered his touch. A piece of paper, wedged like a forgotten playbill between two posts.

Idly, he tugged the paper free, turned it over. It wasn't a paper at all but a photograph. A picture of a man perhaps thirty or thirty-five years, wearing a top hat, a short-tailed black morning coat, and white peg-top trousers. A gentleman equestrian by the looks of him, but there was no horse in view and nothing in the picture that should have interested a ten-year-old boy. An hour later, though, he was still looking at it—or, rather, it was looking at him, revealing new congruencies. The mustache: Hadn't he seen one like it somewhere else? The metal-rim spectacles: Yes, they were just like the ones Father used to wear. The face itself: This, too, like Father's, only smoother and thinner, handsomer.

Morning drifted into afternoon. Kermit clambered out of his hole, surprised to find the game long since abandoned and Ethel sitting crossly by the chicken coop.

"Where have you been?" she demanded.

The photograph lay buttoned inside his shirt. He weighed the possibility of brandishing it like pirate booty, but he couldn't imagine it interesting her—it was just a picture, after all—so he left it in place and removed it only that night when his nanny was taking him upstairs.

"Mame," he said. "Who's this?"

She was an old woman now, and it took her almost as long to stop climbing as to start. With a ragged wheeze, she snatched the photograph from him. Her mouth went ever so slightly slack, and he understood now that this was the response he had been hoping for all along; he was thrilled to have produced it. Mame was silent a good long while. Then, in a voice burred with fury, she said:

"Well, there's some as don't want you to know, child, but that's your uncle."

"I don't have an uncle."

"And what do you know about it? You've got a cousin, don't you? Your cousin Eleanor?"

"Yes."

"Well, that's her father, so that makes him your uncle, Master Know-It-All."

Until this moment, Kermit had never considered the possibility of Eleanor having a father. *Or* a mother. He had assumed she'd come into the world exactly as she was now: tall, clumsy, unparented, a train of pity dragging after her.

"Where is my uncle now?" he asked.

"More questions. He's gone to his reward, that's where he is. There's no help for him on this earth, which means you're not to mention him to anybody, do you hear? Not your cousin, not anybody."

"Why not?"

"Don't trouble yourself with that! You do as I ask."

"Father says I may speak to him anytime I want. About anything I like."

"No," she snapped, leaning into him. "Least of all your father."

"Why not?"

"It was his *brother,* child. Oh, sweet Jesus," she hurried on, "you've made me say too much as it is. Listen, Kermit, you must promise me on this very spot never to speak of him again—to *anybody,* now."

"One more question, then."

"You'll be the end of me. *What?*"

"Tell me his name."

She looked at him. Then, in a voice of unusual softness, she said: "Elliott."

ELLIOTT. A PLAIN NAME made extraordinary by the silence that shrouded it, by the fact that it could never be spoken. And how much more extraordinary that this great and forbidding and all-consuming mystery should be entrusted not to Ted, not to Ethel, not to little Archie—but to Kermit! He and he alone would be the one to solve it.

Oh, but the trail was long, fogbound, twisting out of sight, and he had only two pieces of evidence: a name and a picture. It took him some time to grasp (in the manner of his beloved Holmes) that the very absence of clues was in itself a clue. For if Uncle Elliott's memory had been banished so completely from Sagamore, then surely he had committed some great crime, something that had swept him from civilization's embrace.

If that were so, then there must be a record. Kermit began waking himself an hour early every morning to peruse his father's newspapers and journals. (The Colonel was pleased at his son's sophistication.) But though he forded through many thousands of column inches, he could find no trace of Elliott's name.

The larger world was no more forthcoming. If, by chance, a schoolmate of Kermit's made a menacing allusion to Jack the Ripper or Lizzie Borden or John Wilkes Booth, Kermit might lean forward and, in a confidential whisper, say, "I suppose you've heard of my uncle Elliott," and wait to see what answering chord it produced in his listeners' brains. But their only reply was a crease of bafflement, which he then had to erase by pretending he'd been joking all along.

One thing was growing clear: Elliott's crime, whatever it had been, had not yet taken root in popular lore. Kermit would have to find its after-echoes in Elliott's surviving relations.

Was it any wonder that Cousin Eleanor became a creature of such fascination to him? During the infrequent times she came to stay at Sagamore, Kermit would study her with a clinical intent, as though at any moment some confession or affidavit might come flashing from her. So queerly did he peer that Eleanor, despite being his senior by five years, began quailing a little in his presence and did her best to avoid him.

Clearly, he would find no help in that quarter—and wasn't it possible, he considered, that Eleanor was just as ignorant as he was of her father's infamy? She was only fifteen, after all, and young people were allowed to know so little in this world! Knowledge was the closely guarded treasure of adults, who would tell you things—important things—only if they thought you weren't listening. The key, then, was to linger as long as possible at the edges of their gatherings—their receptions and dinners and after-dinner smokes—to become a connoisseur of whispers, asides, blurts, and retractions. It would be exacting work, to be sure, but by staying patient and keeping his ears open, Kermit might begin to assemble a piecemeal biography.

So he did, working over many months to dredge a whole life out of wistful croons (*Poor Elliott . . . Such a charmer . . . What an end . . .*) and dark mutters (*Drank like a fish . . . Ladies not in his own rank . . .*). There was one point on which all sides agreed: Elliott Roosevelt had been a golden child. Gallant, smart, generous, loyal, witty, polished. Loved by all who knew him. A fine shot, a fine dancer, equally at home in the wilderness and in the drawing room. More gifted by most accounts than his older brother, Theodore, but fatally lacking in Theodore's focus and ambition, with the result that his talents tapered away into idleness, lark, mere recreation. He played polo (like a madman). He hunted tigers in Kashmir, elephants in Ceylon. He married a woman he dearly loved and then amused himself by chasing other women, *many* other women, the less suitable, the better.

He drank. Wine and ale and milk punches and mint juleps and sherry and bitters. He drank whatever was in season or out. He drank to remember or else to forget what he had been.

Oh, it was a sad tale, the saddest—and was there not something about this sadness that jibed with Kermit's own nature? Melancholy had crawled into his pores while he was still in his bassinet and had dogged his steps ever since, had turned him into one of those odd children, palely loitering, shunning talk. "The boy with the white head and the black heart," that's what his own mother had called him, and he had accepted both judgments. He was, after all, the blondest of the Roosevelt children and the most darkened by his own thoughts. He would gladly spend hours in perfect silence, exploring the old stable or deploying his white guinea pigs in battle formations, but there were times, too—whole days, perhaps weeks—when even silence was a burden, when keeping himself free of others seemed like the greatest gift he could bestow on them. These were, predictably enough, the times in which his parents most despaired of him. One night he heard them in the library, talking in the strangled timbre he had come to recognize as his birthright.

"God help me," said the old man, "I don't understand him. So damned moody—heavy in spirit. He reminds me of *him,* you know."

Kermit's skin prickled with surprise. He was obviously the subject of that sentence, but who was the object?

"You are not to suggest such a thing," said his mother in an altogether different voice.

"Oh, for the—it was an *observation,* Edith, not a prophesy."

"It is a terrifying observation. Kindly do not make it again."

Another mystery had risen up. Smaller in scope than the one that had consumed him all these months but linked to it in ways he grasped at once. Who else could they be speaking of but Elliott? *Elliott:* The One Who Could Never Be Named. The one who had come into the world, like Kermit, with a white head and a dark heart and had left behind . . . an example. The kind that made mothers tremble.

By chance, Cousin Eleanor came to stay the very next weekend. To Kermit, she was no longer an object of clinical interest but a secret sharer. For the first time he could see that she was more like him than any of his siblings were: quiet, yes, almost comically solemn, averse to chatter, pained by group games. The experience of playing stagecoach with the Colonel so flummoxed her that she had to retire for an hour of solitude.

Something else Kermit couldn't help but notice: Eleanor was poor. Poorer, at any rate, than he was. Her handkerchief was gray with use, and her brown stockings were torn (Ethel tactfully offered new ones), and one of the bows had come off her kid-leather shoes. She came alone by train, without even a governess, in a carriage that had to be rented at the Oyster Bay station. The driver declined to help her with her bags, but the next day he showed up half an hour early to take her back. Peering through the front window, Kermit could see him reclining against the harness, smoking a cigarette. Hatless and indifferent, looking all in all so worldly that a seed of hope sprang up in Kermit. Leaving by the side door and taking the roundabout way by the windmill and the pet cemetery, he stole up behind the carriage and tugged lightly on the driver's cloak.

"Please . . ." Please, *sir,* he nearly said. "Do you know my cousin Eleanor very well?"

"Well enough, I guess."

"Her family, too?"

The driver looked at him. "I've heard tell of 'em."

"Can you tell me, then? What happened to her father?"

One corner of the driver's mouth rose with great deliberation. "Well, now. Who wants to know? And how does he plan to make it worth my while?"

Kermit began to rummage through his pockets. "I could give you a dollar. And seventy-one cents. And a real, genuine Indian arrowhead. From Cooper's Bluff."

"Arrowhead." The man smiled. "A regular J. P. Morgan, ain't you?"

Kermit held out his treasure in both palms, but the man made no motion toward it.

"I'd be glad to tell you," he said, taking another drag of his cigarette. "All about your precious Mr. Elliott."

Here, at the pitch of discovery, Kermit flinched. None of the questions he had been hoarding would stand clear. The only thing that came from his mouth was:

"He drank. . . ."

"Oh, that he did," agreed the driver. "Worse than any shanty mick, that's what my dad told me."

"How did he die? Did he . . ."

Did he drink the wrong thing? That was the only way Kermit could imagine a man drinking himself to death. Swallowing something bad without knowing it. Cyanide, strychnine.

"He died no better 'n anyone else," said the driver. "My brother used to see him—cripes, this was seven, eight years back—your precious Mr. Elliott; he was living up on West 102nd. Shacking up with some slut, under some made-up name or other. And his wife just barely in the grave. And his *daughter* . . ." Half grinning, the driver cocked a thumb toward the house. "You've *seen* her, haven't you?"

Two things were dawning in Kermit's brain. He disliked this man. And his dislike was actually *feeding* the man, drawing the words from his mouth.

"Well, now, consider the sad case of your Mr. Elliott. All his fine friends have cut him. His money's gone; his fine reputation, that's gone. So what's a gentleman like him to do? Why, he goes and jumps out a window, that's what he does." The driver stole a quick glance at the house. "Even *then* he couldn't finish the job. Held on for a few more days before he kicked it. And what did he leave behind? An ugly daughter and a bastard son. Not a dime to his name. It never fails to amaze me, the doings of the civilized class."

With a light flick, the driver tossed his cigarette butt into the air. It described a high arc and landed just short of Kermit's foot. The boy was about to draw his boot away when the driver grabbed him by the collar and hoisted him off the ground, drew him so close that Kermit's eyes leaked from the tobacco fumes.

"Go ahead," the man snarled. "Tell 'em I told you. Then watch your throat, will you? I got friends *everywhere*."

The man set him on the ground, and Kermit backed away from the carriage. From behind, he heard the front door slam. Out came Eleanor, her crooked, almost elderly figure shuffling toward the carriage.

"Good-bye," she murmured.

Kermit opened his mouth. To warn her, he thought, but the driver's threat still rang in his ears. Even with a loosed tongue, what would he have said that she hadn't already been told?

He wandered in slow circles around the tennis court. Then, feigning illness, he took himself straight to bed and lay there for the rest of the afternoon, feeling the shadows lengthen across his counterpane. He was beginning to grasp why Uncle Elliott's memory had been banished. It wasn't because of how he'd lived his days but because of how he'd ended them. To a man like the Colonel, who worshipped so ardently at life's altar, this must have been the worst betrayal of all: to toss such a gift right back in the Maker's face.

Kermit closed his eyes; his lips traced a silent vow. He would not be Elliott. He would not be the man who jumped out the window. He would not be the photograph in the drawer, the shadowy figure of whom no one spoke. His life would be long, prosperous, crowned with love and success. *This I swear.*

IN FEBRUARY OF HIS fourteenth year, Kermit went alone to Laurel Hollow to hunt for squirrels. The snow lay hard and crusty on the ground, and his breath seemed to freeze and crumble the moment it left his lips. The woods were soundless.

He came at length to the lip of a culvert, through which flowed a small stream, sluggish with ice. A crow started out of a hemlock tree, and Kermit spun toward the sound, then spun back. On the other side of the stream, a man stood watching.

After a few seconds, Kermit realized he was pointing his 12-bore pinfire gun directly at the stranger. Embarrassed, he dropped it to his side, put out a hand in apology. The man put out his hand, too. A different sort of motion: a wave or greeting.

Do I know you? Kermit wanted to ask. But of course he knew him: the mustache and metal-rim spectacles; the top hat and morning coat and old-fashioned trousers. An absurd costume for hunting, but, then, the man had no gun and no clear reason to be there other than to say hello.

He didn't look anything like a dead man should look. Truth be told, he looked in the pink, and Kermit felt no dread at recognizing him. It was more like spotting an old friend in a railway station: the surprise melting into anticipation. Only this wasn't an old friend. And as the implications sank down, a cold rot seemed to rise up in reply.

At last, Elliott gave a courtly nod and a tip of his hat, then turned and walked back up the opposing hill, pausing at the crest before vanishing.

A few months later, Kermit was in the Groton library, half-dozing over his Latin declensions, when he looked up to find his uncle in the chair directly opposite. The same agreeable expression on his face—and, more, an air of politely restrained expectation, as if he were waiting for Kermit to do or say something. Once again, though, the words caught in the boy's throat. He could only stare back and wait for Elliott to doff his hat, rise from his chair, and walk away.

It would have been the height of foolishness to tell anyone. They would have packed him off to an alienist—a sanatorium, an asylum—and what could he possibly say in his defense? That Elliott was incontestably real? As real as the branches of Father's apple tree; the grove beyond Mother's summerhouse; the beach at Cold Spring Harbor—all those places, in short, where Elliott *did* appear over the coming months, dressed as impeccably as ever, waiting as ever for Kermit to . . . explain.

By now the silence that built up during these encounters had become a comfort, because it kept the outer world from rushing in and gave every meeting the feeling of ritual, the more relaxing for being undefined. After a dozen or so times, Kermit ceased to be surprised by his uncle's appearances, began even to welcome them—or, at the very least, accept them. The question of what his uncle expected—this remained in permanent suspension, but Kermit was in no hurry to resolve it. Answers no longer held the interest they had once had.

IT WAS JUST A few minutes past noon on February 27, 1914, when the Roosevelt-Rondon Expedition prepared to launch down the Rio da Dúvida. Kermit climbed into the lead boat. João and Simplício pushed off with their oars, and a second later the current swept them up and bodied them forth. From somewhere far behind him, Kermit heard a single voice calling.

"Good luck!"

It was a voice he had never heard before. He swerved around. On the bridge overlooking the black river stood Uncle Elliott, as natty and unperspiring as ever, waving in his usual droll manner. *Speaking*—that was new. Calling loudly enough for anyone to hear (though Kermit was the only one who turned around).

"Bon voyage!"

8

Bon voyage.

In his mind now, the Rio da Dúvida winnowed down into a long kite string. He held on for dear life as it coiled and wound and then shivered to a stop. Down to earth he floated. On a branch directly over his head wobbled a single bead of dew, growing fatter and fatter as he watched, swelling at last to the size of a globe and only *then* consenting to fall, by the slowest of degrees. Every tree in the forest unfolded its leaflets and reached up to catch the drop— for this was the last water that would ever be—and the drop was glistening with terror, and the air screamed around it, and the jungle opened wide, black and gleaming. . . .

Kermit woke. He felt a pearl of dew sitting perfectly composed on his forehead. He heard the drowse of bees, the flutter of hummingbirds, the dry housemaid scuttle of cockroaches and scorpions. He smelled lilies—water lilies, unpacking their scents. Over his head, like a tiny vulture scouting him for signs of life, a mosquito was circling.

"Go away," he muttered.

In the act of swatting at it, he stopped and stared at his hand. *His* hand, so lately paralyzed. *His* fingers, now swiveling freely in their sockets.

For some time he lay there, entranced by his newness. Then, from close quarters, he heard a groan.

"Kermit . . ."

The old man was stirring. Kermit rolled over, stared down into his father's face. Only it was another face looking back: Thinner, younger, handsomer. A neatly trimmed mustache. A look of polite expectancy.

Kermit squeezed his eyes shut. *Please. Please.*

He opened them again. And there was Father, reconfigured in all his jowliness.

"My spectacles . . ."

"They're right here, Father."

"Are they . . . all right?"

"Yes."

"Not broken?"

"A little crack in the left lens."

"Well. That's the blind eye, anyway."

The old man wrapped the spectacle tips around his ears and levered his torso up. Gazed around at the flowering trunks and the walls of vine melting out of the early-morning mist.

"I don't believe I've been here before."

"No."

The Colonel tweezed a pair of ants out of his ear. "Where are we, do you know?"

"Here," answered Kermit, in an unconscious echo of Luz. "We're here. Far from home."

"And our hosts? Have we been formally introduced? Do we know who they are?"

Kermit was about to shrug, but something snagged in him.

"The Cinta Larga," he said.

He was already reproaching himself as he spoke. He should have known at once. The moment he saw the bark wrapped around their waists. *The men of the wide belts.* Even among other Indian tribes, they were the stuff of myth. Glimpses of them were rare, and few who had crossed their paths had come out better for it.

"Cinta *Larga*," the old man said. "By God, won't Rondon be jealous? He wanted to be the first to see one."

"We are quite blessed, it's true."

The Colonel rested his head in his hands. "Did I dream all that business?" he asked.

"No."

"The jaguar and the . . . the after . . ."

"It happened."

"Hmm," said the Colonel, flexing his arms over his head. "Most remarkable." With Kermit's help, he lurched to his feet. "I don't suppose they offer American breakfasts in this establishment."

"The proprietors keep different hours, I believe."

"Ha," said the Colonel, peering over Kermit's shoulder. "Not so different as all that."

ONCE AGAIN, THE CINTA Larga had stolen up behind their captives in perfect silence and had deftly hooped them around.

"Come to wish us good morning," said the old man. "Very decent of them."

The number of warriors had at least doubled since last night, but the bark belts, the armlets, the hawk-feather headdresses—these were all gone, along with the spears and bows. Except for the liana scrolls around their penises, the men stood utterly bare.

They've disarmed, thought Kermit. *Why?*

Silence held sway for several minutes. Then a series of high-pitched sounds broke from outside the circle as the Cinta Larga women began to poke their heads and arms through the palisade of men's bodies. One by one, the women were pushed back, but in the next instant a boy of ten or twelve, wiry and naked, managed to slip through somebody's legs, and before anyone could stop him, he was crawling toward Kermit and the Colonel on a trail of giggles.

Bellowing, one of the braves—the man from last night with the scar over his eye—snatched the boy and flung him back into the women's ranks. But what lingered in Kermit's mind wasn't the act itself but the spasm that had crossed the man's face when he saw the child—his child?—approaching the strangers.

They're afraid of us.

Maybe the same thought struck the Colonel, for he grasped the folds of his shirt and let loose the full blaze of his smile and, with a flush of Yankee pride, shouted:

"Good day to you all!"

Silence.

"Men and women of the Cinta Larga—and *children,* we won't slight the children—you will observe, I trust, that my son and I are very much among the living. We are, however, a bit banged up. In addition, we are rightfully and manfully outraged by your conduct toward us. Being reasonable and civilized, however, we stand before you, prepared to talk business."

The Colonel had seldom found anyone with whom he couldn't talk business. Even the Colombian students who had flooded his Santiago speeches, screaming, "Down with Yankee imperialism!"—even they, in the end, had given him the respect of their attention.

"Let me preface my remarks by saying this. My son and I do not demand an accounting for your base actions. All we demand is safe passage to the river and reunion with our companions."

The Colonel paused, as if to let the point sink in.

"We are slow to anger, we men of the North, but I think you will find that we do not take lightly any outrages committed against our persons. Nor will our companions. In absence of any word from us, they will beat a fiery path toward this very quarter and will repay any wrong done us two—three—*ten* times over."

How quickly it came back, the old rhetorical grooves. The cheeks, reddened as if by a slap. The jaws snapping off each syllable. The right fist pounding away at the left palm.

"It is clear, my friends, it is manifestly clear, that relations between our peoples have not begun on a sound footing. That being acknowledged, there is no earthly reason why we may not carry forward in a spirit of comity and goodwill. If there has been misunderstanding on your side, if there has been unnecessary and discourteous *aggression* on your side, my son and I stand ready to overlook these offenses in the name of—"

A barking shout rang through the air, and a man stepped forward.

Not the most prepossessing figure, Kermit had to admit. Middle-aged. Small, gaunt, hunched, with a bureaucratic air of suffering. In another world, perhaps, he might have been a pension officer or a bookie, measuring out each day in quires of paper. The only things that announced him as the Cinta Larga chief were the intricate stencils of blue genipap dye fanning across his face and the necklace of wild nuts, large as a life preserver, hanging past his navel. There was this, too: the way he seated himself on his tree-trunk throne. Not the ponderous descent of an emperor but the calm, offhanded motion of a man with no time to waste.

The chief clapped his hands—twice, lightly. Then the tribal circle broke open to admit the bowed figure of Luz. In the light of day, with her softly freckled shoulders and pink nipples, she looked even further removed from the Cinta Larga.

"Senhor Kermit. I am to tell you what has happened."

"We know what happened."

"No. Before you came."

And the two words that followed were somehow more evocative for being in Portuguese.

"*A besta.*"

The Colonel required no translation. "*Beast,* she says?"

"Please," she said. "You shall listen."

THE CINTA LARGA WERE taught early in life to distinguish between two forms of terror: known and unknown.

The job of any child growing up in the forest was to know as many of these terrors as possible. The sound that shakes from the sky before a rain. The snake that squeezes the life from a man. The creature that lies like a log in the water. The frog that kills with a touch. These were all part of the native curriculum and could be apprehended and, with skill and luck, averted. But there was nothing to be done about unknown terrors, for they came without warning and stayed ever out of sight. Only their handiwork could be perceived. The blight that lays waste to a field of manioc. The chill that takes root in the bones. The dream that steals the soul.

The Cinta Larga had remedies at their disposal—shamans, native medicines; these might keep the unknown at bay for a time. Nothing in the tribal lore, though, had prepared them for this latest terror. It came on light feet, and its first victims were toads and side-necked turtles, plovers, wood ibises. The carnage was extreme but tightly contained—not yet outside the realm of experience.

But, in short order, the terror grew bolder, hungrier. Capuchins, hawks, anteaters, peccaries, tapirs—all snatched from their perches and killed, *savaged* in a way the Cinta Larga had never seen. Not just eaten, these creatures, but disemboweled—*emptied*—with only the head left to testify to what they had been.

Surely a thing capable of doing such carnage was no mere animal. Surely it was a terrible spirit, clothed in teeth and claws, loosing its vengeance on the jungle.

At first, the Cinta Larga tried appeasing it with sacrifices. They lined their huts with snakeskins. They strewed the corpses of birds around the village perimeter. They killed a wild pig and left it split open, oozing in the night. The Beast scorned their offerings. It would have the meat it had killed for itself, or it would have nothing.

The killings went on: a sloth; a caiman, snatched from the river's very clasp. And still the Cinta Larga made their sacrifices, praying that they might, alone of all the jungle's inhabitants, be spared.

One evening, one of their girls, no more than six years on this earth, wandered off to collect cacaos. She was found the next morning, scarcely to be recognized. Since then, no one had dared to walk abroad in darkness, and even daylight held a new horror, for who could say when the Beast would strike next?

Even the men were not safe. Only two nights before, one of the tribe's strongest and fiercest warriors was seized in the very act of keeping watch. They found him the next morning, in the vines and brush, so thoroughly consumed that there was no piecing him back together. They left his remains on the spot, and no Cinta Larga would walk there now for fear of meeting the dead man's angry shadow.

The Beast lived and walked and hungered. Most terrible of all: It went unseen. No one—nothing—had ever glimpsed it and lived.

I LIVED.

The thought came flying at Kermit, and a chain of sense memories came right on its tail. The jaguar's terrible howls; the quiet; and lastly the soft, obscene sound of lapping.

Why hadn't the thing come for him? Or the Colonel? Paralyzed as they were, they would have offered far less resistance than the jaguar and considerably more meat. Was the creature sated? Or else too deranged to notice what lay just beneath its nose?

Why? Why am I still alive?

"Luz," he said. "Tell me how long this beast of yours has been preying."

"Since the last full moon," answered Luz.

"But my father and I have been traveling through this region no more than two or three days. We have nothing to do with your beast. Why have you dragged us here?"

"We had to."

"Why, in God's name?"

"To make the Beast go away."

"I don't follow. You meant to use us as a . . . as an appeasement? *Sacrificar?*"

"The very idea," growled the Colonel, translating for himself. "Sacrificing people. They couldn't have found a goat?"

"No," said Luz. "Not sacrifice. Protection. The Beast will see *you,* and he will go away."

"But why?" asked Kermit, incredulous. "Why on earth would you suppose we had such power over the thing?"

"The Beast will kill a mere man, we have seen that. But it must never harm one of its own."

"One of its own?" repeated Kermit.

And as the full import of her words settled over him, a low, mirthless laugh came bubbling out.

"What is it?" the Colonel asked. "What did she say?"

"Well, now." Kermit laid a gentle hand on the old man's shoulder. "They seem to believe that we are beasts ourselves."

"Beasts?"

With a small, tight smile, Luz cupped the vast expanse of Kermit's beard.

More than anything else in that moment, he wanted to explain. That when a man from civilization ventures into the wilderness, he gives up one thing, and this always leads to giving up another. He gives up shaving, and then he gives up his shaving mirror. Then he gives up caring what he looks like, and then he gives up even knowing what he looks like. Or that he looks like anything at all.

But there was no chance to explain. The Colonel had already tipped back his head, and he was roaring with laughter.

"She has taken your full measure, Kermit! You are as bestial a white man as a savage might ever meet."

"Oh, no!" cried Luz. "Not you alone, Senhor Kermit. The people who ride the water with you: They, too, are covered in hair. They also pass in safety. The Beast does not touch them. With you here, the Beast would leave us in peace."

"But . . ." He could feel his breath burning into sound. "We don't *know* this beast of yours! How could we? And you and your people—you left us utterly defenseless before it. We might just as easily have been killed ourselves."

Spinning away, he shouted into the trees.

"This is monstrous! You must see this. We were—my father and I—we were passing *through*, no more. We meant no harm to anyone. If you had left us in peace, we would have journeyed on."

But if he expected Luz to answer him, he would have to wait. Her gaze was already fixed on the chief. For some long seconds, they looked at each other. Then, in a voice almost too low to be heard, Luz said:

"There is more. You should come."

9

Last night's imprisonment had given Kermit the sense of being trapped in a vast fortress extending a mile on every side, with vast complexes of rooms and corridors. Now, in the morning light, Kermit was able to see the Cinta Larga village for the first time in its entirety. There was nothing to look at but a circular clearing, forty to fifty feet across, hacked and scorched out of the jungle's heart, with a dozen or so huts arranged like spokes around a small central plaza and a steeply pitched playa leading down to a stream as black as the Rio da Dúvida and boiling from the winter rains.

You might have fit the whole business into Sagamore's North Room—right down to the bamboo cage in which a half-plucked harpy eagle fruitlessly flapped its wings. Virtually impossible to believe that more than a handful of Cinta Larga could live here, and yet, as Kermit and the Colonel crossed the clearing, some three dozen villagers, acting on some unheard cue, emerged from their huts and began to throng toward the strangers.

Girls swelling with puberty. Mothers lofting their babies onto their heads. Old women with bent spines. A thin, crabbed stalk of a man, older than the sun, reaching with cadaver hands toward the white men. None of them were much taller than five feet, but their curiosity was outsized. They dogged the captives' every step, jostling for better views, filling the air with grunts and clicks. It was like being a Coney Island attraction, Kermit thought, sandwiched between the California Bats and the Electric Seal. *Step up and see for yourselves! The Pale Hairy Hominids!*

The space around him shrank even farther as the villagers closed in, each little incursion smoothing the way toward a larger one. A pat led to a caress, a tug on the shirt to a tug on the trousers. One of the more daring boys plucked Kermit's beard and tried to snatch the Colonel's spectacles right off his face. Then, without warning, the mob fell back. The procession stopped. Kermit looked down. He was standing before a great mound of sticks and ashes and mud, clouded by gnats and mosquitoes. A high, ripe, sweetish scent rose up. The chief barked a command, and, in the next breath, one of the women fell to her knees and began to grope through the muck like a Bowery scavenger, flinging out each new discovery as she found it.

The first thing to emerge was a thigh bone, drizzled with flies. Then a gnawed section of hip. A foot, still half encased in the tatters of a leather boot. And at last the remnants of an arm, flying toward Kermit in a slow parabola.

The same arm he'd seen last night, still curled in an arc of farewell. Thank God there was nothing left to throw up.

"Steady," murmured the Colonel. "Steady now."

But even the old man's equanimity was giving way before the theater of the moment. "Fine dinner they've made of him," he growled. "Bloody savages."

Kermit said nothing. He merely watched as the pieces came sailing, one by one, through the air. A shoulder joint. A breastbone. A section of rib. Each item coming to rest in a different square of earth, in an order that bore no relation to the original anatomy.

And finally, like an afterthought, the head, stripped of all hair, wobbling toward them like a gourd. Unburned but still aflame with astonishment.

"He's not one of theirs," the Colonel whispered. "The skin, do you see? Olive, not copper."

Nor, thought Kermit, was he part of the Roosevelt-Rondon Expedition. Who was he, then?

"Your beast is indeed to be feared," he declared, "if it has created such carnage."

Frowning, Luz tapped the dead man's boot with her toe. "Not the Beast," she said.

"What else would have done this?"

The barest flush in her cheeks. *"We,"* she said. "Us."

THREE SUNS AGO, A group of their warriors had set off down the river's shoreline. They were seeking food, above all, because the Beast had taken so much of the Cinta Larga's prey that they had been forced to travel farther afield.

"In which direction did they travel?" asked Kermit.

"With the water."

"And did they travel by boat?"

"Boat." She blinked several times in quick succession. "We have no boat. We stay always on land."

"And after three days they came across this man."

"Yes."

"Was he alone?"

"Yes."

"Did he run at the sight of them?"

"He did not see. He was . . . ohh—"

"What?"

"He was doing magic. Dark magic."

Kermit stared down once more at that martyred head. "You mean he was *saying* things? Spells, that kind of thing?"

"No, he was touching. *No.*" She corrected herself at once. "He was . . ."

She glanced back at the chief, who swept his arm through the air in a clean, straight slashing motion. The jungle fairly whistled before it.

"The man was *cutting*," said Kermit.

"Yes."

"Cutting the tree."

"Yes."

"Cutting it down?"

Luz shook her head.

"Cutting . . . into it?"

She nodded.

"Did something come out?"

Her eyes swirled with confusion. "*Blood* came out. The blood of this tree."

"And this blood, did it have a color?"

"It was the color of woman's milk."

"White."

"Yes."

"And it was . . . was it sticky to the touch?"

"Yes," said Luz, nodding eagerly. "It *stays*. On the finger. I have seen other trees like it."

Five minutes earlier, Kermit couldn't have imagined doing what he was doing now. And doing it with such a clinical detachment. Picking up that severed arm as if it were a piece of driftwood. Raising it to the light and studying the thin grayish wash that still encased the hand.

"Caoutchouc," he whispered.

Even as he spoke, the Colonel was lurching toward the English equivalent.

"Why, that's *rubber*, isn't it?"

*　*　*

THERE WAS NO OTHER explanation. Somehow—*somehow*—a tapper had managed to work his way upriver even as the Roosevelt-Rondon Expedition was toiling down. How resourceful the poor wretch must have been and how desperate: living on starvation wages, supporting God knows how many children, trolling the wilderness for a tree that hadn't been claimed and stripped and drained by one of his equally desperate brethren.

And having found such a tree, wouldn't he have glowed with holy fire? A perfect beacon for the equally desperate band of Indians stealing up behind him . . .

But, from the horror of that poor wretch's death, a single spark of hope now flew up. For if he had come, others would follow. Wherever there was rubber, there would, in short order, be men.

And this meant—didn't it?—that help was at hand. Closer than Kermit could ever have imagined. It meant the expedition might still be saved.

Why, then, wasn't he rejoicing?

"Luz," he said, setting the severed arm on the ground. "Can you tell me, please? Why did your warriors kill this man?"

"He was our enemy. Our worst enemy."

"Why do you say that?"

"He was one with the Beast."

"I don't understand. He had no beard. He wasn't part of your world."

"No. No, Senhor Kermit. What he was doing to the tree—that is what the Beast does to its prey. This man and the Beast, they are *família*."

"What's she saying?" the Colonel cried. "*Whose* family?"

Kermit's gaze drifted down to the dead man's head. He thought of the tapper's family, waiting for word hundreds of miles away. He thought of Belle, thousands of miles over the sea. A swell of rage pressed against his chest as he felt the heat of these Cinta Larga bodies, smelled the sweat and loam on their skin. He could level one or two of them with a blow, he knew that. But the rest would already be swarming over him—as relentless as those ants—tearing him apart as systematically as they'd rent that rubber tapper.

He knew something else. He knew that as long as this beast continued to prey, he and his father would remain prisoners. It didn't matter how many rubber tappers came calling or how diligently Rondon and the rest of the crew searched. The Cinta Larga would cling to their two captives because . . . because it was *working*. Because, for at least one night, the Beast had spared the village. Because they had no other hope.

And what hope did he and the Colonel have? They had no guns—at least not where they could find them. They had no guides. They would never find their way back. The time had come to bargain for their lives.

And was he the man to do it? Of all the Roosevelt children, he was the least likely to force himself on the world's attention. He could remember attending, when he was ten, one of his father's campaign rallies, in an Albany meeting hall that smelled of sausage. The Colonel had but to speak a few words and the most terrifying of roars would go up from the party faithful, and, rather than dying away, the sound kept building into a kind of bloodlust. It was as if every man and woman in that hall wanted to eat his father alive. When the speech ended and the crowd surged forth to show their love, Kermit was heard to scream, "Don't hurt him!"

Afterward, he asked his mother, "Must Father do that every night?"

"I'm afraid so, dear."

"Will I have to do that someday?"

"Not if you don't want to. Some of us aren't meant to be leaders, you know."

But here, in the midst of the jungle, he was the only candidate. The Colonel, this was plain to see, was in a bad way. The traumas of the past twelve hours had taken their piece of him, and he sat now in the mud, his breath coming in hitches and jerks. Not even enough strength left to swat the stingless wasps that scuttled across his eyes and nose, feeding on his sweat.

Kermit stared into the tapper's eye—and saw the amber-refracted image of himself gazing back.

"Luz," he heard himself say. "I will need you to translate for me."

He was already a foot taller than most of the villagers, but some instinct told him to raise himself even higher, so he climbed onto the remains of an old stump upholstered in wet moss. The words *stump speech* hovered there at the brink of consciousness. And of all the eyes that were now raised to him, none were more astonished than the Colonel's, squinting up through his cracked lenses.

"What in the name of—"

Kermit fanned out his fingers and flung his arms wide.

"Men and women of the forest! Look upon us and tremble!"

Luz stared up at him, hesitating.

"Please," he said to her.

Turning toward the other villagers, she began to translate—in a tone that Kermit couldn't help but hear as wheedling.

"Look upon us," cried Kermit. "We are great and mighty hunters. We have hunted across God's wide earth. We have killed more creatures than there are stars in the sky."

His mind teemed now with memories of Mount Kenya. The moonlit nights. The dry chill of the air against his face. The strummings of the native harps.

"I tell you we have laid waste to cats far greater than the jaguar. Yes, it is so. We have slain beasts with horns as big as a man. We have slain beasts as tall as that tree. We have slain beasts as wide . . ." His hands shivered apart. "As wide as your river, yes!"

Nothing stirred in the faces of the Cinta Larga. But, by all appearances, they were listening.

"I say to you, men and women of the forest, we have eaten the heart of the greatest beast that ever lived. *Roasted it,* I say, in our fires and eaten it whole. And, behold, it was good."

As he spoke, Luz's voice came rippling after his. It was like standing before a massed convention and listening to the echoes of the megaphone man, sending his speech to the farthest balcony.

"Harken unto me, my friends. We will capture your beast. Yes, I say we will! And in return . . ."

Pause, he thought. *Father would be pausing.*

"In *return,* you will lead us back to our comrades. And allow us to go our way, unharmed. We ask no more of you. We ask no less. We ask . . ."

What? We ask *what?*

By now the Colonel would be steaming toward that final terminus, wheels churning, whistle sounding.

"We ask justice."

Luz stopped.

"Pardon, Senhor. There is no word for—"

"That is all," he announced. "Thank you."

He stepped down from the stump. He waited.

For several minutes, nothing happened at all. Then the chief rose wearily from his own stump, waited until every eye was square with his. *Ready to sound the command,* thought Kermit. But he just beckoned with one arm, and without a word, the rest of the warriors lined up behind him and processed to his hut, ducking their heads one by one as they entered.

Not a monarchy at all, thought Kermit, smiling to himself. *A constitutional republic.*

The rest of the villagers began to drift back, in a spirit of resignation, to their morning rounds. Old men propped themselves against trees and whittled bamboo into drills. Women sat with stone bowls in their laps, squeezing manioc root. Children, formerly shiny with mischief, set to weaving baskets and mashing yams.

"Well, now." With a cough and wheeze, the Colonel rose from the mud. "That was first-class oratory, my son. I only wish I could have understood it."

But he must have grasped the import of it, because when the old man spoke again, his voice was thin and hard.

"Do you honestly believe we can do it?"

"We've done it before, Bwana Makubwa."

"You speak true, Bwana Mardadi." The old man took off his spectacles, wiped them on his sleeve. "But, to the best of my knowledge, we have never hunted a beast with no tracks."

10

"ALL BEASTS MAKE TRACKS," SAID KERMIT. "OF SOME KIND."

"So I once believed myself." Taking hold of his son's arm, the Colonel levered himself up. "Let us examine our unfortunate jaguar."

The carcass wasn't hard to find, only a few yards from where they were standing.

"Dear God," whispered Kermit.

Never, outside of a taxidermist's, had he seen an animal hollowed out in such a fashion. Its skin and tissue had been *peeled* off in long jagged strips. Nothing was left but some bones and ripped tendons and the tawny marble prisms of the eyes, from which Kermit's own image stared balefully back. He heard the Colonel's dry voice:

"Not much for sharing, our Beast."

Kermit nodded. "Barely enough here for ants."

"Silly, I know, to speak of a jungle creature being cruel. All the same . . ."

But there was more to the assault than cruelty, wasn't there? To

Kermit's eye, there was an element of terrible *mockery*, as though the Beast wished only to show the emptiness of this jaguar, of every living thing. A life hadn't been taken, it had been erased.

"Well, my boy," said the Colonel. "I am happy to report—or it may be I am ashamed to report—that my time as police commissioner left me with a strong predilection for crime scenes and what may be gleaned therefrom. To *wit*," he continued, with an upward thrust of finger, "we have a crime. We have a *victim*. Now, what else may we say with any degree of certainty?"

"As best I can tell, the jaguar was a male. Though it's damned hard to be sure."

"We'll conditionally agree. What else?"

"We know where he was attacked."

"Just a few feet from where we were so calmly reclining, yes. The rest of our knowledge can be filled in with the most rudimentary understanding of cat biology. Before it met this rather shocking demise, our jaguar was unexceptional in every regard. It was merely doing what jaguars do. Now, tell me, what may we say of the jaguar's assailant?"

Once more Kermit's ears filled with the sound memory of that lapping.

"Our Beast has a tongue," he said.

"A thirsty one. What else?"

"It's strong."

"Quite amazingly strong to perform this kind of savagery on an animal that weighs—what would you say—two hundred, two hundred fifty pounds?"

"Something like that."

"Twice the size of any of the leopards we shot in Africa. Right up there with your small lioness. Yes, when it comes to a scrap, I'd take the jaguar's chances against virtually any other creature in the jungle. But last night our great cat was reduced to . . . *this*." His palm sloped down toward the carcass. "So we know our Beast has the strength of at least *two* jaguars. Perhaps three, perhaps more. What else can we say?"

"Very little."

"I will go you one better and answer, *Nothing else.* That's the queerest part of the whole business. An act of great savagery took place on this very spot, and yet the perpetrator of the act left virtually no trace. It made no cry—none that *I* could hear, at any rate. And it left no tracks. I repeat: *It left no tracks.*"

Kermit's mouth puckered. "Perhaps it rained while we were sleeping. If so, the tracks might have been washed away."

"I had the same thought, but do you see? The *jaguar's* tracks are still intact. We can actually follow his path to this exact point. The Beast, on the other hand, has left not a print, not a mark. Not even a swath of crushed underbrush."

"It might have sprung from a tree. Like a monkey."

"And sprung right back? Against all the rules of gravity? The nearest tree is at least fifteen feet away. Every monkey I've ever seen would take a running start before hauling itself back up. And please keep in mind that the Beast would have had a singularly full stomach last night. It ate and drank an extraordinary amount of jaguar. Do you really see it making such a . . . such a postprandial leap?"

Once more, Kermit found himself staring into the jaguar's dead eye. "Anything strong enough to do this," he said, "makes its own laws."

"Within *nature's* laws, yes. Now, you and I have met our share of carnivores. We've stared lions in the mouth, haven't we? Have we ever come across a mammal that could gouge out—*extravasate*—its prey in this manner?"

Kermit was silent for a time. "What of the mountain gorillas? They're said to be fearfully strong."

"They feast on plants and grubs, Kermit. And make quite a lot of commotion, as you'll recall. If our beast were a gorilla, it would have broken every branch it touched. And left the fattest footprints you ever saw."

"Very well. *Not* a mammal, if you like. Let's posit some kind of raptor. A condor . . ."

"Making not a single cry as it descends. Not even a flapping of wings. No, don't look like that; we were *there,* Kermit. Other than the lapping, the only sound we heard was the jaguar's shriek."

"But, Father, with all due respect, we are no longer in Africa. We are in a new continent with—why, Cherrie alone found two new species of bird last week. Who can say how many other life-forms we might find, given enough time? *New* life-forms?"

The old man looked him squarely in the eye. "I don't recall suggesting it was a *new* life-form," he said.

Kermit stared back at him, coughed up a single mirthless laugh. "*The Lost World,* is that your drift? Well, your Scribner's readers are bound to be delighted. But Conan Doyle may sue."

"The point *is* . . ." And with a vigor that seemed to come from the near-distant past, the old man seized his son by the shoulders. "We are in a strange land, Kermit. *Should we not be braced for strange outcomes?*"

Then, as if embarrassed by his own exertion, the old man let his hands drop to his sides.

"Oh, I know, I know. There's no point speculating. Unless they take us up on your offer, we won't be hunting anything. We'll only be digging a pair of shallow graves. If they grant us that much."

"We will find our way home, Father."

"Of course we shall." He pulled off his spectacles and swept his arm across his face. "Do you know, I think I'll sit down again. If it's all the same to you. What can be taking them so long, I wonder?"

"Damned if I know."

Kermit gazed across the clearing at the chief's hut. From a distance, it was the most serene political caucus he had ever witnessed. No smoke pouring through the door. No pounding on the walls.

No errand boys rushing in with ice buckets and Scotch bottles. From time to time, a squawk or a grunt would break through the hut's walls, but for the most part, the Cinta Larga carried on out of sight and out of hearing.

"Awfully parched," volunteered the old man.

"Me, too."

"Wish we had Juan bringing the morning coffee. How I miss the fellow. Ha! I even miss that grim little Rondon. I shall give him the rudest of embraces when next we meet."

"So you think they'll come for us?"

"Of *course* they'll come. Do you think they would consider, even for a moment, leaving us behind? Why, for Rondon, the publicity *alone* would be torment greater than any mosquito."

Even as he spoke, the old man stared at that jaguar carcass, butter bright in the sun.

"And when they do find us, Kermit, heaven help us all."

ON AND ON THE caucus went.

And as they waited, the sun rose through the hissing mist, and the trees sweated through their bark, and everything blazed green—until noon, when a mattress of cloud burst open into hard, oily drops.

Absently, Kermit reached for his helmet; it wasn't there. He watched the water pool in the bowl of his hands, then tipped it straight into his mouth. Again and again, he drank, and then he tipped his head back and let the water crawl through his skin, through his nose, through his eyes.

The rain was just starting to die away when something began to stir in the hut.

"Huzzah," said the Colonel.

There was only a commotion of palm leaves at first. Then the first Cinta Larga warrior came stumbling out. Another followed and then another—in an unbroken, nearly comical chain, disgorged from that tiny hut like a knotted handkerchief from a magician's hat. Last of all came the chief, moving in strange arcs of abstraction.

"What *is* the fellow doing?" the Colonel whispered. "You don't suppose he's drunk?"

The chief made a clicking sound, and, from nowhere, Luz came running. She bent her ear to the chief's mouth. Then she turned to the white men and, with a broad smile, announced:

"Está concordado!"

It is agreed.

"You will kill the Beast," she said. "In exchange, you will be freed."

"Freed how?" asked Kermit. "Escorted back to our party?"

"Yes."

"And they will agree not to harm us. Or anyone in our company."

"This they have agreed."

Kermit looked at the Colonel, then back at Luz.

"Very well. We accept."

Luz turned to the assembled throng and gave an emphatic nod. And of all the reactions the Cinta Larga might have had to this declaration, this was the one Kermit least expected: absolute silence.

Perhaps, he thought, the villagers hadn't yet grasped the full nature of their new arrangement. Or else they had simply absorbed the details, without fuss, into their understanding of things. As he gazed around at their creased, solemn faces, Kermit couldn't help but recall the whistle-stop tour he'd taken with the Colonel during the '04 campaign. "Little jaunt through Pennsylvania Dutch Country," that's how the old man had described it, but one day, as the sun was starting to sink behind the mountains, the Colonel suggested they stop in one of the coal towns along the train line. Was it Centralia? Ashland? Kermit couldn't summon up a name; he remembered only what they found when they got there.

Night was falling, and the men had just come out of the mines, carrying their dinner buckets. Some of them were still wearing their carbide lamps. Their faces were so thickly coated with coal dust that it was impossible to say which were fathers and which were sons, just as it was impossible to tell mothers from their grown daughters, for all the women had the same skeletal frames, the same deep etchings around the eyes and mouth. The same *stare:* parched, fathomless.

In any other part of the country, the Colonel would have whipped the townsfolk to a froth just by showing up. (Even people who hated him couldn't resist a view.) Here they greeted him with the silence of monks. They knew who he was, all right, but he'd come, like any other politician, offering hope, and that was something they couldn't afford anymore. So they looked at him the way you look at anything that's gotten between you and where you need to go. Wondering: *Will it go away by itself?*

So it was with the Cinta Larga. They lived not in the El Dorado of Western imaginations but in the Amazonian equivalent of a coal town, where every day began and ended in struggle. When a pair of strangers offered to kill a beast for them, they didn't pound one another on the shoulder; they made no swelling shout or triumphal cry; they merely looked. Anything else was a waste of energy.

The villagers' silence stretched out for more than a minute and was broken first by the caged, half-plucked eagle, stuttering from its slumbers, and then by Luz's low, embarrassed murmur.

"They are waiting," she said.

"For what?" asked Kermit.

"They would like to know—oh, what is—how you will *proceed.*"

I'd like to know, too.

Kermit looked at the old man. Then, feeling the clutch in his gut, he remounted the tree stump.

"Luz," he said. "Please translate."

Their opaque faces seemed to converge on him, pinning him into place.

"Men of the forest! We have agreed to hunt and kill your beast.

Hear me now, though, when I tell you: We cannot kill it with only thunder sticks, and we cannot kill it by ourselves. We do not know your forest. We do not know your *world*. We require a guide."

"*Um guia?*" whispered Luz.

"*Sim. Um espião. Um líder.*"

He was bracing himself for another two hours of negotiations, but Luz answered at once.

"*Você via me aceitar.*"

You will have me.

And, again, just enough of the Portuguese reached the Colonel to provoke a reply.

"She's offering herself? For such a business as this? That's perfectly barbarous."

"My father," explained Kermit, "is greatly afraid for your safety."

"He need not be. This is my home. I know it as well as anybody. I will be as safe as you. It is possible," she added, with the trace of a smile, "that I will be safer."

The old man was not to be persuaded. "We are to *drag* this young girl into harm's way? Is that what you're telling me? Dear God, Kermit, it would be like endangering your own mother—your sisters. It cannot be countenanced."

"I'm afraid it must."

"Nonsense!"

"Father, listen to me. Luz speaks true. As a native, she is far from helpless. And she and I share a language. Can you imagine trying to communicate with one of *them*?"

"I don't care." The blood came flushing to his face. "You must ask—you must *demand*—that these savages serve up an able-bodied man. Look at them standing there! These brave warriors, letting a woman face down their enemy. They ought to be ashamed."

Bending toward Luz, Kermit lowered his voice to a confidential croon.

"In recent days, Father has not been so *spry* as he would like.

To compensate for his weakness, do you think we might engage one of the village menfolk?"

He thought at first that she failed to take his meaning, but just as he was about to rephrase, she said:

"They have thought of this."

"Yes?"

"Thiago will join us."

"Thiago . . ."

Turning around, Kermit scanned the palisade of warriors, waiting for someone to answer to the name. But the only reply was a vague flurry behind their ranks—a stir of limb, registering so faintly it might have been a mile off. The next moment, a boy was elbowing his way to the fore.

Kermit blinked. It was the same boy who'd come crawling out to them that morning. He stood now in the greenish-yellow light of noonday, no more than twelve: reedy, tight-muscled, hands lightly flexed. As dark as the other children, but immeasurably lighter in spirit. Among the grim faces displayed to the white men, his alone seemed to cherish some prospect of pleasure in their company.

"*This* is Thiago?" asked Kermit.

"Yes," said Luz.

She didn't look at the boy, nor he at her. They didn't even resemble each other so very much. It was simply the way they angled their bodies to the world, bracing for the next collision. They belonged together.

"A child!" squeaked the Colonel. "This is beyond sufferance."

"Father—"

"He is a boy. A *stripling*."

Kermit took the Colonel by the shoulders, drew him close. "We cannot set the conditions, Father, you know that."

"Nor are we obliged to accept them! Not when they run counter to all rules of civilized conduct."

"We are not in civilization."

"Civilization is not a *place,* Kermit, it is . . ." The spit flew from the old man's mouth. "It is a practice. A way of living one's life—meeting one's *death,* if necessary. Have I not taught you this much?"

Smiling, Kermit lowered his forehead until it was touching the old man's. "I was eight years old when I went on my first hunt."

"You shot a reedbird. And with no small amount of collusion on my part."

"And I had as much fear in my heart as this boy here. Maybe a good deal more," he added, glancing back at Thiago, whose mouth had parted into the ingredients of a smile.

"Eu sou forte!" the boy shouted. I am strong. And to make the point, he flexed his biceps in the manner of every boy who has ever aspired above his station.

The Colonel was unmollified. "For the love of God, Kermit, where is the lad's father? I should like to meet him. I should *very* much like to broadcast my opinion of him to the world."

"Luz," said Kermit. "Does Thiago have a father? I mean, among the living."

And because she made no reply at first, he again thought he had misspoken.

"I will look out for Thiago," she said. "You will look out for the old man. We will be well."

The Colonel took one look at Kermit's face, then walked to the edge of the clearing. For several minutes he stood there, staring into the jungle's purpling shadows. And the whole time, it was fair to say, the entire village watched *him,* waiting to see which way he tended.

"So this is how it stands, Kermit. You and I are to place ourselves in the jaws of death with no one in our corner but a child and a slip of a woman."

"It would appear so."

The old man nodded, twice, rubbed his eyes under his glasses.

"Well, now," he said. "I suppose we have made do with less."

"That is so."

"Then tell them . . . tell them we are thoroughly delighted—we are *enchanted* with our new hunting party. We could have chosen no better. No, not if Selous and Cunninghame were taking up arms with us."

"My father accepts," said Kermit, bowing his head an inch. "We do, however, require that our weapons be returned to us."

"Weapons?" echoed Luz.

"How else shall we hunt?"

"I am not certain. What weapons do you mean?"

"Why, our rifles, of course. Surely your men took them when they—when they so kindly invited us here."

"Espingarda. I am sorry, Senhor, do you . . . can you . . ."

Kermit curled his hands around an invisible barrel, raised it to his eye. A simple bit of mime that, in this case, required no translation, for the Cinta Larga shook their heads and flared out their fingers and hopped from foot to foot, as though the earth had turned to brimstone.

"They seem disinclined," murmured the Colonel.

"Luz, you must explain to them. We cannot put ourselves in the Beast's way without some protection. Some way of killing the thing."

"We have weapons here."

"Spears, yes, and sticks. Bows and arrows. Useless to us."

Unusable, he added to himself, eyeing the massive peach-palm-wood longbows that lay stacked against a woodpile. It would take him half a week just to bend one.

"If we give you these rifles," said Luz, "you will use them to hurt us."

"No. We won't. You have our word on it. As gentlemen."

She tucked her lower lip under her teeth. "I am very sorry, Senhor Kermit. I do not think we can give these to you."

"Then there can be no agreement. You will have to kill your own beast."

Her eyes tightened. Then, with a strange, half-shambling gait, she made her way back to the chief. She murmured in his ear, stood back, and waited. And Kermit waited, too, for the public declaration he felt sure was coming. A yes, a no. A shout, a clap.

But the chief's reply was strictly private. He grabbed Luz by the arm, hissed a few words in her ear, and shoved her away. Stumbling in the mud, she set down a hand to regain her footing. Then, gathering herself, she crossed back to the two captives.

"You may have your rifles, Senhor Kermit. But if you use them on any of our people, things will go bad."

"What do you mean, *bad*? With whom?"

"With me," she answered flatly. "And . . ." Her head leaned a fraction of an inch toward Thiago. "I will be plain with you. If you should kill any of our people, they will kill us."

No words came to him, not at first.

"Luz," he said. "I am sorry for you. Your people have taken an evil course. But tell me, please. Why do they suppose we should *care* what happens to you?"

She tucked her eyes to one side.

"It is not that, Senhor Kermit. It is that *they* do not care." And then she reached through his beard all the way to his chin and cupped it lightly. "We must care for ourselves."

11

THE DEAL WAS STRUCK.

In token of their new standing, the white men were granted the use of a hut: small and bare and recently swept, no more than twelve paces from the stream. Whether the hut was already vacant or someone had been evicted to make room, Kermit didn't ask. He did, however, offer a silent prayer of thanks as he and Father crawled out of the dazzling light of the plaza and threw themselves into a pair of hammocks that creaked and rocked beneath their weight.

Food, too, was offered without asking. A manioc pie, in roasted banana leaves, sending up a smoky musk that was more pleasing than the actual taste. "Touch of salt would do wonders," said the Colonel. But it went down quickly enough and another soon followed, and a young girl ran to the stream to fetch water, and the water was cool and tannic and laid down a prickly balm in their throats.

From his hammock, Kermit gazed through the doorway at the noon blaze. The shadows bled across the land like ink. Even the Cinta Larga had sought shade. A stack of turtle shells lay baking in the sun, and at the perimeter of the clearing, a jabiru stork perched on one leg, its beak resting grievingly on its breast.

This last sight was so strangely captivating that Kermit didn't at first hear the spindly rustle from the other side of the hut. Twisting around in his hammock, he found, framed in the doorway, the villager who had reached out to them that morning: the old man with cadaver hands. He was even eerier now: his eyes clouded over, his corduroy neck wobbling, his mouth hanging open in folds of ruin.

"Good God," said the Colonel.

The man gasped and dropped to his knees and began to crawl toward them.

"*Coo,*" he whispered.

"What's that?" the Colonel said. "What's he saying?"

"*Coo . . . roo . . . peera.*"

And having spoken the name, the man spent the next minute coughing it back up. In fragments of no particular order.

"*Peer . . . coo . . . roo . . .*"

Then he stopped. Puzzlement flashed through his eyes as he began to slide away from them—with shocking haste, for a hand had fastened around his ankle and was hauling him into the sunlight, and where the old man had once been, Luz now stood. Just enough of her face was in the light for Kermit to see its lacquer of triumph.

"I am sorry," she said. "He disturbs you."

"But he wasn't troubling us."

"You must not listen to Bokra, Senhor Kermit. He is not one of us. Bad things are in his heart."

She nodded once and left.

"Egad," muttered the Colonel. "That's no way to treat your elders. Dragging them out like old polecats. Odd business, though. The fellow went to some lengths to speak to us. I only wish we knew what he was driving at. How did it go again? Coo-roo—"

"Curupira," said Kermit.

The old man gave him a wry look. "It strikes a chord, I see."

"It's a name, that's all. From native lore."

"Mythical?"

"Well," said Kermit, "I suppose one might call him a demon."

"And what exactly does he do?"

"Guards the forest."

"From what?"

"From us." Kermit's mouth cracked into a half smile. "From men."

"All men?"

"Those who hunt for food, it's said, are given free run of the place. But those who hunt for pleasure—well, he won't stand for that. It squanders his bounty. So he lays traps for them."

"Traps?"

"He baffles them. Sends them down the wrong paths. Addles their brains so thoroughly, they . . ." Kermit shrugged lightly. "They never come back."

"Sounds more like an imp than a demon."

"I only repeat what I hear."

"So the local legends say nothing about him carving open creatures? Draining them of all their innards?"

"It does seem strange that he should turn on his own creation. That would run counter to his purpose, wouldn't it?"

"Ha!" A fine cloud of spittle flew from the Colonel's teeth. "Perhaps you haven't read the Old Testament of late. Quite a lot of creators getting snappish with their creations."

Kermit stared out the hut opening, where a pile of peeled bark lay baking in the sun. He could feel the heat squeezing his eyelids down.

"There is one other thing," he said.

"Yes?"

"They say Curupira's feet are backward."

"And where does that get him, I wonder?"

"It keeps hunters from tracking him."

"I see." The Colonel brought his hands together. "A demon that sends its enemies running in the opposite direction. Now, that's what I call cunning. I shall have to forward the idea to the secretary of war. All the same," he added, "I would wager this Curupira brute has never met hunters like us."

But what sort of hunters were they?

In Africa, over the course of one year, they had killed five hundred twelve beasts between them, including seventeen lions and eleven elephants. They had taken pride in their nicknames: Bwana Makubwa and Bwana Mardadi. Great Master and Dandy Master.

Mankind was incontestably better off for their labors. Hadn't they donated many of their trophies to science? Hadn't they helped to make the Museum of Natural History an African wonderland? But there was no use pretending that altruism woke them up every morning or set them dreaming every night. Their days had been festivals of blood and sinew and muscle. They had wolfed down elephant-trunk soup; they had toasted slices of elephant heart over a fire. They had watched Nandi tribesmen circle a lion and drive spear after spear into its flanks, fling themselves on its prone form, and hack it to pieces. One way or another, they had lived in the marrow of things, and they had been utterly free. As happy as they had ever been.

"Senhor Kermit," said Luz. "The chief is ready to see us."

THE GREAT MAN STOOD in the full painted glare of the sun, his arms folded, his head sagging. Between his legs, like something he had just extruded, lay the white men's rifles. The message was clear. If they wanted their thunder sticks, they would have to kneel before him.

This they never would do. On that point Kermit was resolved.

Indeed, he was already calculating how long the impasse would last when he heard the Colonel's wheezing chuckle.

"Very well, Your Majesty."

With a groan, the old man stooped and handed Kermit his Winchester, then stooped once more and grabbed his Springfield.

"Ah, yes," he said, using the gun to prop himself up again. "The old medicine. Wasn't sure I'd ever see it again. I think I'm feeling better already. Oh, but give it an eyeball, would you?"

Kermit peered down the barrel, locked and unlocked the rear bolt, and then, without thinking, began to raise the Winchester to his eye. From nowhere, it seemed, a covey of Cinta Larga warriors converged on him, their hands on their longbows.

"Luz," he said. "Tell them I am not firing."

"They do not like it when you point."

"I understand, but please explain to them we cannot shoot. We have nothing to shoot *with*. We will need our cartridges."

A crease sketched itself across Luz's brow. *"Cartuchos?"*

"It's what holds the . . . the bullet and the gunpowder, and the point is, without cartridges, the guns won't work. We won't be able to hunt."

Luz looked at him, looked back at the chief.

"There was a bag," Kermit insisted. "When we were *brought* here—we had a bag with cartridges."

Even as his impatience mounted, a wisp of hope sailed up. The cartridges were still in that clearing, only a hundred yards from camp. They would have to go back for them.

Then—from some great abstract height, it seemed—a canvas bag landed with a plop at Kermit's feet. Inside it were a dozen smokeless powder cartridges with soft-point bullets.

"Well, now," said the Colonel. "That's five for each of us, and a pair left over. We shall have to aim true, eh?"

The chief watched them for some time longer, as though he was trying to satisfy himself of something. Then, unfolding his arms, he murmured a few words and stalked away.

"Sentimental old fool, isn't he?" said the Colonel. "Never mind, we've quite enough to do as it is. Before we go, Kermit, I should probably tell you which way my thoughts have been inclining. It seems to me we must dispense with the fantasy that we will simply stumble *over* this Beast in the course of our wanderings. That would be a deeply unlikely prospect even if we knew what species it was and could isolate it in its native clime. Making it even unlikelier— well, as these savages have already told us, it follows the perfectly sensible practice of attacking by night. Oh, I suppose, if we were extremely fortunate, we might catch it *slumbering*, but that's the stuff of boys' adventure, wouldn't you agree? What I propose, therefore, is to examine the *other* crime scenes."

"Other?"

"Well, we have two human corpses, do we not? Left exactly where they were killed. Some time has passed, but if we examine the grounds thoroughly enough, we may just find that this Beastie of ours has left behind, well, some clue or other to its identity. Something we can use to prepare ourselves for when it next comes."

"Assuming it does come."

"Oh, it will," said the old man, with a grave tilt of his head. "Mark my words, it *will*. Nothing in the least retiring about it. It's tasted blood, and it wants more. Now, I seem to recall that the most recent human victim was . . . one of their own braves, is that so? Dragged a short distance from the village. No better place to start our inquiries, as I'm sure you'll agree, so the only thing left to say is *chop, chop!* Wish we'd gotten an earlier start; the day's already half gone. . . ."

Kermit looked slowly around. He was ashamed to admit it, but he had expected more of a send-off from the village. The day was infernally hot, though, and the Cinta Larga were busy doing what they always did: surviving. Hunting and fishing, yes, and gathering firewood and peeling and grating and pounding the poison out of their manioc root and carving new arrows and feeding their babies. There was no one left to wrap a nut garland around Kermit's neck or kiss him on the cheek or shed the smallest tear.

The Colonel, for his part, could barely be restrained. "What in heaven's name are we waiting for? Much to do, *much* to do. Are you ready, Senhorita Luz? Oh, hold on a bit, here's the rest of our party."

With the mincing steps of a court page, Thiago came toward them, carrying only a walking stick and a sharpened end of bamboo. His face was a mask of solemn purpose, until he got within five feet. Then, with a squeal of joy, he turned his stick into a rifle and swiveled it from side to side, spraying invisible rounds.

"Ga-boom! Ga-boom!"

"Ha!" shouted the Colonel. "An artilleryman, is it? Just you wait, young squire, you'll get your turn soon enough. Now, if you wouldn't mind, oh, disarming for a second, I must ask a great kindness of you, young Thiago. Are you marking me? You must agree to stick to me like a burr. Like a *burr*, I say. Otherwise, I shall become hopelessly lost before another minute is out. What do you say?"

Thiago had enough presence of mind to grasp that something was being asked of him. After a brief consideration, he nodded yes.

"Well, that's splendid. Now, if you'd be so good as to walk to my *right*. Just like that, yes. It's the only spot I have any peripheral vision at all. But you needn't worry: I may lack vision and speed, but I *compensate*. Oh, I'm the doggedest old cuss you ever saw."

Some things, it seemed, really were universal. The look of wonder, for example, that crossed Thiago's face as the Colonel's words showered down on him. It was the expression the old man tended to produce wherever he went in the world.

"And do remind me to tell you about the first time I went hunting buffaloes. Why, it was raining hard enough to drown a rat. You couldn't tell what was buffalo and what was *water*. It was touch-and-go, I don't mind telling you, but, to my great good fortune, I had a fine associate name of Cadmus *Swallow.* . . ."

So they walked, the old man and the boy, until they reached the forest wall. The boy used his bamboo knife to hack out a crevice in the vines and then push himself through. The old man followed.

"All will be well," said Luz. "I believe this."

And she, too, disappeared into the jungle.

Kermit stared after her. Then he looked back.

Someone was watching them go, after all. It was Bokra, the old man with the marbled eyes, holding in his arms the half-plucked harpy eagle. Freed from its cage, the bird showed no inclination to take flight but simply nestled against its protector's shrunken chest, cooing and purring. The old man stroked its balding skin with his cadaverous fingers and, just as Kermit was about to turn away, began unexpectedly to cackle.

"Curupira!" he called. "Curupira!"

12

As soon as Kermit entered the forest, the light vanished like a breath. But the mosquitoes—what else had they to do but follow? For some two hundred lengths, Kermit waved them away in the mechanical, hopeless fashion of a jungle traveler—until he realized he was swatting only air.

He stopped, inspected his surroundings. No breeze had risen up. The air was every bit as hot. The trees still rose in their vast smooth columns, blotting out any thought of sun. But the mosquitoes were gone. And so were the gnats and flies and bees. Every flying torment had abandoned its post—and headed straight to a darkened heap some twelve feet off.

There rose to his nostrils now a rich, hot, sweet scent. The unmistakable scent of decaying flesh.

"Dear God," Kermit whispered to Luz. "They couldn't forsake tribal custom for once? Bury the poor fellow?"

Luz shook her head. "You must not touch a man who is taken by evil spirits. The same thing could happen to you."

"It's barbarous," the Colonel muttered. "Leaving a man to rot like that. Listen, now, Kermit, we mustn't let the boy see."

But Thiago had been at the head of their party from the start, and he was looking down at that body without a tremor or recoil, surveying its flaps of rotting skin . . . its shreds of bone and tissue . . . that *head* . . . tilted back and wrenched open, as if to roar away the insects that circled it in a frenzy of ardor.

The Beast, though, hadn't left much for the bugs to feast on. Muscle, heart, liver—all were gone. The man had been peeled open and scooped out like a tin of sardines. The only organs that remained were his eyes, and, under the ministrations of heat and bacteria, even these had melted into black craters, staring out of a mustard-colored mask.

"*Somebody* was hungry," said the Colonel, half-grimacing at his own callousness. "Quite a dismal crime scene, I'm afraid. No light to speak of, many hours of decay. I doubt even the finest Manhattan coroner could tell us exactly how the fellow died."

"So many causes of death to choose from," added Kermit.

"It would help just to know if he was insensible from the start. Or did he fight the whole way? Was there some—some coup de grâce the Beast administered?"

"And where did all the blood go?"

For all its decomposition, it was the cleanest corpse Kermit had ever seen. Not an ooze or seep anywhere.

"Well," said the old man, "we know the answer to that one. Our Beastie's a drinker. Damn me, though, it kills in a way I've never seen before. Beyond malevolence, more like . . ."

"Comprehensiveness."

"Yes. Just so. The thing doesn't want simply to kill. It wants the *whole* of its prey."

From high above them, a brood of cicadas broke into a grinding whir, as shocking as a steam whistle. Turning, Kermit found

Luz, ten paces off, her hands moving at angles. Only hours later would he realize she was genuflecting.

"Can you tell us about the victim?" he called.

"What do you wish to know?"

"How old was he?"

"He was young. A man, but young."

"Eighteen? Nineteen?"

"Young."

"You say he was one of the men keeping watch that night."

"Yes."

"Did anyone see him attacked?"

"No."

"Did he cry out?"

She thought. "There was one shout. Very short."

"And then silence?"

"Yes."

"And he was dragged here?"

"Yes."

"By what path?"

She pointed to the ground. "This one. The one we came by."

Kermit's eyes widened. So the path they'd been traveling had been specially carved for them by the Beast itself. But as he looked back, the only signs of violence he could see were bent-back shrubs . . . tiny disruptions in the carpet of humus. . . .

"Did they find anything near the body?" he asked.

"Such as what, Senhor?"

"Markings. A piece of hide."

"I cannot say. I wasn't there."

He had to fight the impulse to shake her.

"The men who found him," he persisted. "Did they say anything about what they found?"

"I heard them say something. To the other women."

"Yes?"

"They said the Beast must have come from above."

"Why?"

"There was nothing leading away from the body."

"No tracks?"

"None."

Against his will, Kermit's eyes swung to the vertical, followed the bole of the nearest tree some one hundred feet, all the way to its crown, where the tree threw out its side branches and gathered into a dense matting of vine and leaf.

"Aerial," guessed the old man. "Is that what they're thinking?"

"Something like that."

"Oh, very well, then. Search the skies all you like. You won't find it, I tell you."

"It makes as much sense as any—"

"Kermit, what's the biggest bird you've ever seen?"

"I don't know. Albatross?"

"And how long would you suppose its wingspan to be?"

"Ten, twelve feet."

"And what's the biggest thing you've ever seen it pick up?"

"Not sure, really. Largish fish . . . a squid, maybe."

"So you're telling me there's a *bird* out there so large, so powerful, it can drag a full-grown man through underbrush and foliage—*dense* foliage—thirty or forty yards with minimal protest and then have its way so utterly with him that"—the old man gestured to the corpse—"*this* is the result?"

"I'm not saying anything. I'm just trying to make the evidence fit."

"And what would a fine detective like your Mr. Holmes say in such a case? If the evidence doesn't fit the theory . . ."

"We need a new theory."

"Precisely."

"For my part," said Kermit, "I'd settle for more evidence."

Even in the jungle's churchy gloom, it was impossible to miss the gleam in the old man's eye.

"You anticipate my very thought. Ask Luz if she'll take us to the other body."

But her eyes didn't exactly light up at the request. "There will not be much to see, Senhor. It was only a child."

"All the same."

"It is farther, much farther."

"How much farther?"

"Oh . . . many minutes, Senhor. Perhaps an hour."

The words "no matter" danced on Kermit's tongue. Then he saw how the Colonel was beginning to sag, subtly, against the trunk of a silk-cotton. How the earliest signs of vacancy—the old Cuban fever—were shining from the old man's eyes.

"Father . . . if it's all the same to you . . . maybe Luz and I should go on, just the two of us. You can go back to our hut and rest."

"*Rest?*" The Colonel swayed into erectness. "Nonsense. You're as bad as Cajazeira. I mean to conclude this business, even if it kills me."

"But the heat, Father. And your leg. You can barely stand on it."

"Oh, be quiet, will you? I'm feeling fitter every second! And with this *Leatherstocking* here"—the old man gave Thiago a tiny cuff on the cheek—"we shan't travel any farther than is strictly needed. Lay on, I say."

The footing was hard, the way narrow, but true to the Colonel's prediction, Thiago threaded a sure line. A *trail,* one might have called it, but it was impossible for a non-native to pick out the markers. A bent branch? A macaw feather? A slick of moss? Somehow the boy beat on.

Now and again, the sibilant accents of insects came whispering down. But by and large it was *their* tread they heard, *their* breath. *Like a dream,* thought Kermit. No, *the* dream: the staple of his childhood slumbers. Once again he was walking down the long, empty, amplifying halls of a house—not his house, not anyone's—and every hall led to another, and nothing intruded, and nothing resolved.

In the dream, of course, there was never any question of stopping. Here in the jungle you could pause if you so chose, and each time you did, you would find evidence, incontrovertible, that you weren't alone. A snail as big as your fist. Ruby dragonflies hovering over stagnant pools. A sulfur-colored butterfly, flying past like a swallow.

Once, leaning against a tree for balance, Kermit found a mantis, four inches long, holding a fly in its spindly arms as if it were a peach. He could actually see the fly passing, mouthful by mouthful, down the mantis's glassy neck.

"Come," he heard Luz call. "We don't have far to go."

Minutes later they were descending to a stream bridged by a fallen tree. The Colonel teetered to a stop.

"All apologies. Do you think we might stop a bit?"

Shameful, really, the hissing retort that rose up in Kermit now. *I told you! I told you!*

He saw Luz whisper something to Thiago. At once the boy snatched up a palm leaf, folded it into a bowl, and lowered it into the stream, then carried the water back to the Colonel.

"Ah," said the old man, his mouth wincing open into a smile. "It's . . . it's a Gunga Din. . . ."

Thiago grinned back. "Gunha. Deen!"

"Yes, that's a . . . Naturally, I don't expect you to . . . recognize all my allusions. . . ."

"Who is Gunga Din?" asked Luz.

The two men looked at each other, oddly bashful.

"*É um poema,*" Kermit answered at last. "You wouldn't have heard it."

"A poem?"

"Yes, by a Rudyard Kipling."

"Who just happens to be one of Kermit's best pals," the Colonel volunteered.

"Father—"

"You've stayed at the man's house, haven't you?"

"I hardly think—"

"What is this poem about?" Luz asked.

Kermit shrugged. "It's about—how would you say it?—*um menino de água*. A water boy. Only he's a man, I suppose. His job is to bring water to the English troops while they're fighting."

"This Gunga Din is English?"

"Uh, no. He's Indian. From India, I mean."

"India . . ." She let the name rest on her tongue. "And he helps the Englishmen with their fighting?"

"In a fashion, yes."

"And who are they fighting?"

"Well, other Indians. It's a bit hard to explain."

"Whatever you're telling her," called the Colonel, "don't ruin the ending! You know how I hate that."

"At any rate," Kermit explained, "Gunga Din's job puts him in great danger. But he bears this danger willingly, although the men he serves are sometimes unkind to him."

"Why?"

"Because of . . ." He glanced from Luz to Thiago and back again. "Because of his skin."

"And what is wrong with it? He has scars or sores?"

"No, it's just that, being Indian, he's a bit darker in hue than the . . . than the Englishmen."

Luz nodded, said nothing.

"But the point *is*," Kermit rushed on, "the whole *moral* of the poem is that one shouldn't judge a man by the color of his skin. That he might have quite noble qualities underneath. It's really . . . I've always considered it Kipling's most democratic verse."

He struggled to translate this last bit, but Luz gave the impression of having left the subject behind. Reaching into a sisal bag, she drew out a handful of Brazil nuts—already shelled, thank God—and poured a ration into each of the men's palms, then divided the rest between Thiago and herself. For some minutes they sat there, chewing, feeling the heat pile on them like sediment.

"Here's an idea!" the old man cried. "Why don't we do the whole poem?"

Kermit squinted at him. " 'Gunga Din,' you mean?"

"We could perform it right here. It's a short piece, after all; wouldn't take more than a minute or two. What do you say, Kermit?"

"Why would we do such a thing?"

"Because that's what leaders do," the old man snapped. "They lift the spirits of their troops any way they can."

He might as well have said: *That's what men do.*

"Then lift them on your own," said Kermit. "I don't recall the words."

"Oh, that's all right," said the old man, all breezy. "Between us we'll manage. With Kipling, it's like an old tune. Once you get going, the words just pour out. But how are we to enlist our fellow conspirators, I wonder? Thiago, my boy! Oh, I know you can't quite make out what I'm saying, but I want to assure you that you have the most important part of the whole poem. Yes, you will recite the central part of the poem—the *refrain,* yes. It's the height of simplicity. You need but shout the man's last name three times. In your best barracks growl. Like this: *Din! Din! Din!* Can you do that?"

"Deen deen deen."

"A very fine first effort, but a touch lacking in the volume department. Do you think you might . . ."

The old man cupped his hands around his mouth, and the boy responded with three shrieks loud enough to startle a parrot into flight.

"*Deen! Deen! Deen!*"

"Ha! A voice crying out in the wilderness. A *prodigy* of bel canto production. Dame Nellie Melba would sob for joy. Now then, Mademoiselle Luz, *you* shall be responsible for what I like to call the capper. Oh, no need to look so pained, it's simply the man's full name. *Gunga. Din.* If I'm not mistaken, it's the closing rhyme of virtually every refrain. Er . . . *repetir,* if you'd be so kind."

Luz cast her eyes to one side. "Gunha . . . in . . ."

"Extraordinary. Duse herself could do no better. Now, then, Kermit, how's your Cockney?"

"Better than yours."

"I don't doubt it. You perforce will be our narrator, if you don't mind carrying all the linguistic freight. The rest of us will chip in wherever necessary, won't we?"

"And what will *you* do?"

"*I*"—the old man propped his rifle in the sand and hoisted himself to his feet—"shall be the conductor. Master Thiago, if I might have that pointed . . . *thingie* of yours? Thank you very much."

Rapping the bamboo knife against a neighboring tree, the Colonel pushed out his chest and, in his best carnival barker's voice, addressed an invisible throng of onlookers.

"Ladies and gentlemen! On behalf of the Jungle Philharmonic and La Comédie Brazilienne, it is my great and unspeakable honor to present the following unparalleled theatrical spectacle. Directed by: *Us*. Starring: *Us*. And being that this ain't no vaudeville, kindly refrain from applauding until we are duly done and finished. I give you now . . . the great . . . the awe-inspiring . . . Kermit the Magniloquent!"

The old man swung an arm toward Kermit and backed away, softly clapping. The seconds piled on top of one another as Kermit stood there, feeling the familiar clutch in his chest and throat. This was exactly the kind of public spectacle he had always dreaded as a child. Playing his mandolin in the North Room, with brother Quentin plunking along on the piano, and rows of beneficent adults, drowsily nodding. He remembered stiff collars and tight shoes and hair combed as far down as it could go—the curdled complacency that piled on top of every chord. *Darling, aren't they? Precious* . . . Quentin enjoyed the attention, but to a boy like Kermit, it was a whole season of penitence packed into half an hour.

"Father, I really don't think—"

"Please." Luz braided her fingers into a supplicating knot. "We should like to hear, Senhor."

God, how does the poem even start? Something about beer and gin, wasn't it? His mind swirled with fragments of dialect. Then, with a swiftness that astonished him, the pieces clotted into lines, and the words began to cascade from his mouth.

> You may talk o' gin an' beer
> When you're quartered safe out 'ere,
> An' you're sent to penny-fights an' Aldershot it;
> But if it comes to slaughter
> You will do your work on water,
> An' you'll lick the bloomin' boots of 'im that's got it.

One line sped into another until he was riding the poem like a flume, all traces of self-consciousness washed away. Fascinated, he felt the stillness that lay just beneath the words—*his* stillness; *his* calm. With something like pleasure, he watched the Colonel carve the air with his bamboo baton. He watched the foreboding disappear from Luz's and Thiago's faces as they accepted their cues and spoke their lines and, with a flicker of surprise, wove themselves into the larger texture.

Soon a competitive camaraderie took hold. Kermit screwed up his eyes and gave each line an extra flourish of East End. Thiago, in the midst of shouting his "Deen deen deen," executed a deft little jig, like a tin soldier. Luz improvised some stage business of her own, sinking to one knee and extending her palms like a salver as she crooned, "Gunha deen . . ."

On they went, adding embroidery with each stanza—a rising inflection, a dip of the head, syncopation—their spirits growing higher even as the poem grew sadder. By the time Gunga Din had dragged the wounded narrator to safety and been drilled with a bullet for his pains, there was almost no containing them. Kermit leaped onto the nearest rock and, in the ripest of cadences, declaimed the penultimate lines:

> *Tho' I've belted you an' flayed you,*
> *By the livin' Gawd that made you,*
> *You're a better man than I am . . .*

Upon which the Colonel, waving his arms in a symphonic frenzy, brought all the voices together for the final syllables.

"Gun—ga—dinnnnnn!"

Like any good chord, its resonance depended less on noise than agreement, and so thoroughly were they in tune by this moment that the sound knifed upward, through the strata of heat and humidity, and charged straight for the sky. Long after the sound had ended, they were following it with their eyes.

"Thunderous applause!" bellowed the Colonel, flinging up his arms. "Flowers by the thousands! Mind your heads; the long-stemmed roses can kill. Oh, but let's not forget our *bows*! You first, Master Thiago. Like this, *entende?*"

Not only did the boy understand, he became so enamored of the movement that he kept repeating it, flopping up and down until the blood rushed to his head and the rest of him followed. As he lay there in the sand, every quarter of his reedy brown body shook with laughter—such a violent commotion that the air bent before it and then bore it outward in waves, and before another two seconds had passed, Luz and Kermit and the Colonel were every bit as convulsed. A *new* chord now, not quite so in balance as the last one but richer and warmer: the Colonel's rooster cackle somehow forbearing to drown out Thiago's snigger and Luz's breathy chuckle. It was the sort of laughter that drew strength from itself and forged higher.

Oh, it died away, as such noises must, but the sensation it left behind—this, too, was familiar to Kermit. He had known it as a child, sitting with his family on the Sagamore veranda on a summer night, watching the sun drop over Long Island Sound. On such an evening, the thrashers would have been out, along with the indigo buntings and bobolinks and catbirds. (All the Roosevelt children had been thoroughly schooled in bird calls.) And Kermit would feel his lids sagging beneath some combination of exhaustion and satiation, and for just a few seconds, maybe, he might feel himself in step with everything around him.

He would never have guessed, of course, that this same feeling could be so easily exported, could reestablish itself right here in the middle of the Amazonian jungle with people who had, until this very day, been unknown to him. It was a mystery almost too deep to sound.

The Colonel, for his part, was sufficiently buoyed to sketch out a limping form of quickstep, which he accompanied with a whistled rendition of "Garry Owen." "Old marching tune, Thiago. Very popular with the Fighting Sixty-Ninth. Now, my feet don't quite *bound* as they used to, but you get the idea, don't you? Yes, that's it, exactly! Oh, he's a hopper, this one! How I wish I had a fife."

Smiling, Luz sat in the stream's sandy margin, half in shade. After some consideration, Kermit joined her, relishing the feel of cool water against his sore-pocked flanks. Together they watched a helicon butterfly flicker and dive.

"Your father is very kind," said Luz. "He loves children."

"All people." *As long as they do what he says,* Kermit added silently, reproaching himself in the next breath. "My father is a great man," he muttered.

The stream was cool and deep, but a few shafts of daylight leaking through the canopy lit up the streambed like an aquarium, disclosing crowds of small fish, silver and blue and gold, darting and jostling.

"Luz, might I ask you something?"

"Yes."

"Is Thiago yours?"

She waited some space before nodding.

"And was he born here? In this forest?"

Again she nodded.

"You have lived here some time, then. You yourself."

Her eyes pinched together, as if she were rounding up a sum. "I was twelve," she said.

"When you came here?"

"Yes."

"And you came from . . ."

"Out there."

"Ah, yes. Just like me."

He was quiet awhile, following the migrations of the fish.

"I confess, Luz. You have dealt a serious blow to our pride."

"How is this?"

"We believed—my father and I, our comrades—we thought we were the first white men to come to these parts. We thought no *civilizado* had preceded us. It seems we were mistaken."

"My father was not a *civilizado*. Not in truth. He was a missionary."

"Jesuit?"

"No. No." She smiled, just a little. "Father never belonged to any church. He said it was between God and him."

"I see."

"One day—I must have been eleven; yes, eleven—God came and told him he must find the ones who had never seen the light of Christ. God said that was the surest way to heavenly reward. For all of us."

"Did God tell him where to look?"

"He said only to go north by west. From Tapirapuã. So my family, we took everything we could, and we left. We traveled for months. Forests and plains. When the mules died, we . . . we just walked. And every time we found a settlement—Indians, I mean—we would ask them: Have missionaries been here? And if they said yes, we would have to move on. Father wanted always to be the *first* man of God. He wanted to find the . . . the—"

"Virgins," prompted Kermit.

And regretted it as soon as the cloud swept over Luz's face.

"I don't—"

"What I meant is, you found a virgin river. Where no one else had been."

She nodded. "A black river. *Rio do Inferno,* that's what my mother called it. Father was very glad, though. He said, 'Imagine, Luz. We have dropped off the map. There is only God and us now.' He was very happy about this. We traded some beads and trinkets for a boat. It was nearly the last of our possessions, but Father said God would provide."

"And so you came downriver?"

"We tried. On the second day, our boat—the rapids took it, and it broke on the rocks. So we had to walk. It was hard. Father was a very good hunter—like you, Senhor Kermit—but there was little to eat." She took up a stick, stirred the stream's sediment into a cloud. "Mother died. I don't even know how. She went very fast. We buried her by the river."

"And then you kept walking?"

"Yes."

"How many days?"

"I don't remember. There's so much I don't remember."

"Do you remember meeting the Cinta Larga?"

She leaned forward, hugging her breasts to her knees. "You say *meet*, Senhor Kermit. I don't know what you mean by that. We did not *see* them."

"So you heard them?"

"Yes."

"Every night, I suppose. Before sunset."

She nodded. "Father, he would leave them presents. Little nothings. We had nothing to give. A shoelace, a bit of yarn. Things like that. Whatever we left, it was always gone the next day."

She stared into the water, her head sinking to her knees.

"And then one day we went to look, and the gift was gone and—and *they* were there. Just *there,* from nowhere. I thought they were ghosts. But Father was filled with joy. He got on his knees and gave thanks to God."

She fell silent.

"You don't need to go on, Luz."

"No, I was trying to remember how they looked to me then, that's all. They had their arrows drawn. I had never seen such big arrows. We hid behind Father, but he made us come out and face them. He wanted them to know we came in peace, so he . . . he gave them his knife. It was the only weapon he had."

Her face began to wrinkle.

"They didn't know what to make of it, Senhor Kermit. They had never seen metal. They kept passing it around, and then one of the men—by accident—he *cut* himself with it. A little—what's the word?—*entalho.* On the thumb. All the men, they gathered around to watch the blood come up on this man's thumb. Drop by drop. And this same man . . ."

She paused.

"This same man went to Father, and he . . . he drew the knife across Father's throat." Her own hand mimicked the motion, a swift, clean incision. "So much *more* blood. I don't think the man expected that. He thought it would be like the blood on his finger. I remember he—he *jumped* back, but the blood got all over him. I remember I was looking at this man, and I was looking at Father, and with all the blood I didn't—I wasn't sure who was . . ."

Her head tilted gently to one side as she fell silent again.

"That knife," Kermit said. "What happened to it?"

"They kept it. They were afraid of it, but they kept it. His Bible, too. They thought it had dark magic in it, so they were afraid to destroy it."

She stared into the stream awhile longer, then snapped her head back.

"My brother and sister. They were kept, too, but they died. It was a blessing, I think. They were younger than me. I believe this was God's kindness."

From somewhere in the forest behind them came the high raucous squawk of parrots.

"And you were married?" he asked. "To one of the village men?"

"One could say *married*." Her mouth twisted into something like a smile. "I was fourteen when I had Thiago. A baby with a baby."

Kermit stared down at his rotting boots. He was going to say . . . what? How sorry he was? But in the next second she was laughing.

"It is very strange, Senhor Kermit!"

"What is?"

"I have always dreamed I would tell this to somebody. In my own language, not theirs. And now . . ." She shook her head. "I never thought how it would *change* things—to speak them aloud. I listen to myself—*ele cortou sua garganta*—*minha mãe*—*makreu*—I think I must be talking about someone else. I think I must *be* someone else."

He said nothing, only watched the fish darting and whirling at the bottom of the stream. He felt her hand on his arm.

"Do you ever feel that way, Senhor Kermit? That you are not who you are?"

He was saved from answering by the shrieks of a howler monkey. In reply, the parrots set once more to squawking, and the chirring of the locusts swelled to its highest volume.

"Well," said Kermit once the noise had subsided. "Let's be off, shall we?"

13

THE COLONEL BY NOW HAD JIGGED HIMSELF INTO A NEW STATE OF exhaustion, and as he reached for his rifle, his left leg crumpled and sent him toppling forward. He might have formed quite a heap in the sand if Thiago hadn't put out a hand to arrest him. For several seconds, they hung there in a quivering suspension before the Colonel straightened himself.

"Thank you, my boy. Must have put my weight on the wrong *joint*. Out of joint, that's me! Help me walk it off, if you'd be so kind."

The boy took the Colonel's arm, and together they marked off segments of six feet at a time, the Colonel gamely dragging his leg behind him and Thiago keeping the grave, self-possessed pace of a sanatorium nurse.

"Your father," said Luz. "He is not well, I think. His leg."

"Old injury," Kermit answered. "He was struck by a trolley— *um carrinho*—some years ago. It threw him, oh, thirty feet—banged up his shin something fierce, it never really healed. And then just a few days ago he struck the same shin against a rock. It's bad now, getting worse." The heat began to rise in his voice. "If he stays here much longer . . ."

He'll die. The words were more stunning for not being spoken.

"You take good care of him, Senhor Kermit."

"Well, I—yes, I am responsible for him, naturally." He felt a faint tinge in his cheeks. "You must feel the same about Thiago."

"No," she said after some thought. "You will say I am a bad mother, Senhor, but I believe Thiago is strong. He will make his own way. He must."

Kermit watched the Colonel limp along the foreshore. "My father is strong, too," he said. "The strongest man I know. But there are things that lie outside our control."

"What things?"

"Well, this Beast. It's stronger than all of us combined. We'll need all the wits and weapons at our disposal, and even then we can't be sure of . . ."

He watched her face soften into a grin.

"What is it?" he asked.

"Nothing. I enjoy to hear you talk, that is all."

"Perhaps you don't appreciate the severity of our situation. There's a very good chance we will all be dead before this day is out. I don't think it's too much to . . . to ask that . . ."

And even as he spoke, he was conscious of the play of light on her eyes.

Play was the wrong word. The light had to *work* to make it through all those layers, and it came back changed. Not like Belle's limpid blues, he thought, transparent from top to bottom.

"Time to go," he said abruptly.

"As you wish, Senhor."

ON THE OTHER SIDE of the stream, the forest grew darker and danker. Dead sticks crunched beneath their feet. And rising through the gloom and ooze was a grove of trees, hung with pale globes that, in the tomblike pall, appeared to glow with their own light.

"Cacao," said Kermit.

"This is what she came for," Luz said. "The little one."

"Why such a distance for a cacao pod?"

"Her mother was sick. The cacao is medicine."

The image dug into some soft part of him. A young girl, traveling far from home, loading pods into her basket. Did she hear the thing coming for her? Did she run?

Luz had come to a stop. Directly ahead, a pair of butterflies with crimson-spotted wings rested on a pile of kindling. They stayed no longer than a breath, but they seemed to leave behind some particle of luminescence, for in the next instant Kermit saw that the kindling was an arm. And a leg. And something that might have been a head.

"Oh," he said.

This time, Thiago declined to charge forward—declined even to take another step—and by some instinct of protection or solidarity, the Colonel remained at his side. It was left to Kermit to approach the body.

The jungle had done its work. Only the bones and the still-vibrant fall of hair could be reliably called human. Everything else was a squall of black, bubbling with flies and ants. Kermit could manage no more than a few seconds of looking at a time. But with each new glance he came away with something.

"Same pattern of attack," he said, with affected ease. "Skin peeled away. Internal organs removed. The muscle tissue gone. Looks to be the same modus operandi, wouldn't you—Father?"

The Colonel had turned away.

"Are you all right, Father?"

"They left her here," he said, clipping his syllables. "Her mother, her father—they left her here to rot."

"Luz explained it to us. They believe the body harbors bad spirits. It's part of their lore."

"Hang their lore. This is a child. *Was* a child."

Gingerly, the old man knelt by the corpse and picked up one of her hands.

"Rigor mortis should have passed by now," he muttered.

With great care and delicacy, he unfolded the dead girl's fingers, one by one. The hand opened to reveal a thatch of hair, damp as oil in the sickly white expanse of skin.

The Colonel coiled the hair around his index finger and raised it toward the sky.

"By God," he whispered. "She got a piece of it."

"Are you certain?"

"As certain as one can be. If the poor girl was clutching something at the moment of her death, doesn't it stand to reason it belonged to her attacker? Why else would she have curled her fingers around it? Brave little thing, she went out fighting."

"Perhaps it's her own hair."

"But look at the color. Can you see? Brown. *Reddish* brown."

He dropped the hairs into his son's palm. They were coarse to the touch and surprisingly cool.

Kermit lifted them toward the half-light of the canopy. Grains of yellow and gold peeped through the brown.

"No sign of blood," he said. "They likely weren't torn out by the roots."

"Oh, I doubt the creature even felt it happening. He had larger matters on his mind. All the same, Kermit, this is awfully encouraging."

"Encouraging?"

"I ask you: What is hair?" The old man clapped him on the chest. "What is hair if not *corporeal*? Don't you see? We're no longer treating with spooks or hobgoblins. Be gone with you, Curupoorah, or whatever your name is. This Beast is a thing of *our* world." He seized his Springfield around the barrel. "If it's flesh we're vying with, then I give us a fighting chance. What about you?"

Kermit said nothing. It occurred to him, though, that things of flesh—of this world—could be quite as terrifying as the other kind. Not for the first time, he remembered Elliott waving from that bridge. Looking as corporeal as anyone.

Bon voyage.

"Shh," hissed Luz. "Listen."

Kermit's senses sprang open. He heard a cry of immense outrage, swelling over a period of seconds and then strangling down into something thin and quivering, no less eloquent. It was the sound of suffering.

The sound stopped, and for a few seconds they stood in place, letting its echoes settle over them.

"How far, do you think?" the Colonel asked.

"No more than a quarter mile."

"My sentiments exactly. From what direction?"

Here they couldn't agree. The Colonel favored retracing the ground they had just traveled, but Kermit pointed toward a thick copse of myrtles with leathery leaves the size of elephants' ears.

"There," he said. "I'm sure it was there."

"Thiago can lead you," said Luz.

She knelt until she was level with the boy, and from her mouth came a patois unique to the two of them: a mosaic of Portuguese and Cinta Larga (or so Kermit assumed), spiced with dumb show. Thiago listened gravely but with glittering eyes.

"Siga me!" he cried.

Follow me.

"Makings of a general," the old man murmured. "Lay on, Macduff."

The sound by now had fallen away. The jungle was still as death as they followed the boy through a forested tunnel so narrow that the trees jostled them as they passed. The path led down to a hollow studded with granite boulders, then climbed again. Within a few minutes, they were standing in a clearing: a tiny bay of light, in the center of which stood three or four silk-cotton trees, as bare and gray as stone walls. Around them the jungle walls pulsed and breathed. The sibilation of insects was like the sound of the sun striking the earth.

Thiago stopped, listened.

"Well?" said the Colonel.

The boy put up a finger. As if on command, a new sound welled up from the jungle interior. No, thought Kermit, not a new sound at all. He had heard it last night. That eerie lapping, quick and bright and metallic. The sound of an animal drinking its fill.

He peered through the spindles of trees. The light, as it poured from above, was peeling away the jungle's gloom, layer by layer. The shades parted to reveal a rough outcropping, strangely tawny in the greenish-black surroundings. As Kermit watched, the outline suddenly shifted—jerked—and now that sight converged with the sound, and he understood that he was looking at something animate. Something that had just killed.

He felt a tap on his shoulder. The Colonel was backing away, beckoning him to follow. Together, they retraced their path until they were standing once more in the granite hollow. Only then did the Colonel allow himself to speak.

"Highly promising," he said. "You didn't happen to notice the thing's color, did you?"

"Reddish brown." Kermit's fingers uncurled. The tuft of hair, so lately imprisoned in the dead girl's hand, lay sheathed in his palm. He'd been clutching it the whole way without knowing it.

"Hard to say what species it is." The old man blew on his spectacles, rubbed them with his sleeve. "From the color, I'd wager it's some kind of simian."

"Possibly."

"Do you think it saw us?"

"As far as I can tell, it never turned its head."

But, then, Kermit hadn't seen a head.

"Very well," said the Colonel. "What's our best course of action?"

The very casualness of his tone was itself an excitement. It had been like this in Africa. Every time they came within shooting range of some prized creature, everything slowed down: movement, breath.

"Conditions are good," Kermit said. "If he'd gone farther into the jungle, we wouldn't have such a clear view of him. He's— what?—twenty, thirty paces off?"

"Give or take."

"That's as clean a shot as we're going to get. We have to take it."

"But if we miss him," said the Colonel, "or wing him—"

"Then he'll run, sure as Sunday. Even wounded, he'll outpace us."

"How do we keep that from happening?"

Kermit frowned, tapped the stock of his Winchester. "We circle him. Give me a few minutes to get round to the other side. When I give the signal, you draw your bead and fire. If he turns and runs, I'll be waiting for him."

"So *you'll* fire the next round—"

"And you the next. We'll keep at him until he's brought to ground."

"Aim for the head?"

"If you can find it."

The old man nodded. "Then let us pray we shoot true, you and I. We've precious few bullets to spare."

"Senhor?"

Luz had followed them back down the path; Thiago was close behind.

"What is happening?" she asked.

"What's happening?" echoed Kermit, unable to keep the tension from his voice. "We're going to kill your Beast for you."

"We will help."

"Just stay out of sight, that's all. We need to keep the field as clear as we can."

A hush of incredulity crept into her voice. "You wish us to *hide*?"

"Stay low, that's all."

"For how long?"

"As long as it takes. A few minutes."

"And why should we do this, Senhor?"

"Because!"

She crossed her arms against her breasts. "That is not an answer."

"It's the only answer I have." But already his brain was floundering for something more persuasive. "Thiago," he gasped. "Someone must watch over him. Make sure he's all right."

The argument might have been more telling if the boy weren't presenting every bit as skeptical a front as his mother. They matched each other sneer for sneer, and all Kermit could do was turn his back on them and march up the hill, praying they wouldn't follow.

They don't understand. I have a plan.

But as soon as he gazed on that solitary reddish-brown shape in the jungle shadows, his plan began to sprout holes.

How could he possibly circle the thing without its knowing? How could he count on it running toward him at the first whiff of danger? For a few seconds, he hovered there at the forest's brink, feeling the veins in his wrist and neck swell. He took a breath, pulled apart a mesh of vines, and stepped through.

In at least one respect, Fortune smiled on him. The canopy on this side of the clearing was unusually thin, and so the light, rather than vanishing, merely diffused, allowing him to keep the creature at all times in his peripheral vision. But how slowly he progressed! Terrified of alerting his prey, he had to pry apart the overgrowth inch by inch and carry himself over branches and fallen trunks with the greatest possible deliberation—as if he were crawling across an ocean floor.

By now the lapping sound had given way to something more intimate: a voracious *gnawing* that made Kermit's innards writhe.

Yet as he clawed his way through the foliage, pushing away sticks and pods and the desiccated remains of a wasp's nest, this sound became an anchor—a comfort, even—reassuring him that he was *here* and the Beast was *there*.

An additional comfort: his Winchester, black and inviolate, swimming through the watery green.

Had it been five minutes since he'd left? Ten? Had he traveled twenty yards or thirty? It no longer mattered. All that mattered was keeping that sound in his left ear. Then, when the sound's angle bent, he stopped and braced himself against the peeling bole of a laurel tree. Slowly, he turned back toward the sound.

And saw nothing.

A prickle of panic seized him. *Where the hell is it?*

His eyes ranged up and down the lines of trees, looking for motion, a flash of color. He scanned the canopy's upper stories, and he was just starting to retrace his steps when something flickered into his line of vision.

It was a head—pale, still, and astonished—attached as if by whim to an empty cavity. A tapir, Kermit thought. Only the barest chassis of a tapir, stripped to its component parts. And into that devastated cavity the Beast—if Beast it was—had plunged its head with the fervor of a lover.

There was a bubble, a shudder. Then, with infinite slowness, the creature raised its head. Kermit's stomach contracted to the size of a pebble as he stared at that tangle of hair and blood and entrail, almost indissoluble from what it devoured. It was as if the creature, not yet sated, had turned to consuming itself.

With an obscene gargle, the Beast now lifted one of its own appendages and smeared it across its head. From the morass of tissue and plasma, a pair of eyes emerged. A shock of perception—*intelligence*—scanning the terrain.

Kermit drew back. Breathed in a draft of air and slowly expelled it. The Colonel was on the other side, concealed in some makeshift blind, waiting for Kermit's signal. Now was the moment.

What had the old man said? "Let us pray we shoot true." Kermit raised his tongue to his palate, but the tongue was dry, obdurate. It wouldn't signal. He wetted it with his lips, then tried again. Nothing. *Nothing!* He took another breath, then tried once more, and this time his tongue unbent itself enough to emit a series of staccato clicks, which flew one after another through the leaden air.

It was the squirrel's call he had been making all his life. Father would know it anywhere, but the *creature*—the creature had never heard such a sound before. It cocked its head, listening for more. Then it lurched upward and took a long step toward Kermit—when, from the woods behind, a shot rang out.

Father's first volley. Not in the head, as Kermit had hoped, but the shoulder. Startled, the creature let out a shriek and spun around, frantically canvassing the vines and boles. Kermit raised his rifle, positioned the thing in his sights.

Now, he thought. *Before it runs.*

But its next motion was neither forward nor back but *up*. With a velocity so fierce it was as if the laws of gravity had been instantly and absolutely abrogated, the creature flung itself straight into the overhanging branches.

Kermit gritted his teeth, muttered an oath. Once the creature was in the canopy, there would be no tracking it down. But then he noticed that the noise above his head was expanding. Branches were shaking; leaves were raining down. The creature wasn't retreating, it was merely seeking a faster and cleaner route to its next prey.

Kermit could just make out its outline, swinging from branch to branch with its one good arm, moving straight in the direction of the shot. Straight in the direction of the Colonel.

"Father," he whispered.

And then he was bellowing.

"Father! It's coming to you! It's coming to you!"

Kermit stumbled toward the clearing, slamming into trunks, tripping on buttresses. He heard another shot ring out, but the creature, undeterred, kept thrashing its path through the leaves and vines.

"Father!"

A third shot. The canopy went still.

Kermit stopped, strained his ears. Then he heard a stifled cry. A human cry.

With the butt of his rifle, Kermit hacked and bludgeoned his way through the last three yards of undergrowth, and as he tumbled back into the clearing, the rays of sun came at him like knives. He rubbed his eyes and, through a caramel haze, saw . . .

Something that looked like his father, sprawled on the ground beneath a grunting bloody mass of fur and leaves.

Luz and Thiago had thrown themselves on top of the creature. They were pummeling it with their fists, pounding for all they were worth, and yet so little did they trouble the thing that it had only to shrug to fling them off—with such a sickening force that Thiago was left in a tiny ball on the ground and Luz sat half insensible against a tree.

Now the creature was free to focus on its prey. With horror, Kermit noted the mottled pink of his father's face . . . heard the breath leaching out in broken measures. . . .

"No," Kermit growled. "You won't."

His rifle was already raised, his cheek was pressed against the stock, his finger was curled around the trigger.

Steady. Steady.

The bullet was so loud, it was as if it gutted the sky clean through. The creature screeched, grabbed its side, then tumbled over, rolling two or three times in the dirt before falling still.

For several seconds the old man lay there. Then, with a barbed groan, he levered himself up, squinting in the naked sunlight. "Have you . . . have you seen my—"

My glasses, he was going to say. Only there was no time to finish, because the creature was erect once more—alive, yes—and flying straight in Kermit's direction.

In his short life, Kermit had seen cheetahs, lions, antelopes, wildebeest. Never, never, never had he seen a creature—a wounded creature at that—move with such velocity. He had no time to reload, no time even to breathe or brace, so the collision, when it came, seemed to vibrate all the way down to his individual cells. When consciousness returned, he was flat on the ground, the creature was on top of him, pinning him to earth, rendering him just as helpless as the Colonel had been. His brain was clouded with pain. He could feel the creature's saliva sting like acid against his face.

Well, there it is, he thought. *Get it done with.*

It was no different from how he'd felt in that river, the water speeding him along, all thought of rescue abandoned. He was resigned. Ready. But then he opened his eyes and found himself staring up into a pair of eyes so layered with anguish and fear that, in what he assumed to be his final moments, Kermit was visited with the curious desire to comfort his killer.

There, there. It's all right. . . .

For some indeterminate length, they stared at each other. Then the world exploded around them.

It was a single shot, loud as a cannon in Kermit's ear. The creature's eyes sheeted over. Its frame rippled with spasms as it loosened its grip and tipped its head back. There was one last shot, and the weight fell away, and with a choked cry Kermit rolled himself up, already groping for his gun. In the clearing stood his father, pale and grim, the smoke curling from his rifle. Next to him, Luz and Thiago. At their feet, the still figure of the creature, its eyes popped open.

"God have mercy," the old man muttered.

Luz knelt down by the creature and peered into its eyes. *"Morto,"* she whispered.

"No," said Kermit. "Don't—"

In the very next second, every orifice in its face sprang open, and from out of its midsection a great plume spewed, catching Luz squarely in the face, blinding her and throwing her on her back.

With one final spasm of energy, the creature flung itself at her. As they rolled across the ground in a hideous embrace, the cry that issued from the creature's throat was more terrible than anything Kermit had ever heard. Rage and sorrow and terror and all the darkest emotions distilled into a wailing shriek that scattered every last parrot from the trees and left Kermit and the Colonel too transfixed even to lift their rifles. It was Thiago who kept his eye clear. Thiago who strode silently forward and plunged his bamboo dagger into the creature's back. Drove it in again and again and again until, with a gurgle and a gush, the beast collapsed in a sodden jumble of limbs. Even then Thiago continued to plunge the dagger, like an axman felling a tree, each stroke a declaration of will—until Kermit caught the boy's arm in mid-strike.

"Thiago . . ."

The boy's face was clouded like a night sky. His knuckles shone white and veined around the bamboo shaft.

"*Mamãe,*" he said.

Luz, virtually unrecognizable in her raiment of blood, staggered to her feet and drew him toward her.

"*Meu bebê,*" she cooed, softly teasing the dagger from his fingers. "*Meu grande homem.*"

The Colonel sank to his knees and lowered one ear to the creature's mouth—or at least the part of its head that most resembled a mouth. For upward of a minute, he knelt there, unmoving, listening for a breath. Then, with a pair of light snaps, he declared:

"*Now* it's *morto.*"

14

"W<small>HY</small>, K<small>ERMIT</small>," <small>SAID THE OLD MAN</small>. "Y<small>OU'RE SHIVERING</small>."

Of course I'm shivering, Kermit wanted to say. *It's freakishly cold.* He was actually following the trajectory of the breath from his mouth, expecting it to freeze in the air above him. But when he looked around at the others, he realized he was the only one trembling. Even Thiago was as still as a barber.

"And how is our brave lad?" asked the Colonel, lowering himself to the ground until he was looking directly into the boy's face. "All well?" he asked.

Thiago, without even quite knowing what was being asked of him, nodded.

"Little titan," said the Colonel, jabbing him lightly on the jaw. "Let us speak not of Gunga Din, let us speak of Horatius at the bridge, yes! I do not traffic in hyperbole. And the doughty Miss Luz!" He dragged a handkerchief from his pocket. "The Fearless, the Indomitable. I hereby proffer you a means of cleaning your person. *Para lavar,* my dear Luz."

She, too, nodded her thanks and began to wipe her face. The blood came off in thick daubs, like grease from a griddle.

"*Obrigada,*" she said.

The sun had shut itself behind a cloud, and in the melt of afternoon, the clearing seemed to be liquefying and evaporating around them. From every precinct of the jungle, insects swarmed forth, gossiping over their newest feast.

And yet how strangely that feast now loomed. No matter what angle Kermit came at the carcass from, no matter how much he pored over it, he couldn't put his finger on the part that didn't *work*. Then he heard Thiago murmur:

"*Pequeno.*"

That was it exactly. *Small.* Ludicrously small. As though some prankster had crept up behind them, stolen away the Beast, and substituted this . . . tiny changeling, a fraction of the original's size.

"Why, it's no more than three feet," whispered Kermit, kneeling by the creature. "Head to toe."

"Most curious," agreed the old man.

"More than curious, Father, we were—we were *helpless* before this thing. Utterly captive. Are we to believe this . . . this little *thing* created all this havoc?"

Kermit sat back on his haunches, squeezed his lids down to half-mast. "Luz," he said. "Give me the handkerchief."

Feeling a bit like a sculptor, he began to gouge away the layers of mud and blood from the creature's head. With each stroke, more and more features revealed themselves: a short snout; a scraggly beard; a pair of wide-set nostrils; two rows of humanoid teeth.

It was Luz, peering over Kermit's shoulder, who delivered the first verdict.

"*Bugio.*"

"What's that she said?"

"A howler monkey, Father."

"*Howler?* Are you certain?"

It was the eyes that gave it away finally. Solemn, dignified, ineffably wounded. It was a look no other monkey had.

"I don't understand," said the old man. "I've *heard* a howler before."

All these weeks in the jungle had made the Roosevelt-Rondon Expedition well acquainted with the cry. That shriek, fierce and guttural, penetrated for miles. Unmistakable, yes, and nothing like the unholy noise that still rang in Kermit's ears.

"Well," said the Colonel with an abbreviated sigh. "At least we know why it didn't leave tracks. Howlers are strictly arboreal, aren't they? It's why we've never been able to kill us any."

"They're also vegetarian."

"What's that?"

"They eat leaves and berries, Father. Just like gorillas."

"Ah, yes." The old man pinched his glasses up the bridge of his nose. "Apparently *this* howler begs to differ."

Once more, Kermit studied the creature's eyes, trying to remember how it had looked in its final moments, but the image was already blurring.

"There must be a scientific explanation," said the Colonel. "It might have acquired some pathogen or disease. Hydrophobia, perhaps. I've seen rabid dogs become quite extraordinarily aggressive."

"Have you seen a dog that could take down a jaguar? Devour it in minutes? Devour a full-grown man?"

"Well, not *yet* I haven't. Confound it, though, Kermit, this is a new world, as you said. A new *species*, for all we know. I daresay our friends at the Natural History Museum would—hello, what's this?"

Out of nowhere, it seemed, a stripe of blood had trickled down the old man's left eyeglass, bisecting his range of vision.

"Gad," he said. "These head wounds have a way of bleeding, don't they?"

"Father."

"Never mind, Kermit, it's just a cut. Nothing to get womanish about."

"No, it's . . ."

A crater. There was no better word for it. A hole the size of a silver dollar had been carved from the old man's forehead—driven, as if by an auger, through the skin all the way to the subcutaneous tissue. Very nearly to the bone. Luz was mopping the wound, but the blood kept flowing, so she rustled up some leaves from the forest floor—mahogany and buriti and spiny fern—and, with quick fingers, tore them and ground them into a poultice, which she glued together with her own spit and plastered over the wound. The work of no more than a minute, and still the blood came streaming forth.

"Não se mova," she snapped.

"Luz has instructed you not to move, Father."

"Oh, fine. I won't even breathe, how's that? You know, it's the queerest thing, Kermit, I don't remember the creature even touching me. Ugh. Another minute or two, I should have been just like that jaguar. Well, that's all right, if all we come away with is a few scratches, we must consider ourselves damned lucky."

Kermit surveyed their party: the Colonel with his seeping plaster; Luz with her raiment of blood; the ugly violet bruise just above Thiago's left eye. If any of them had been lucky, it was Kermit himself. No contusions. Nothing twisted, broken. Why, then, of all of them, was he the dullest in spirit?

He watched Luz bring out more Brazil nuts, saw Thiago fashion a ewer of couratari leaves and ferry over drafts of water from a nearby creek. He listened to the reams of words the Colonel cast forth between each swallow, watched the bright gnash of his teeth. *Yes,* Kermit remembered. *This is how it's supposed to be. After a kill.*

In just a few minutes, they would be returning in triumph to the Cinta Larga. They would be hailed as heroes. They would be escorted back to the expedition, brimming with tales of their latest adventure. Wouldn't their comrades be amazed? Wouldn't Father's readers at Scribner's gasp and clutch their cultured pearls when they heard of the Beast with No Tracks?

But none of that mattered so much as this. The expedition would travel on, and Kermit would reach the end of that accursed river, and, come June, he would be a married man. Married to the grandest girl in the world.

Why couldn't he relish such a prospect?

"Why are you such a gloomy Gus?"

On any other night, if Kermit were to sit in the front seat of his father's Haynes-Apperson Model 19, he might have been left alone for upward of two hours to smoke his cigarettes or recite Villon poems from memory or listen to the crickets and the ovenbirds. But tonight was different. Tonight Belle Willard, with the tenacity of a coonhound, had sniffed him out in his burrow, and she was now giving him the full blaze of her attention.

"You were quite right to run off," she was saying. "Squeak, piggy, squeak is a childish sort of game. Even for a summer evening."

"It wasn't the game. And I'm not being gloomy, not on purpose. I just like to get away every so often."

"And now I've gone and ruined it."

"Not at all."

"Are you quite sure? Would you care awfully if I joined you?"

He looked at her. "In the car, you mean?"

"I've never sat in a Haynes before. Only Packards."

"But I'm not . . ."

She was already walking around to the other side, her oyster dress flashing like scales in the moonlight.

"Do you need help?" he called.

"With what?"

"Climbing in."

"Of course not."

There was a rush of silk, a cloud of lavender perfume, and suddenly she was there, only a few feet away, in the darkened interior. It occurred to him how close to scandalous it was: a young man and a young woman sitting in a car together. On a night such as this. There could only be one reason. . . .

But that's not the reason. I didn't even ask her.

"Shall I leave the door open?" she asked. "Cooler that way."

"Certainly."

The silence wove around them.

"It's quite all right," she said. "We don't need to talk at all."

"No."

"What I mean is, *you* don't need to talk. I can do all the talking for both of us. Unless it's disagreeable."

He shook his head, softly gripped the steering wheel. "I'm sorry to be such a trial," he said.

"Not at all, Mr. Roosevelt. You merely strike me as . . . ohh, one of those brooding, *sensitive* sorts of souls. All hidden depths."

"Too well hidden, I think."

"Ah! You have graduated from taciturn to inscrutable."

To his own amazement, he was laughing. He could actually feel his breath on his hands.

"I'm so very afraid of being a bore," he confessed. "To you in particular."

"If I were bored, Mr. Roosevelt, you would be the first to know."

He was silent again, but only for a moment.

"You talk about depths, Miss Willard, but the question I ask sometimes is: What if there *aren't* any depths?"

"I'm afraid I don't follow you."

"*Inside* us, I mean. What if there aren't any depths at all? Just a great drop? Just nothing at all. . . ."

He couldn't see her face in the dark. He could only sense the tiny recoil in her willowy figure. But before he could apologize, she was rallying.

"In *that* case, Mr. Roosevelt, we shall drop together."

LOOKING BACK, IT WAS clear this was no grand affirmation on her part but an extension of her sociability. It was clear, too, that this was when he had begun to love her. And what better sign of his love than this? That when his thoughts should be tending toward the Beast, they kept sliding toward her. To that oilskin packet of letters pressed against his chest. Line by line, committed to memory as surely as Villon.

I don't know how, or why you should love me—perhaps because I too have prayed,—& been unhappy—and now you love me and my heart is very full—What have I done that God should choose me out of all the world for you to love—but as He has done this, so perhaps He will make me a little worthy of your love.

He closed his eyes and imagined her, as he so often did, on their wedding night. Prying her like a pearl from the shell of her gown. Tracing the long white stem of her neck . . . past the clavicle, the sternum . . . that first inkling of cleft . . .

Only today the fantasy didn't play out as usual. The trail darkened as he descended it, and the breast that peeped from behind the dress's folds was not Belle's—and the lips, parting to drink his, those weren't Belle's, either. . . .

"I hope it's tasty," said the Colonel.

"Sorry?"

"The Beast, I mean. As soon as we've brought him back to the village, I say we throw him on the fire. I reserve for myself first crack at the shanks."

"And what of our duty to the expedition's sponsors?" Kermit permitted himself a smile. "To science?"

"Oh, science is all well and good, but it won't fill a man's tumtum, will it?"

The Colonel pressed his hand against his belly and shouted with laughter. Like a virus, the laughter was carried from Luz to Thiago. For a time, they seemed actually to be lobbing it back and forth, seeing which of them could toss it higher.

"Dear me," said the Colonel, giving his eyes a wipe. "This must be the jolliest hunting party I have ever been part of. Wouldn't you agree, Kermit?"

"Absolutely."

"Well, enough levity. To quote the walrus, the time has *come*. We must put our heads together and determine how best to convey our Beastie back."

Of course, thought Kermit. They couldn't just leave the thing here. The chief, the entire village, would expect tangible *proof* of their deliverance. And with Thiago busy guiding them back and the Colonel barely able to walk, the job would have to fall to Kermit and Luz.

The chief problem was finding some comfortable arrangement for sharing the burden. Though they trussed the monkey's arms and legs with lianas and strapped it to a branch, the difference in stature between the two bearers caused the weight to shift back and forth, knocking each of them off balance. At last, in a fit of pique, Kermit slung the creature around his neck—like a sweater on a warm day—shuddering at the touch of its clotted fur.

"Let's be off," he muttered.

"Are you quite sure, Kermit? It's not too heavy?"

"I shall live."

He was twenty feet down the trail before his father called after him:

"That's quite a hair shirt!"

They took a more direct route back to the village, but it was even barer of comfort. Dead leaves, uprooted trees, broken branches, mummified husks. The wreckage grew higher and higher—rubbish and lumber twining with dried foliage and dead creepers. The only intrusion of color was a morpho butterfly, startled from an uprooted tree, gone like a memory.

Welcome to paradise.

But, ahead of him, young Thiago beat his usual path through the brush and, whenever the mood seized him, sang out, *"Deen! Deen! Deen!"* And Luz answered with her low, throaty chuckle, and the Colonel cried, "Ladies and gentlemen! Thiago the Magnificent! Thiago the Trailblazer!" And their laughter swelled and ebbed and mysteriously swelled again—until the Colonel gave out a sharp cry and dropped straight to the forest floor.

"Father, what's wrong?"

"Oh, just some thorn or other. Damned thing's gone right through the sole of my boot. No worries, I'll have it out in a wink."

But the wink turned into something longer, and the more Kermit waited, the more he felt the creature's weight on his back. His lips were chapped. His feet were sloshing inside his boots. His hands were as crinkled as if he had dipped them in a soda bath.

"Nearly got it," said the Colonel.

With a rasping grunt, Kermit flung the dead monkey from his shoulder, sank to the ground, and then jerked up again as the abscess on his buttock flared. Just ahead, he could see Thiago and Luz standing as still as fawns in the smoky light.

"You seem awfully down in the dumps," the old man said.

"Tired, I expect."

"Who could blame you? Are you sure you won't let me carry the creature for a bit?"

"We were wrong, Father."

"What's that?"

Kermit fingered the sweat out of his eyes. "We thought the Beast hunted only at night."

"Well, yes. That's true."

"We also thought it attacked only one prey at a time."

"So we did." The old man grunted slightly as he dug his fingers

into his foot. "Because that's what the preliminary testimony suggested, Kermit. Now that we have the testimony of our own senses,
any theories we previously entertained must give way before our
enlarged knowledge. Whether we like it or not, we have stumbled
across an entirely new—or at least a radically altered—life-form.
Unknown to Western science in all its particulars. We may only
record what we see and"—he squinted down at his bare foot—"let
Dame Reason sort out the rest."

"Dame Reason."

"Will you kindly tell me what is vexing you so much?"

"I don't know that I can." Kermit leaned back against the smooth
brown bole of a laurel, angled his chin to the sky. "Do you recall
what you said before, Father? How deuced unlikely it would be if
we simply *stumbled* over the thing?"

"Did I say that?"

"You said it would be 'the stuff of boys' adventure.'"

"Well, yes, so it would be if we'd found it *slumbering*. But, as
you'll recall, the Beast called itself to our attention."

"So it did. And in a place where we would be sure to see it."

The Colonel's eyebrows drew down. "Something's not squar-
ing for you."

"Something, yes."

"You surely can't believe we killed the wrong animal."

"No. It was the right one. It could be no other."

"Then what can be the trouble?"

Kermit frowned, curled a vine around his finger. "It was
just . . ."

"Yes?"

"It was too easy, Father."

"*Easy?*" The old man's mouth made a perfect hoop. "Do you
call the four of us being nearly killed—do you consider that *easy*? I
have enjoyed considerably easier days."

"What I mean is, the chronology is off."

"Chronology . . ."

"Do you remember in Africa how long it took us to bag your lion? *Days* we spent looking. And yet today—today we travel into a jungle and, in the space of a few hours, we stumble across a creature that has eluded the mighty Cinta Larga hunters for weeks. What are we to call that? Beginner's luck?"

He could see the bull-like flare in the old man's nostrils.

"Kermit, I must tell you. I have never known anyone more afraid of succeeding than you. Since you choose willfully to ignore what we've accomplished, let me refresh your memory. We took it upon ourselves to find a beast. We *found* said beast. More than that, we caught it red-handed—red-mouthed, red-*everythinged*. We observed with our very own eyes its velocity, its capacity for destruction, its bloodthirst. We . . . we *effaced* it from the company of the living. Now, I don't know about you, but I call that a job well done, and I don't much care how long it took us to do it. We're not paid by the *hour*, you know, like some pipe fitter or stevedore. We're hunters."

Kermit ran his hand down his face. Why had he even said a word? There was no way he could have conveyed the look in that creature's eyes. Or explained that, of all the animals he had ever killed or helped to kill, he had never felt such tender feelings as he did toward this one. And that this tenderness was, under the circumstances, so awkward, so unmanning, that it was almost as good as poison.

"Enough!" he snarled. "I wish I hadn't brought it up."

"Well, you don't have to sulk about it."

"I'm not."

"I can excuse many things in a young man, but *sulkiness*—"

"Father, I promise you I am completely and utterly . . . sulk-*free*. I'm as happy as a clam. Look, I'll dance, shall I?"

Kermit set his foot on a shivered length of wood, felt it sink beneath his weight. He brought up his other foot and began to hop, lightly and brightly, like a hare.

"Don't be silly, Kermit."

"Not silly. *Happy*, Father."

"You look like a damned fool."

"A *happy* fool. Embracing his success."

In the next breath, he was dropping.

Through the wood, through the ground that lay beneath—straight into the earth itself.

15

THERE WAS NO TIME TO PROTEST, NO TIME TO REACT. HE WAS conscious only of the ground closing around him . . . the friction of ants and sand against his skin . . . and then suddenly the absence of friction. He blinked. Coughed out a bubble of surprise.

Some ledge or outcropping must have risen up to catch him. He swung out his arms in a wide scissoring arc and felt only a great suspension. From some remote region, the Colonel's voice came straining down.

"Kermit! Can you hear me?"

The fall must have shaken the wind from him, for it took him some time to raise his voice above a whisper.

"Here I am!"

"Are you hurt?"

"I don't believe so."

"Can you climb out?"

Once more, he swung his arms through the darkness. Nothing.

"I can't be sure. . . ."

"Senhor Kermit!" called Luz. *"We will send for help. We are not far from the village."*

"Steady, now!" shouted the Colonel. *"We will come back as soon as we can. Don't move an inch, do you hear?"*

As if he could. The darkness had closed even more tightly around him—without becoming any more tangible. Carefully, he extended his leg . . . kicked once . . . twice. On the third kick, he made contact with something. A piece of granite or schist, jarred loose by his boot. For some twenty or thirty seconds, he listened as it caromed downward, sending up tinny after-echoes.

The darkness began to rustle.

A rasp, a shudder. A scattering of squeaks. Then they were on him.

Raking his limbs, tearing at his clothing, scurrying up his trouser legs. They probed him. They *hungered* for him. And, even as he beat them away, he felt the first prickings of teeth on skin.

WHAT A FOOL. WHO but a fool would have blundered into a colony of vampire bats?

For his stupidity, he was now being repaid a hundredfold. The bats were thrashing his hair and jerking his shirt and diving into his crevices, and for a second or two he had a sense of being borne aloft, writhing and helpless.

"No," he heard himself say. "No."

Groaning, he peeled them off one at a time (shivering at each caress) and flung them into the darkness. He punched, he kicked, but it was like striking at shadows; they absorbed every blow and came right back, hissing and squealing.

Never had he known blood to flow so freely. It coursed down him in thick stripes, smearing his eyes, tincturing his lips. Through the blood, he could feel the lapping of their tongues. A thousand tongues.

Yes, they were drinking him as cheerfully as a cardinal in a birdbath, and still his arms and legs kept flailing. Not out of any hope or plan but from barest instinct.

He was, for that reason, slow—unconscionably slow—in grasping the change in his situation. In understanding that his limbs were flailing at air. That he was alone again.

All the air pent up inside him came rushing out. The bats had gone.

Had they simply returned to their slumbers? Or had they never even woken up?

Blood was everywhere: on his cheeks, his ankles, his wrists. Yet he couldn't see any of it. Even when he dipped his thumb in one of his cuts and held the thumb to his eye, the darkness folded around it.

And now, from that same darkness, something came gliding toward him.

Squinting, he made out the rudiments of a form clothed in black. He saw an outstretched arm, a pair of softly kicking legs. A face, as dapper and imperturbable as the first day Kermit beheld it.

Elliott.

Kermit pressed the heels of his fists against his eyes. Pressed harder and harder and, when the pain was more than he could stand, pulled his hands away.

Elliott was gone.

Nothing presented itself to his senses now but the dripping of water against stone. The sound built and built until Kermit began to imagine that it was eating away, inch by inch, the outcropping on which he sat. Soon, though, the dripping was replaced by a new sensation: an icy current of air rising up on either side and wreathing him. The same species of cold that he had felt an hour earlier, standing over that howler's carcass. It crawled through his pores, burrowed down to his bones.

"Show yourself," he growled. "Show your damned self."

Yet if he had been pressed to say to what or whom he was speaking, he couldn't have done it.

"Kermit!"

Gasping, he threw back his head. It was the old man's voice, chiming from above.

"We're sending a rope for you!"

No . . . He was shouting, but they couldn't hear. *Stay away.* But the cold had stopped his speech at its root.

"Kermit!"

With that last blast of sound from his father came the first inklings of thaw. It began slowly—a tiny flush of sensation in his extremities—and then it grew. His nerves quickened. His blood thrummed.

"Father . . ."

He was still barely audible. He had to draw in a long draft of air and send it flying upward.

"Father! I'm here!"

Something dropped through the darkness. He fastened his hands around it. A rope. Where in God's name had they found a rope?

"Grab hold, Kermit! We'll pull you up!"

He looped the rope around his legs and waist and gave a tug. The rope tautened and swung him outward. For several seconds he hung there, dangling over the void . . . but the rope held, and a few moments later he was rising. Already shielding his eyes because the jungle interior, after the darkness of the cave, was like the blaze of a foundry. Through the apertures of his fingers, he gazed at four Cinta Larga braves.

Not braves at all. *Boys.* No more than fifteen or sixteen. Their fathers too busy, presumably, with hunting and fishing to trouble themselves with rescuing a white man, so they had sent their striplings, who were incandescent with bravado until they laid eyes on Kermit. In the next second, they were falling back in confusion.

"Lord above!" said the Colonel. "What happened to you down there?"

Kermit squinted at his hands. Half a dozen pocks of blood, still declining to clot. More on his forearm. He could feel a half dozen more on his face alone.

"Bit of a quarrel," he replied.

The Cinta Larga lads were studying him now from a great remove.

"Luz," he said. "Would you be so kind as to thank these gentlemen?"

"There is no word for thanking, Senhor Kermit. That is for *civilizados*." She scraped a handful of moss from the bark of a couratari tree. "For you."

He had no idea what to do with it, so Luz performed the honors, calmly sponging the blood from his face and neck and arms.

Through it all, he could feel his heart racing as furiously as ever. Only it wasn't his heart at all but a flapping bat, trapped in the breast pocket of his shirt. Two inches long, its mouth parted as if to scream.

He cupped it in his palm, watched it drag its tongue frantically across its own body. And then watched Thiago pluck it away and carry it to the cave opening and, after a brief pause, let it drop.

By now the Cinta Larga lads had taken notice of the dead monkey that lay where Kermit had flung it. No one had identified the thing, but something about its twisted, trussed figure must have communicated status, for the lads drew even farther back.

"Ha!" said the Colonel. "They need a bit more work in the mettle mines, don't they?"

"Never mind," said Kermit. With a grim and ironic smile, he snatched up the howler and wrapped it once more around his shoulders. "Perhaps," he said to Luz, "these gentlemen would be so good as to show us the way."

* * *

THEY WERE JUST FIVE minutes outside the village when the Colonel, intently fingering the fog from his lenses, said:

"You gave us quite a scare back there."

"I'm sorry, Father."

"No, I'm only . . ." The old man wrapped the glasses around his ears. "I'm just glad you're all right. Can you imagine me telling your mother I lost you down a hole? *Oh, but don't worry, dear, he should turn up in China any second.* No, hold on, it wouldn't be China at all. Well, never mind. The point is, you're back among the living, for which I give inordinate thanks."

Kermit's boots were pressing half a second longer into the forest floor. The monkey's weight was beginning to tell. With a grunt, he tossed it to the ground.

"Father, may I pose a question?"

"Of course."

"Strictly hypothetical."

"Of course."

"What if we didn't kill the Beast?"

The old man slowed to an amble and then stopped. "Dear God, Kermit."

"Hear me out, please."

"I *have* heard you out. You admitted yourself it could be no other."

"I know. That's why this is strictly an intellectual exercise. To pass the time, if you like."

"Pass the time."

"For argument's sake, let us suppose that the animal we killed was *indeed* the animal that killed the girl, the young man, all those other creatures. We can agree on that, yes?"

"Mmm-hmm."

"But what if the *Beast* was something other?"

"Something other. So we've gone back to Coo-roo-whoever-he-is? I'm afraid this has ceased to be an intellectual exercise, Kermit."

"Father, do you remember when we were standing over that creature?"

"Of course."

"Do you remember how cold the air was?"

The Colonel's head moved with great deliberation from side to side. "I remember seeing you shiver. I don't recall there being any proximate cause."

"I'm telling you, Father, the air around me grew quite bizarrely cold. *Polar*."

"Very well, you felt a chill of some sort. Touch of malaria, perhaps; we've all had to—"

"It wasn't that."

"Or else it was your *blood* running cold. Don't you remember that lion we cornered on Mount Kenya? *There* was a cold moment. Thirty yards off, mane bristling, teeth showing. I had to hear the crack of the Winchester before I was quite sure I was breathing."

"No, Father. *No.* This was something different. Not malaria, not exactly fear. I can't define it; all I can say is I *felt* it. And not only there; I felt it in the cave."

"And again . . ." The old man made a tray of his hands. "Where better to experience a sudden drop in mercury than in a cave?"

Kermit let his head dangle. Let the breath come tumbling out. "That may be," he said.

"I don't mean to make light of your . . . your sensibilities, my boy, but the notion that one man might experience a climatological shift that somehow escapes his fellows—well, I hope you see that's difficult to countenance."

"Certainly."

Ahead of them, their Cinta Larga escorts had stopped to wait. Kermit could see their small square outlines in the purpling shadows.

Had he gone mad? Was that it?

It wasn't the first time the thought had crossed his mind. For many years, after all, he had been consorting with the specter of his dead uncle. But, if anything, he had come to view that as some private understanding between the universe and him—just another compartment to be sealed away from the others. Here in the jungle, the compartments were starting to leak.

"Listen to me, Kermit." The old man rested his hands on his son's shoulders. "You've been through an ordeal; we all have. I suggest—no, before you say another word, let me exhort you to *rest*. That is all. Rest. Give yourself time, and then come at this again. You'll be amazed at how different things appear. A calm, *relaxed* mind may discern connections that an agitated mind cannot. Wouldn't you agree?"

Kermit looked at him. "Of course."

"That's the spirit, my boy. Now, let's get a move on, shall we? They're all waiting for us, and we've precious little light left. You're quite sure you don't need help carrying the Beastie?"

"Oh, no." Kermit stooped once more and took up his freight. "I hardly notice it."

PART TWO

OUT OF
THE JUNGLE

16

IT HAD ALWAYS BEEN A SAGAMORE TRADITION THAT WHEN ROOSE-velt boys returned from their hunts—and they would have roved at best two or three miles from home—they would receive no hero's welcome. Indeed, they would receive no welcome at all, unless it was the maid beseeching them not to track mud through the foyer. The Colonel himself would wait until evening to query them about their exploits, and each of his questions would be so pointed and exact that whatever embellishments the boys had thought to add would peel away like burned skin. At which point their father would say merely, "Well done." And if one of those squirrels or rabbits should turn up at some later date on the dinner table, the old man might drawl, "This was yours, wasn't it, Archie?" and that was that.

All of this to explain why Kermit, though earlier hoping for a hero's send-off, was neither surprised nor offended by the lack of ceremony that greeted them when they returned. Their teenage escorts had run ahead with tidings, but the only figure that greeted them as they staggered out of the jungle was the chief himself. He sat on his tree-trunk throne with an air of dolorous expectancy, his eyes hooded, his head listing. If he was surprised to see Kermit bleeding from every quadrant and the Colonel limping after, his sole response was to let his head sink another inch.

Even when Kermit dropped the howler monkey at his feet, the chief's face didn't alter. He studied the carcass as if through a lorgnette. He muttered a few inquiries at Luz. Every angle and line of his body pronounced itself unpersuaded.

Of course, thought Kermit. *He's having the same reaction I had: The thing is too small!*

On impulse, Kermit tipped the creature onto its back. A puff of breath escaped the chief's throat as he beheld the belly soaked in blood and entrails . . . the wrenched-open jaw with its harvest of bloodstained teeth . . . the fierce and unnatural twist to the neck, as if the howler were already craning toward its next prey.

But what caught the chief's attention—what drew him off his stump and made him bend down for a better view—were the eyes. No longer awash in pity but violently popped open, fluorescent with rage. Even in death, they seemed to live, to *hunger.*

The chief rose with a shudder. For another minute he held his peace. Then he made a queer circling motion with his fingers. From his mouth came a series of rapid clicks, which were taken up across the village, staccato clusters that returned as a succession of shouts, the shouts thickening into bodies. Within a minute, every last Cinta Larga was sprinting toward the matted, blood-soaked creature that lay sprawled and broken in their plaza.

Man, woman, boy, and girl, they crowded round, not in any clear formation but with a clear intent. Having taken their fill of the spectacle, they began to move in a kind of maypole dance, linking hands and whirling in an undulating circle around the dead animal. The bolder ones sallied forth and bathed the carcass in volleys of spit.

One of the Cinta Larga braves lifted Thiago above the crowd, and from there the boy was passed from shoulder to shoulder, his limbs dancing, his face a trance of joy. Around and around he went, until one of the company abruptly pulled him down. It was the same man who had kept Thiago from crawling toward the strangers that morning, and he was no happier about their presence now. With a grunt of suppressed outrage, he threw the lad over his shoulder and strode back to his hut.

"Oh, no," said the Colonel. "That won't *do*. See here, my good fellow! I suggest you—"

He had taken a single belligerent step in the man's direction when Luz came flying toward them.

"No. No. *Seu pai. Seu pai.*"

The Colonel scowled. "What's she saying?"

"It's the boy's father," said Kermit.

"Oh! Reasserting the old paternal privileges when it suits him. Never mind that he sent his son into the jaws of death. I wouldn't mind having a word or two with—dear Lord . . ."

An aged woman with stained skin and freely swinging dugs had tottered toward them. Her face was folded over her toothless mouth, and a bowl was squeezed against her cantilevered hip.

"Please," said Luz. "She would like to treat Senhor Kermit's wounds."

Reaching into the bowl with her stubby fingers, the woman scooped out a mound of ocher paste and applied it in thick dollops to Kermit's face and neck and arms—wherever the bats had taken hold. The effect was instant. The heat in his skin changed to a caress.

"Please," he said, fighting the urge to embrace the woman. "Tell her she is very kind."

"She wishes to do this, Senhor. She believes you are a miracle."

He very nearly laughed.

"No, it is true," said Luz. "You have helped to kill the Beast. More than that, you have descended to the depths and come back. No men have done this before."

"Well, who can deny it?" said the old man when it was explained to him. "You're a veritable miracle worker, Kermit! Even if you do look a trifle geisha in that makeup. Now, will you kindly ask our interpreter when we might expect to return to our comrades?"

The query produced the faintest shadow in Luz's eyes.

"Is there something wrong?" Kermit asked.

"No, Senhor. The chief has said . . . he is very sorry to say to you that it is too late to take you back."

"Too late?" Kermit gazed at the yolk of the sun sinking behind the trees. "We were abducted in less light than this."

"But by the time they reached your friends, it would be dark, very dark."

"I don't give a damn if it's midnight. I mean to hold them to their word."

"No, Senhor, you must see this is a sign of their respect. Truly. If by chance you were to be lost on the way, this would be a very bad thing. For you and the honor of our tribe."

"Honor." The word trickled like wormwood down his throat. "You can tell them, Luz, that this is not honor. It is the *opposite* of honor to keep us here after we have fulfilled our agreement."

"I cannot blame you for being angry, but I swear to you the Cinta Larga will do what they say. They have great respect for you both, Senhor. That is why they wish you and your father to be their *convidados*. For our *festa*."

"Party?" interrupted the old man. "*Guests?* What can she be talking about?"

Two translations assembled themselves in Kermit's brain. The first was simply: *We are at their mercy.* He took the more diplomatic tack.

"The chief wishes us to postpone our departure until tomorrow morning so that we may join him tonight for a celebration."

He searched his father's face, waiting for some sign.

"I . . . regard . . . this . . . as . . ." The Colonel hammered his fist into his hand. "Downright neighborly, Kermit!"

"You're quite sure?"

"If the price of our freedom is some bowing and scraping and speechifying—well, I've had to endure much worse, believe me. You may tell His Majesty that we accept his gracious invitation but that we insist on being up with the dawn tomorrow. Oh, and see if they can fetch us some snacks in the meantime. I'm hungrier than a flock of birds."

HERE WAS THE SUREST sign that they had risen in the village's estimation: Instead of getting manioc, Kermit and the Colonel were proffered a roasted armadillo, still simmering in its clay pot. The only thing that kept them from swallowing it outright was the mechanical difficulty of tearing off chunks small enough.

"Bit like turtle," said the Colonel, squeaking his finger along his teeth.

"Or chicken."

"*Food*. That's what it tastes like."

They were still eating when the rain came.

All these months in Brazil, and Kermit never failed to be stunned by the speed of the storms. You saw a cloud lazily snarling over your head and then, before you knew it, the trees were writhing, and the sky was roaring, and you were done for.

They were barely in their huts when the rain massed into a cataract. No more than twenty minutes in duration, but it left behind a heaving fog that took with it most of the remaining light. Kermit could feel the drowse on his eyelids, the sag in his bones. . . .

"Time for a swim!" shouted the Colonel, stripping off his Army flannel shirt and his khakis.

"Father?"

But he was already gone. Striding through the village, clad only in his underdrawers, white as a summer cloud. He stumbled down the playa and marched right into the black stream—giggling at the first shock of cool water. Farther and farther he waded until, slipping on the stream bottom, he sank altogether, only to pop his head through the surface a second later.

"Up he comes!" shouted the Colonel. "Like a fat cork!"

By now a cluster of children had gathered to follow his progress. And the combination of his porcine squeal and his hairless porpoise torso, shining from the water, released something in them. They began to point and shriek, and when the old man, using his forearm as a blade, sent a spume crashing on their heads, the shrieks redoubled.

The effect on the rest of the village was not galvanic but incremental. Which is to say that three of the Cinta Larga women paused in the midst of chopping wood, and the glaze of abstraction on their faces lifted a little as they watched the children dart forward and fling gallons of water at the stranger. And though he splashed back twice as hard, the children came back even harder. The battle raged on. The laughter mounted to the sky.

"Kermit!" cried the old man. "Come in!"

The younger man hesitated. He thought of what might be lurking beneath that surface. The piranha with its bellicose jaw. The sharp-spined, blood-sipping candiru. The pirara, the piraiba. Oh, Cherrie had cataloged all the risks—stingrays, electric eels, caimans—but the events of the day had chipped away at enough of Kermit's reticence that, before he could talk himself out of it, he was kicking off his boots and tearing off his shirt. With a stifled cry, he flung himself headlong into the water.

The stream bottom caught him sooner than he expected, but he propelled himself back to the surface and was rewarded with a wall of water that caught him full in the face. Gasping, he saw the grinning spectacle of Thiago.

"You little devil," murmured Kermit.

He shoveled up two handfuls of water, but the boy was already spinning away.

"Don't let him escape!" the Colonel shouted. "He has no respect for his elders!"

Moving with exaggerated slowness, Kermit and his father began to circle the diving, darting boy, closing the noose tighter and tighter. But every time they sought to capture him, Thiago wriggled out of their grip or found a new hole to squirm through, and the hunt would be taken up again, half in jest, half in deadly earnest—such an entrancing spectacle that the other children fell utterly quiet before it. At last, after a succession of ducks and feints, the Colonel succeeded in collaring Thiago from behind and, with a bellow of triumph, tossed the boy straight up in the air. For a second or two, Thiago seemed to hang there, his arms and legs limp with delight, before crashing back into the water. And now the watching children broke their silence, clucked and howled and slapped the water and banged their wrists together.

Spent, Kermit found himself floating a little farther downstream. The water felt feathery against his skin. The sky was a lilac gray. He was glad—*glad*, yes—that they weren't leaving tonight.

He wondered how he would ever begin to describe this day to Belle. Phrases flitted across his mind. *The experience of . . . of repaying evil with good . . . of delivering a grateful people from their oppressor . . . is quite the most singularly rewarding . . .*

No. Maybe it was better to start with the Cinta Larga mothers, who had never quite left off their work—whose faces had never quite cracked open into smiles—but surely some ray of light had been breathed into their darkness. Surely they grasped at some unutterable level that two strangers had risked life and limb on their behalf.

It's true what they say, Belle. The feeling one gets at such times really can't be put into words. . . .

Belle.

His hand scrambled toward his chest. The oilskin envelope containing her letters was still there.

"Senhor!"

Luz was standing on the near shore. No more than ten feet away but looking very far off indeed.

"You must be very clean," she said.

He saw then that she was smiling. More freely than he had ever seen.

"Come in!" he called.

"We may not, Senhor. Women are not permitted to bathe with men."

"Oh, but I'm a monster, not a man."

She smiled again, shook her head.

"Well, in *that* case," he declared, "I shall come to shore."

Her head was bowed as he strode out of the water. They exchanged no words, but as he carried himself back to his hut, he noticed that she was following him.

"The children," she said. "They love your father."

"Oh, yes," he answered with a snort. "It's always been that way, you know. He was always the most popular of all the fathers. He was the only one who ever played with us. *And* our friends."

"Very nice."

"No matter how much muck and mire we got into, he'd wade right in, come back every bit as filthy. When we lived in the White House, he used to break off cabinet meetings—"

"Ministério?"

"The point is, he would interrupt his business—his very important business—and go scrambling with us along Rock Creek, up and down rocks. Little cliffs, really. He wasn't afraid of anything. Or, if the weather was bad, we'd make obstacle courses in the White House hallways. We always had the grandest time with him."

"He is still half a child."

"It's true."

More child, in fact, than Kermit had ever been. Once again he pondered the destiny that had linked him, through mere biology, to such a man.

He and Luz sat quietly in the hut, listening as the cries of the village youth gave way to the noises of the jungle. Toads. Crickets and cicadas. A parrot or two. And some strange lamentations that Kermit had still not learned to identify. What was it Cherrie had said? "Always talking, this jungle. About nothing at all."

"Your rifle," said Luz. "Can you . . ."

"Yes?"

"Can you tell me how you fire it?"

"You mean you've never shot a rifle before? Not even as a girl?"

"My father could not abide guns, so I am as stupid about them as any savage. I noticed . . . there was smoke that came out."

Kermit picked up his Winchester, felt its rind of moisture. "That's just the powder burning," he said. "Of course, you don't want too much smoke or you won't be able to see your target, in case you need to shoot again. There's also a bit of *resíduo* that comes out. A kind of soot."

"And the sound," she said. "Why is it so loud?"

"Why, because you're making a . . . a great explosion. A little *bomba*."

He thought of that day in the Sudan when they had surprised a rhino lolling on its side, its hide black in the sun. As soon as the Colonel stepped out of the bush, the rhino jumped to its feet. Too late. The first bullet went through its lungs. It wheeled, blood spuming from its nostrils, and galloped straight for them. The Colonel fired off his Holland, and Captain Slatter fired, too, with his one good hand, and the chord made by their blasts was the single loudest sound Kermit had ever heard in his life.

"Luz," he said. "Would you care to hold the rifle?"

"Oh, no."

"I don't mean fire it. I mean *hold* it. Here."

He pressed the Winchester into her hands.

"Don't be afraid," he said. "It's not the devil's plaything; it's a means, that's all. To an end. Now, just . . ." He reached over her shoulder. "Point the barrel."

"I am still afraid, I think."

"*This* hand goes . . ."

Hooping his fingers around her right wrist, he guided her toward the crook between the stock and the trigger guard.

"And the other hand goes around the *cano*, yes. Now you"—slowly, he drew the rifle toward her—"bring your cheek to the stock . . ."

He was standing directly behind her. Unable at first to distinguish the smell of gunmetal from the smell of her hair.

"And now," he said, "you're ready to aim."

"How?"

"Look through the sights."

"Yes . . ."

"And bring your target into alignment. Do you see that cicada on the wall?"

It was the size of a small rat, with a lantern for a head.

"I see it, yes."

"Frame it in your sights. But don't focus on the bug; let it become a blur. Focus on the sights instead."

"Very well."

"Is your target in view?"

"Yes."

"Well, then . . ."

Her finger curled around the trigger and quivered there. Kermit leaned in to her ear.

"Ready," he whispered.

The veins startled up from her hand. The trigger drew back. She jerked her finger free and flung down the rifle.

"Pardon me, Senhor."

"For heaven's sakes," he said. "I only meant to show you the thing."

"I know, Senhor. I pray you will forgive me."

He snatched up the gun, tossed it on the hammock.

"Perhaps you should go," he said. "I am sure you have better things to do."

She only lowered herself to the hut floor and watched him.

"All this humidity," he grumbled, wiping the stock on his trousers. "Hell on a rifle."

"Yes."

"One doesn't want the thing to rust."

"No."

He cocked one eye, peered down the barrel. Dabbed away some fouling.

"Tell me about Thiago's father," he said.

She was silent awhile.

"What do you wish to know?"

"His name, for example."

"Anhanga."

"And you are—I don't know what to call it—the *esposa* of Anhanga?"

"One of them."

"Ah."

A sly smile spread across her face. "I did not mean to shock you, Senhor. Here a man may have as many wives as he likes. If he can make them marry him."

"And how did he make you?"

"I was not his choice," she answered simply. "I believe he regrets it. He speaks often of trading me."

"Trading?"

"This is permitted, too. If a man sees a girl he likes, he may trade her for the wife he has. Or something else of use. A new belt. Some bows."

"And the *old* wife has no say in this?"

"Not if . . ." Luz paused. "Not if she is like me—from *out there.* Oh, but it is not just the men who do this, Senhor. I have known girls to take lovers of their own or lie down with other girls' men. They can do this so long as their husband does not become *uma piada*—something to laugh at."

"But you are not permitted to do this yourself."

"I have not wished it."

A spinster's logic, he thought. Yet here she was, the sap still rising in her. Had she been screening herself from the sun all these years, she might easily have slipped on a summer frock and walked into a Gracie Street cotillion, and no one would have been the wiser.

"Luz. What do you mean when you say Anhanga never chose you?"

"I was given to him."

"Why?"

"Because he killed my father."

Something tightened in Kermit's throat.

"They handed you over to your father's murderer?"

"Yes."

"But that's barbaric."

"No, Senhor. For them, it was the right thing. It was *justice,* as you say, though they didn't have the word for it. I never questioned. I suppose I was glad they let me live. And ashamed, too, to *be* alive. Probably I should have died with my father, or with my brother and sister. But I didn't." She began to scrape the dead skin from her toe. "When I gave birth to Thiago . . . I bled very much, but I lived, and Thiago lived. It made me barren, but I cannot complain, Senhor Kermit. It was God's doing."

"After all you have endured, Luz, why would God punish you?"

"Oh, no!" she exclaimed. "Not me. Them."

And, without warning, she rose and walked toward him. He could feel her breath stirring in his beard.

"It is all part of God's plan, Senhor, I believe that. I believe he sent the Beast. I believe he sent *you*."

"For what possible reason?"

"Ah, well." She shrugged. "If I knew this reason, I would be God."

They were silent once more as the shadows deepened around them.

"You should know, Senhor. Thiago is not the name they gave him. It is the one I use."

"Well, it's a fine name. A saint's name."

She nodded. "The first apostle to be martyred for his faith. It is there in the Book of Acts. I like to read to Thiago from the Bible sometimes."

"So they let you—"

"Not from my father's Bible. They buried that long ago, as I said. I recite from memory." She smiled. "This is what comes of being a missionary's daughter. Bits and pieces—whole chapters, even—come back word for word."

"No doubt."

"Thiago knows much Portuguese. He can make his way in the world. The world out there."

Kermit looked at her. "I am glad to know it," he said.

He was conscious, even as he spoke, that this was not the right answer. She leaned toward him and hooped her hands around his wrists.

"Senhor Kermit."

"Yes?"

"I wish to ask you something."

"Of course."

"When all this is done—when you leave here—I would like you to take Thiago."

Slowly, gently, he peeled her fingers from his wrists. He looked into her eyes.

"That is a large request," he said.

"I know."

"I don't even know how we could accomplish it for you."

"You need not worry. I will make it happen."

He slumped down on his hammock, kneaded his scalp. "The boy's father . . ."

"You're right. Anhanga would not approve. He would rather die, I think. But I will make certain he is not there when the time comes." Once more she pressed her hands in his. "The rest," she said, "is up to you."

17

"A BEAUTY, ISN'T IT?"

The Colonel nudged his elbow toward the sky, where a fat moon sat just above the parapet of the trees, pouring down bluish light on the palm fronds, on the crowns of the Cinta Larga huts, on the crooked old tree huddling over the stream. They were seated on the village's western extremity, not too far from the ancestral burial grounds.

"These savages are awfully good at making fires," said the Colonel. "Have you noticed? Even the wettest wood raises a flame."

He gave the embers a light kick—and then, with a wince, pulled his leg back.

"A spasm," he explained.

"Let me see it."

With a grunt, the old man rolled up the cuff of his trouser leg. There, on the soft inner portion of the lower thigh, was the abscess, slowly colonizing, bulbous with pus. And something Kermit had never seen before: a ringlet of bumps around the base of the knee. Each bump about the size of a fish egg.

Maggots. Feeding and flourishing just beneath the skin.

"Is it bad?" the old man asked.

"Oh," said Kermit, gently rolling the trouser leg back down. "I've seen worse. One of Fawcett's companions, do you recall? Came down with espundia. All the flesh around his mouth and nose rotted away. He looked like a leper by the time he made it out."

A grim smile played across the old man's face. "It appears we are all engaged in a grand competition. Mere dysentery will no longer suffice. One must contract something truly exotic." He touched the abscess through the cloth. "Perhaps Cajazeira can give it another lance when we get back."

When we get back. Not a touch of uncertainty in the old man's tone. If only the firelight hadn't brought out all the fissures in his face.

"Kermit. You know what I'm going to say, don't you?"

"You needn't."

"I am merely *stipulating* that if anything goes wrong tomorrow—not that anything will, but if for some reason I can't make it back to camp—there are to be no extraordinary measures on my behalf."

"Father."

"You are to *leave* me, Kermit, do you understand?"

"Don't—"

"It is my sincerest wish. You know the family credo. We are buried where we fall."

Kermit scratched the underside of his boot. Smiled sadly. "Surely, Father, we might wait until you are fallen."

"I don't intend to wait. Not when it comes to that."

Kermit nodded, said nothing. But from the corner of his eye, he scanned the old man from head to boots. Wondering where the morphine vial was.

"Father," he said. "You do know what Mother would say."

"I do."

"And you know what *I* say." He clapped the old man's shoulder. "You're to come home with us. Even if I must carry you all the way."

"Ha!" Grinning, the Colonel squeezed his son's hand. "That would be a mortal strain even for Hercules. I shouldn't wish it even on President Wilson."

They laughed softly.

"Suppose," said the Colonel. "Suppose we were to follow that stream there. Follow it all the way to its natural end. Do you suppose it might take us back to the river?"

"To *a* river, surely."

"Well, never mind," he said. "We must take the Cinta Larga at their word. Tomorrow morning we will be back with our comrades. That is what Miss Luz has told us, and I choose to believe her."

Kermit poked a stick into the fire, watched the shower of sparks billow up.

"Luz has asked something of us, Father."

"Yes?"

"She would like us to take Thiago."

The old man glanced up. *"Tomorrow?"*

"Yes."

The Colonel absorbed the news. Then he, too, took a stick to the fire.

"I can't see the boy's father permitting that, can you?"

"Anhanga? No, he would not."

"Nor would the Cinta Larga."

"I wasn't intending to ask their permission."

"So you have already given your promise."

"I've promised nothing."

Tiny blue and yellow lights came blazing out of the forest. Fireflies, blinking in no clear pattern.

"Kermit, please understand. I should be the first to stand by your side in any battle, however quixotic."

"Quixotic?"

"Which leads me to my next point. Even if we found a way to spirit the boy away without the Cinta Larga knowing, oughtn't we . . ."

"Yes?"

"Consider what's best for the lad?"

"You mean *this,* Father?" With a sweep of his arm, Kermit circumscribed the whole village. "Day after day, living hand to mouth? Cuffed and beaten and despised? His mother bartered back and forth like a mule?"

"Kermit—"

"These aren't noble savages, Father. Yes, we had a fine time splashing around with their children, but those children will grow up to be abductors and murderers. Cannibals. Rapists. You can't honestly believe his life is better for being lived here."

He could actually see the heat rising through the old man's skin. "If you please, Kermit, I have eyes. I can see what the boy is up against. But civilization is not an unmixed blessing. Think of the diseases he might contract. The social barriers . . ."

"And when have you ever honored those barriers, Father? When have you taught *us* to honor them?"

"I am speaking of the boy's capacity to overcome them. He has never learned to read or write. This is the only life to which he has been trained. Isn't it possible it's the life to which he's best suited?"

Kermit leaned back on his elbows. "Then we must be counted his greatest enemies, Father, for we are putting his world on a map for everyone to see. Do you think, once we've charted this river of ours, the rubber tappers will be far behind? The telegraph builders? The railway men? They will all come." His heart was clanging inside him. "We may take him to civilization now, or we may wait for it come to him. If I'm not mistaken, the latter course rarely ends well."

There was a long silence.

"I'm not sure either course ends well," said the Colonel. Sliding his hand through his hair, he tweezed out a pair of lice—crushed them idly between his thumb and index finger. "But what a firebrand you are, Kermit! I should have engaged you to speak at the last convention."

"You know I would have hated that."

The old man nodded. "I'll grant you this, though: One Thiago is worth a dozen Cinta Larga. Give me a few hours with him, he'd be a champion pugilist. Give me a few years, I'd get him elected to Congress."

"You can't make him president, I'm afraid. The Constitution."

"Oh, I'm sure we could find some other country to suit. Panama, maybe." The old man's eyes gleamed in the firelight. "And there's no harm in being *vice* president, you know. That can turn out quite well."

"Point taken."

Above their heads, indigo clouds as large as continents were squeezing out runnels of color. But the only color Kermit could see after a while was black, a swoop of black wings. Without ever abandoning his seat or shifting position, he fell fast asleep—like an old man nodding on a porch—and might have slept straight through till morning had the smell of pork not crawled into his nostrils. He woke with saliva dripping from his mouth. The Colonel, all gums and teeth, was standing over him.

"Our feast awaits."

THE CAPTURE OF THE Beast was not the only exciting event to take place that day in the circumscribed world of the Cinta Larga. Only an hour or so later, one of their men had surprised and killed a peccary. Not just any peccary, either, but a *caitetu munde*. At four feet in length, it was nearly twice the size of any other boar Kermit had encountered.

To the village shamans, the appearance of such bounty so hard upon the Beast's slaying was conclusive proof that the spirits of darkness were appeased. So, while the Beast's carcass had incited paroxysms of relief, the arrival of the peccary—wrapped around poles, carried by a delegation of village braves—was a time of pure rejoicing. The entire village gathered in the plaza, squatting in jagged rows, all freshly painted in red uruku and arabesques of dark-blue genipap. The dead peccary, roasting in a column of fire, made a great crackle of fat and flesh.

As each section was cooked, one of the village women hacked it away; another threw it into a heap in the center of the plaza. The villagers rushed in, lunging and grabbing. Children fought alongside their elders, mothers snatched from mothers, yet the mood never veered from festive, and every diner, upon taking his fill, threw back his head and let out a cloud-shaking belch.

"That's all right," said the Colonel. "I wasn't so very hungry."

"Aqui," said Luz, bearing two ceramic bowls.

In one sat the peccary's foot, still hooved. In the other, the severed head, seared into a carbon mask.

"To express his thanks," Luz announced, "the chief wishes you to have these."

"O chefe!" answered the old man. "Be sure to send him our thanks for these delicacies. We are delighted to partake."

He wasn't being diplomatic. He grabbed the peccary's foot and waved it at the chief, then tucked right in.

"Mmm . . . just like a slab of Virginia ham. Try some, Kermit. . . . You haven't even touched the head. . . ."

But Kermit couldn't get past the Cinta Larga themselves, with their greasy hands and smacking lips and their faces shining in the firelight. Now and again, Kermit would find the chief's eye resting on him, and for the sake of politics he would raise the boar's head to his mouth and make a show of eating. At last, one of the village boys crawled over and, with a grin of complicity, seized the head for his own.

As the bowls were cleared and the peccary's carcass rendered, a shaman strode forth in a headdress of hawk's feathers. Someone else began pounding on a hollowed-out log, and someone else cooed into a bamboo panpipe. A woman took up a deep wailing chant. From the darkness now came men in outsized animal masks, fashioned from tree bast: A squirming snake. A springing jaguar. A yellow-eyed owl fluttering from post to post.

"These are the demons," said Luz, leaning in to Kermit's left ear. "They are angry at our village, and they have sent the Beast to harm us."

"Dear me," said the Colonel. "This must be some sort of Amazonian mystery play. I see a lizard, a toad. And that's the most fearsome by-God butterfly I've ever encountered!"

Now growling onto the stage came an actor in the largest mask of all, covering face and torso, incorporating elements of the howler, yes, as well as bits from all the other masks: owl talons, snake coils, jaguar teeth. Screeching and slavering, he rent the air with his claws, then ran straight for the audience, pausing at the very brink of hurling himself at them.

"A fine Beast!" declared the Colonel. "If a bit larger than the original."

Two more masked actors swept onto the scene and arrayed themselves on either side of the creature, ready to do battle. The smaller of the hunters had a floury face, a pair of lion's eyes ringed in ellipses, and a single row of teeth, as large as pickets.

"Well, who's *that* supposed to be?" the Colonel asked.

"*É seu pai,*" whispered Luz.

"What did she say? Somebody's papa?"

"Just some obscure local deity, Father."

"Well, I'll tell you what. Whoever it is, he's giving that Beastie a good hard thumping. And that furry thing next to him, who's that?"

Me, thought Kermit.

A mane of light brown hair. A long scraggly beard. An air of gloom to even the most violent acts. Yes, they had captured him quite well.

The two hunters began to pound the Beast on its snout. Then they grabbed it by its arms and spun it in a wide circle, the drum keeping time the whole way. Dizzy, outmatched, the Beast fainted. The hunters, seizing their advantage, pretended to stomp it into submission. As the Beast released its last cries, a round of cheers went up from the crowd, none louder than the Colonel's.

"Well done! Hooray!"

There were no curtain calls. The actors simply stripped off their masks and tossed them, one by one, into the great fire.

"They are sending the spirits home," Luz explained. "If you keep them too long, they grow even angrier with you."

Kermit felt a slight chill as he watched his own mask melting in a hot blue flame. The last part to disappear was his eyes. Eyes that had been, for as long as he could recall, an obscure torment. He could remember mornings at Groton, standing before the long walnut-framed glass on his dorm-room door and scrutinizing, with a feeling of mounting dread, his own demeanor: milky, stunted, unthreatening. It seemed to him now that his whole life had been an attempt to escape that face of his.

And so he had, he thought, watching his simulacrum vanish in the flames.

The last thing to be piled atop the fire was the genuine article: the dead howler itself, still hog-tied, carried out on a litter of sticks and waxy leaves. The onset of rigor mortis had stiffened it into a kind of sculpture—like a piece of wood beaten on by the sea, all twists and joints. The villagers gave it the greatest possible berth as it passed—made no sound, lobbed no spit in its direction. The whole ceremony had the solemnity and precision of a flag-folding, as the litter bearers positioned themselves alongside the pyre and swung the creature once . . . twice . . . then flung it clear. A second later, the flames had swaddled it whole. There was a curious stuttering, a low hiss, a puff or two of sepia smoke. From the depths of the fire, the aroma of roasting meat billowed forth, replaced in short order by a bitter, tarry scent that was the perfect translation for the compacting ball of bitterness in the fire's heart.

And so the creature burned. Quickly, efficiently—comprehensively—as if it were in the greatest of hurries, as if the only thing still holding it on earth was the awestruck gaze of every last Cinta Larga. The fire popped and keened and coughed, but the silence on every side of it held fast, and when the last remnant of monkey, the last black blot of tissue, was consumed, the Colonel's gravelly tenor could be heard clear to the other side of the village (though he barely spoke above a whisper).

"Well," he said. "*That's* all over with."

BUT THE POSTMORTEM CELEBRATION was just getting under way. The chief rose from his throne and gave three soft claps. In perfect synchronicity, three village men glided into formation and began to stamp out a rhythm with bamboo pounders. Drum and pipe took up the chase, and the villagers caught the pulse and passed it through their feet. Three women entered the formation, and the steps grew more intricate, the chants deepened, the pipe shrilled higher, the drummer pounded harder. . . . Kermit didn't even grasp the din that had risen up around him until he saw the Colonel flapping his mouth.

"What did you say, Father?"

"I said somebody must have told them about our ancestors!"

"Sorry?"

"They have brought us a little Dutch courage!" The old man held up a wooden jar. "If I'm not mistaken, it's fermented!"

Kermit didn't have the heart to tell him what the fermenting agent was. He'd seen the native women spitting into that same jar.

"Try some!" the old man said.

Kermit lowered his face to the jar opening. The smell was surprisingly agreeable: clean and crisp, the barest hint of carbonation. He took a sip. Then another.

"Not bad," he allowed.

"Careful! You're spilling."

But he kept drinking, all the way to the bottom, until the last bit of froth was dripping from his chin.

"Christ . . ."

He staggered to his feet, expecting every eye to be on him. But no one noticed, not even the Colonel. And this was worse, somehow, to be standing like this, the froth dripping from his chin.

"I'll be . . . I'll be back shortly. . . ."

How long it had been since he'd gotten good and potted! Just a few swallows, and he might as well have been back at the Porcellian Club, tipping an old chest of drawers out of the casement window. Weaving and listing, he made his way back to the hut, but the prospect of configuring his body through that low entranceway was too much, so he dropped to the ground and rested his head against the hut pole. The lights dimmed around him. He slept.

Then woke again—how many minutes, hours, later? There was no way of knowing. He could only say it was night—still night—and someone was coming toward him, shuffling through the mud and dust.

Bokra. The crazy old man with marbled eyes. Carrying something that was impossible for Kermit to identify until, with a silent and definitive click, the thing snapped into focus.

It was the harpy eagle, lying utterly still in the old man's arms, its half-plucked wings wrapped like husks around its breast, its eyes blazing and sightless. No blood, no sign of violence. Tears swarmed like rain from Bokra's white eyes as, with jittery grunts, he extended the dead bird toward Kermit.

"No . . . I can't . . . I'm sorry. . . ."

Then Bokra was gone, and it was raining again. Or it might have been the old man still weeping. Kermit slept, and woke to a new world.

18

He was wet all over.

To his own amazement, he was standing in the muddy playa on the rim of the village swimming hole. The moon had carved a crater from the black water, and in the reflected light, he could make out a humped figure on the far bank. Its head was bowed in an attitude of piety, and from its throat came the strangest of sounds. Like a handful of lead shot rolling down a chute.

With a coo of surprise, Kermit looked down to find, squeezed in his hand, a torch—already swinging toward the sound. There, in the crosshatch of moon and firelight, a giant anteater sat drinking, its serpent tongue flickering in and out of the stream. Stung by the light, the anteater paused, reared up to its full four feet—stood there for minutes on end, its nostrils twitching in a perfect fury, the rest of it utterly still, right down to the bristles, which were flexed and ready. Then it inched its head back and a shudder rippled up its spine, so that for a second or two it was writhing like an oak in a wind.

Or was it only mimicking Kermit? For he was shaking inconsolably now. And the air was crackling, and the stream was bubbling and curdling—and *cooling,* with shocking speed. Barnacles of ice glittered from the depths, and scallops of snow shouldered up, and the water flowed more and more slowly until finally it sheeted over into glass.

Kermit's breath was congealing into smoke. At his feet lay his rifle—his Winchester, yes—coated in rime. He picked it up. He turned slowly around.

And found a new village. A village he had never seen before.

Snow had piled in banks against every hut, crowned every roof, mattressed every path and clearing. Ice mist snarled toward the sky.

Where am I?

The glare of the moonlight on the snow was so dazzling he had to spider his hands across his eyes. Through the angle of his second and third finger, he found the one creature that seemed to have escaped the spell. A small figure, weedy and dark, shuffling through the snow.

It was a boy. Bundled in a wool coat a size too small. Dragging behind him a sled. Crying softly to himself.

Kermit knew exactly why the boy was crying. He had been in a snowball fight with his older brother, and the snowballs had flown faster and harder until the older brother had clocked him with a hunk of ice—hidden under snow—and the boy had begun to cry, and his brother had told him he would never be a man like Father if he cried every time he got a clout. He had turned and run, wishing every harm on his brother—his father, too—himself most of all. And now he was trudging home on the very plain of despair.

Kermit grasped it all in the space of a second. For the boy was him.

He had gone out with Ted on a winter afternoon just like this, out to Cove Neck, and had come back in this exact fashion, every finger and toe blazing with cold, his face splotched with shame. Wanting to be swallowed whole.

It's all right. The words trembled on the grown man's lips. *Come, now, little fellow. . . .*

But the boy padded on, sniveling into his mittens. Then he stopped and dropped the rein of the sled and pulled the stocking cap from his head and opened his mouth.

To cry, or so Kermit thought. But the mouth kept widening. It stretched past the cheeks, past the ears, until there was nothing on the boy's shoulders but a chasm, and from the depths of that emptiness there came a roar. Like nothing Kermit had heard before. Clamorous and echoing and afire with ancient rancors.

He felt his finger tighten once more around the trigger. He raised the rifle. He settled the boy in his sights.

The stock was dry and powdery against his cheek; the barrel was as warm as skin. With an agonized deliberation, his finger squeezed down. It was here, at the exact point of equilibrium, that everything was lost.

Without warning, his boots lost their purchase in the snow. His legs went out from under him, and the rest of him followed, and the boy's roar gave way to a scream, neither human nor animal. The noise ratcheted inside his ears as he lay on his back, staring up at the stars, each star catching a small piece of the scream and sending it back.

He wasn't cold anymore.

He turned his head to one side. There lay his torch, still blazing on the packed earth. Not a flake of snow. Feet, shoeless feet, were galloping past him. Over him.

"Senhor Kermit."

Luz stared down at him.

"I . . ." His lips cracked open. "I have . . ."

He raised himself to his knees, looked around. The village had shrugged off its mantle of snow. The moonlight was funneling down into a single column, and the forest was as black and blank as before.

He ran his hand along the rifle. Had he fired? No. No, he hadn't.

How many cartridges did he have left? Three? Two? Who were all these people? Why were they all awake in the middle of the night?

"Luz," he said. "Tell me what's happening."

"There was a cry, Senhor. The people are gathering now."

"Gathering? Why?"

"To call out the names."

He stared at the Cinta Larga men as they strapped on their armlets, at the women clutching their babies, the children toting crude dolls and whittled sticks. Only now did he understand. They were congregating before the chief's hut for a village census. To see who was missing.

In a soft, uninflected voice, the chief called each name and waited with folded lips for the answering call. In solemnity and cadence, it was oddly similar to a commencement ceremony, and Kermit was amazed to find his mind dancing back to Groton ("the Christ factory," Arch always called it). The Reverend Peabody in his alb and cotta. The plangent rhythms of those Mayflower names.

Except these weren't Mayflower names. Noara . . . Takakrorok . . . Teptykti . . . Kentyxti . . .

As Kermit stood listening, the chief lingered on one name, waited for an answering call, said the name again. When no one answered to it, this was the name that was passed from tongue to tongue.

"Anhanga . . . *Anhanga* . . ."

Luz's eyes met his.

"I must go to Thiago," she said.

"Must you?" A strange half smile crawled through Kermit's lips. "I mean, why worry the boy unless you need to? Anhanga may have—I suspect he's just wandered off. I've done much the same thing myself at night."

Only not in the jungle. Only a fool would go walking at night there. And the Cinta Larga were no fools. Even now they forbore to launch a search party until the sun rose. There was nothing to do, it seemed, but wait. Since Luz showed no inclination for company,

Kermit went back to his hut. But the Colonel was still snoring away—he had managed to sleep through the whole alarum—so, rather than return to his hammock, Kermit seated himself against an acai palm and waited. From time to time he fell into a doze, thin and dreamless, but, each time, his head snapped him back.

Through heavy lids, he caught the first glimmers of light. First a pale aureole around the moon and then, from behind the forest, a swell of orange, turning the shadows into a tracery of fronds and boles. Somewhere, a vanilla vine was blooming.

The Cinta Larga rose without a word. Within minutes, the village was as empty as an old flask. Kermit took up his rifle and, with no clear intent or plan, began to wander through the clearing, circling hut after hut, waiting for something to snag his eye. At length, for want of an anchor, he settled on a path he had never noticed before: a wide, well-hewn gap in the jungle front. The villagers had done a fine job of keeping the jungle from reclaiming it: Even a man as tall as Kermit could travel down it without a care. The path kept its course—and concluded after ten or twelve yards in a plot of scorched, stamped earth pocked with holes and ligatured with roots. The Cinta Larga garden.

On any other morning, the village women would have been here, dragging the manioc and yams from the earth and stacking them in baskets. Today, it was only Kermit, swatting gnats and bees and spiderwebs and staring at the point just beyond the garden where a thin, tiny, jagged figure crouched in the early-morning shadows.

At the sound of Kermit's boots, the figure swung toward him. A pair of marbled eyes swam out of the darkness. A small haggard face, a toothless mouth.

Bokra.

He had fallen to his knees in an attitude of pilgrim piety. It was only when Kermit drew nearer that he noticed the pomegranate-like stains on Bokra's hands. Noticed, too, the trembling in his limbs and shoulders.

Something's wrong. . . .

Then his eyes traveled to the region just below Bokra. Something human lay there. A hand. A foot. An elbow, a knee, the remains of a shoulder. With strange stubbornness, his mind resisted the idea that these things might once have been parts of a whole. It took seeing the look on Bokra's face to make the connection.

"Oh," Kermit whispered. "Oh, God."

He grabbed for his rifle. But there was nothing left to fire at, was there? Only an accounting to be made. So he pointed the barrel to the sky and squeezed off a round.

Bokra shrieked and fell backward and lay cringing in the mud, muttering the same untranslatable word again and again. Around him, the forest swarmed into life. Flies went diving and wheeling, monkeys screamed, birds washed out of the trees in waves. The ground actually shook—human *feet* converging—and no tread was more familiar to Kermit's ear than the one closest to him. That quick, delicate, light-footed gait that had led him through the jungle and back.

Thiago.

For the first time, Kermit recognized the disemboweled man on the ground, recognized the crop of black hair, the still-intact eyes—and, over the right eye, a white scar where the eyebrow should be. Kermit had seen an eye just like that on one of the village braves. The brave who had dragged his son away from the white men. The brave who would have done anything to keep his son from leaving. . . .

In that exact moment, Thiago came bursting through the trees, and Kermit caught him in his arms and angled him away from the body.

"*Não importa,*" he whispered. "*Não faz mal.*"

Never mind. It's all right. But from every quarter, the Cinta Larga were emerging, bows drawn, torsos tensed, and, unlike Kermit, they needed only a second to determine what had happened and who had done it.

"Bokra!" they shouted. "Anhanga!"

Kermit looked down at Thiago. The boy's face was slack and rubbery, and his eyes had turned to the basest metal, but the reassurances kept flowing from Kermit's mouth.

"It's all right. . . . Never fear. . . ."

19

BOKRA LOOKED NEARLY DEAD HIMSELF BY THE TIME THEY DRAGGED him back to the village. His face was drawn and gray, and his arms hung uselessly by his side as the braves threw him into the center of the plaza and kicked him about the ribs and thighs.

Luz came forward now to claim her son. She lowered her forehead to his and gazed straight into his eyes. Then she kissed him, once, on the tip of his nose and led him away.

"Muito triste," Kermit called after them.

Very sorry. But they kept walking.

From the chief's hut, a single bark rang out. The braves stepped back, and a silence fell over the village as the chief, wiry and coiled, advanced on the condemned man. He muttered as he walked, and with each step the mutters grew in volume and coherence, until they assumed the shape of a chant or recitation. *A bill of attainder,* thought Kermit, enumerating every last crime.

"Good God!" The Colonel came stumbling out of their hut, twining his spectacle stems around his ear. "What's all the hubbub?"

"It's Bokra, Father."

"That crazy old bugger? What's he gone and done?"

Kermit paused. "Murdered someone."

"Who?"

"Anhanga."

The old man gave his head a shake. "You mean to tell me that little blind spaniel over there overpowered Thiago's father? Impossible."

"They caught him in the act," said Kermit. "Red-handed. Red-*everythinged*."

He stopped and slowly shifted his gaze toward the jungle.

"You don't seem persuaded," said the Colonel.

"Father, how would you like to view another crime scene?"

"Before breakfast? Very well, I'm your man."

IN KEEPING WITH TRIBAL practice, the body of Anhanga was left exactly where it was. Indeed, no Cinta Larga would ever again lay eyes on it. The garden would be relocated; the trail would grow over; the jungle would gather the corpse back to its bosom; children would be warned never to wander there for fear of waking Anhanga's shadow.

The two white men, however, had no such inhibition, and since no one stopped or even noticed them ducking down the garden path, they were able to find the body in a matter of seconds. They had only to follow the hivelike hum of insects whirling around Anhanga's ravaged face and strafing the walls of his abdominal cavity.

"Remind you of anything?" asked Kermit.

The old man came to an abrupt halt. Then, in a soft and wondering gait, he began to circumnavigate the body.

"This can't . . ." He lifted his voice to a more urgent frequency. *"This won't do!"*

"It's been done."

"We killed the Beast. We saw it die."

"I know."

"We saw it crackling in the damned fire!"

"I know."

The old man leaned back against a trammel of epiphytes. "I can only think this is some—some gruesome sort of *prank*. It's the only possible explanation."

Kermit studied the tatters of his boot. "How would Bokra have carried out such a prank?"

"I dunno, ask *him*. Perhaps he poisoned Anhanga first. Disabled in him in some way, then . . . dragged his body here and set about . . ."

"But the blood, Father."

"What of it?"

Kermit squinted up at the canvas of sky. "I beg you to recall that howler. Recall how it looked in the moment of its death. It was filthy, yes? Drenched. Fairly *robed* in blood. I was there, Father; I saw it *plunging* its head into its prey's cavity."

"And your point, Kermit?"

"My point is that disemboweling something—some*one*—emptying them out like that is not a clean business. It stains; it contaminates."

"You said yourself Bokra had blood on his hands."

"*Only* his hands."

"Oh, bother, Kermit. He might have . . . *washed* himself, I don't know."

"Washed himself with what? His hands? Father, imagine you've stumbled across some body in the jungle. You don't know whether it's alive or not, so what do you do? If you have any sort of human feeling or curiosity, you kneel down. If you're not too faint of heart, you *touch* the thing. All you need do is touch it once or twice, and you'll have as much blood on your hands as Macbeth."

The Colonel vised his hands around his skull. "That still doesn't explain why Bokra was here in the first place. You're telling me he just happened to find a body that everyone else missed?"

"I just happened to find it, too, Father. And Bokra had more reason than I."

"What reason?"

"Ecce avis," said Kermit.

The morning shadows still lay thickly enough on the ground that the old man had to stare for several seconds before he discerned the corpse that lay next to Anhanga's. A half-plucked harpy eagle, bundled into itself like a dead pharaoh.

"Bokra came here to bury his friend," said Kermit. "Only he never finished the job."

The Colonel stood for some time, scratching his whiskers.

"Well, you've still one problem, my boy. If Bokra didn't kill Anhanga, who did?"

"The Beast."

The old man closed his eyes. Tilted his head forward.

"Dear God, Kermit."

"Father, please hear me out."

"I have *heard* you out. There is no point in—"

"No, you must listen. What if we *didn't* kill the Beast? What if we only killed the thing that harbored it? What if the Beast is something . . . separate? Something that *survives* the death of its host?"

"So we're back to spirits, are we?"

"Not spirits. Not necessarily."

"Then what?"

"I don't know! Perhaps it's some kind of *virus* that infects a particular creature, drives it to commit terrible savagery."

"And when the host dies?"

"It moves to another. All it requires is some . . . some living creature to sustain it. It doesn't matter what."

"Then where is it now?"

"I don't know. If I *knew,* I would—" Kermit stared at his empty hands. "It's *somewhere,* Father. That much I believe. It's biding its time, it's . . ."

It's in one of us.

The thought flashed on him with such force that he nearly buckled. His mind flew back to yesterday's tableau: Four hunters standing over their quarry. Kermit bruised and Thiago battered. The old man punctured and leaking from the brow. Luz, painted head to toe in blood and viscera. Surely any of them could have been infected. Any of them might be walking around—at this very moment—with that seed inside.

And yet how monstrous to even imagine such a thing!

"Tell me something, Kermit. If you hadn't seen Anhanga's body, would you still believe the Beast was alive?"

"Yes."

"Why?"

Kermit paused. "Intuition."

"Can you kindly be more concrete?"

"I *can't.* I can only tell you I *felt* it, Father. Last night. And down in that cave. And standing over the howler . . ."

"That chill of yours."

"No, it's more than that. This *creature,* Father, this Beast, it seems to speak to me—or else I'm able to *hear* it in some fashion. It's as if—I don't know, as if we're eavesdropping on each other."

"Eavesdropping." With a grim smile, the old man joined his hands behind his back. "Why should you, Kermit—alone among mortals—be so magically attuned to this Beast? Is there some manual you've been studying? Some spiritual *medium,* perhaps, has been blessing you with the fruits of her instruction?"

"I appear to have a certain . . ."

"What?"

"Quality."

"Which is?"

"Receptivity."

"Well, that's vague enough. To *what* exactly are you so receptive? I myself am most curious."

Would it have ended differently if Father had imparted a different emphasis to the word *curious*? If he hadn't lashed it with that whip of scorn? Perhaps then Kermit wouldn't have felt such a sting. Perhaps he wouldn't have hurried onward the way he did—past any hope of returning.

"I see Elliott."

The old man took a step to the side. "You—"

"I know it beggars the imagination, Father. I know we're not supposed to know of him or speak of him, but I've—I've *seen* him! Dear God, a good dozen times. Starting when I was thirteen. I've seen him at school, at home, in the woods. I saw him when we first started down the river; I saw him in the *cave*. For the longest time he's been trying to tell me something or else warn me—*prepare* me. Now I think maybe it has something to do with this Beast, only I don't know what. I don't—I don't know *anything*."

As he spoke, he never once looked at his father. There was no need. Everything he needed to know could be heard in the old man's tremulous voice.

"I cannot conceive of a more obscene joke than this."

"It's not a joke."

"You have transgressed every boundary of decency."

"Transgressed, yes, but not decency."

"Well, then, if you are not indecent, you are mad."

The very word Kermit feared. It landed inside him with the tiniest of explosions.

"I blame this jungle," fumed the Colonel. "It's worked some hideous transformation on you. And here—here!—is the fruit of your malady. Bizarre and outlandish theories. Outrageous, wholly *fabricated* encounters with a man you have—I have never . . ."

The old man wrestled himself into silence, but a second later he was breaking out with even greater vehemence.

"You should never have come on this expedition in the first place! I should never have allowed it!"

From the village, all sound had died away. Kermit imagined every last Cinta Larga cupping an ear, straining to make out their quarrel.

"*Allowed* it?" he said.

Even he was unnerved by the calmness in his own voice. He took a step toward the old man. He felt a smile etching itself in acid across his face.

"Do you truly believe I wanted to come here, Father? Do you *sincerely* believe I had nothing better to do than chase after you and . . . and tramp down this horrible . . . deadening . . . *soul-killing* river and starve and suffer day in and day out? All so you could have your little place in the gazetteer—your—your little burst of elderly glory—your *scope*?"

"Don't look at me," answered the old man. "I never asked you."

"Oh! Oh, no, a great man never *asks*, does he, Father? He has minions to do that for him. A great man need only command—*conquer*. If one country doesn't want his canal, he finds another country that will. Makes a *new* country if need be. If one country doesn't want him to be its *president*—"

Stop! he was beseeching himself. *Too far.*

"—well, then, a great man just finds a new country he can preside over. The world is chockablock with new countries, isn't it, Father? All ready to lie at your feet."

The old man was gazing at him now in a kind of awe.

"I may be mad, as you say, Father, but not mad enough to be your vassal for one second longer. I have my own tiny little scope, my own humble, *humble* career—I know how low it ranks in your eyes—and I have a woman who loves me, and *I'm to be married in June!*"

With that, every last particle of rage and thwarted desire seemed to rise up in a great smoking column.

"Only I *won't* be married in June, will I, Father? I'll never leave this accursed jungle, and why? Because you decided you had to go and shoot some monkey in a tree!"

"The men were starving, for God's—"

"You knew the rules! We weren't to leave sight of the camp. But mere rules don't apply to the great Theodore Roosevelt, do they? He writes his own rules. And his son—his docile border collie of a son—*trails* after him, as he's been doing his entire pathetic life."

Kermit felt the last atoms of force draining from him as he dropped onto a tree stump and folded his head in his hands.

"And look. Look where it's got us, Father. We've reached the place where conquest ends." He swung his arm toward Anhanga. "Unless you can colonize *that*."

No words now. No movement. Kermit sat with his head lowered, like a schoolboy bracing for the cane. But all the Colonel could manage before he stalked off was a strangled cry.

"Sharper than a serpent's tooth!"

LEAR, THOUGHT KERMIT. *THE perfect choice.* From his chest rose a dry, mirthless chuckle.

A day ago he would have trembled at the idea of driving away his father. But perhaps he was better off alone. He had questions to consider, didn't he? And he was the only one willing to consider them.

Question number one: Why would the Beast have chosen Anhanga? Out of all the Cinta Larga, why him?

Question number two: How had the Beast done it? Surprised him in his hut? Killed him on the spot or dragged him here—snuffed him out before anybody knew he was missing?

This crime scene was even more hopeless than the last. Whatever square of earth had escaped the trodding Cinta Larga braves had been swept clean by Bokra's body as they dragged him back to the village. The least disturbed element of the whole site was

Anhanga's eye, which the morning light had wrapped in a gauze of amber, indissoluble from the sweetly souring scent that rose from each pore.

Kermit squatted down, uncurled the fingers of the dead man's right hand, then the left hand. Nothing. Still squatting, he scanned the middle distance: surges of black and green that, on closer scrutiny, became riggings of liana, robes of leaves, epiphytes hanging like twine. His knees were cramping now, his eyes dulling over. He was no longer even sure what he was looking for—until he found it. The something that didn't belong.

A single print in the square of earth by Anhanga's left shoulder. A *hand*print.

Not the stubby fingers of a Cinta Larga, either, but longer, thinner. *A* civilizado's *fingers,* thought Kermit. And before he quite grasped what he was doing, he pressed the tips of his own fingers into the indentation. Felt the mud retreat at his touch . . . and then felt it swell back, so that for a second or two the earth seemed to be folding around him.

He drew his hand back. Stared at the smear of black on the tips of his fingers, then looked down again, half-expecting the print to be gone. But there it was, stamped like a star in the jungle floor.

I have you, he thought.

20

LUZ CONSPICUOUSLY ABSENTED HERSELF FROM ANHANGA'S funeral. It was his favored wife who strode into the center of the plaza and, with a long trailing moan, sank to her knees. For several seconds, she held her peace. Then she began to claw the earth around her, flinging it up in clouds, hissing and writhing as a group of children circled her and showered her with pothos leaves.

A gray rain cloud squatted over their heads and broke open with a gun burst. Blue flames flickered down through the trees, and Anhanga's wife, bent under the force of the rain, smeared herself with the newly hatched mud as the children tilted their faces to the sky. Only there was no sky to look at, because the rain had chased it all away.

Kermit stood under the overhang of his hut, watching the water pound down: a million tiny fists. He knew Father was waiting inside—he could hear the sighs and wheezes. He knew, too, that if he went in now, he would be expected to apologize—that was the way of the world. The apology would be accepted or it would not. Conversation would resume or it would not. Somehow they would get on again—or they would not. It was amazing and terrifying in equal measure that the bond of a lifetime could be breached by just a few hasty words. That prospect pressed so hard on him now that he could neither stay nor leave.

From inside, he heard his father say:

"Oh, I know how it is. Don't think I don't."

Such a soft voice! Kermit couldn't help but lean toward it.

"When *my* father died, I tell you, I bawled like a baby. And me, a college boy! Humiliating . . ."

As quietly as he could, Kermit crept through the entranceway. The Colonel was sitting up in his hammock, with his back turned, talking above his usual speed.

"I couldn't help myself. Father was the greatest man I ever knew. Do you know, more than two thousand people came to his funeral? Not just society swells, no—newsboys, *orphans*. Young mothers. All the people he helped in life."

From the shadows, Kermit picked out the seated figure of Thiago.

"There was so much grief—on every side—I said to myself, *Surely the world can't go on. Surely it will have to stop, a second or two.* And when it didn't—ha!—I recall being quite cross." He paused for a moment. Then his voice slipped into a huskier register. "I lost a wife, too. She was lovely. The loveliest. Her name was Alice."

Kermit lowered his head. It was the first time he had ever heard that name spoken.

"She died quite young, Thiago, and I thought I'd died, too. Yes, when they—when they closed the coffin, I said, 'Are you sure I don't belong there?' The only thing I could do was go away. As far as I could. Well, never mind. The point *is*, you see, I found another wonderful girl. Edith is her name. Four wonderful children, as different from one another as summer from winter. That's what I mean when I say God finds a way, doesn't he? To heal what's inside? And someday . . . someday . . ."

Kermit took a step into the hut's interior, but the old man didn't see him.

"What a quiet boy you've become, Thiago! Do you know you remind me of my son? Kermit, yes. Silent just like you. But rash! In Africa, he was daring to the point of recklessness. Ran down and killed a giraffe all on his own. A hyena, too. Stopped a charging leopard within six yards. Oh, I don't mind telling you my heart was in my throat more times than I can—what time is it, anyway? I've quite lost track. . . ."

Kermit cleared his throat. The old man's head swung toward him.

"Ah! There you are, my boy!"

No mistaking the upward inflection of the voice. The Colonel was happy to see him.

"Have a seat, why don't you?"

In the light from a small, sputtering fire, Kermit could see his father's parched lips, glassy eyes, the blotches of pink in his face.

"As you can *see*," the Colonel was saying, "I've been doing my best to comfort the poor lad. He lost his father, did you know?"

"Yes. I did."

"Oh, but he's tough as flint, Thiago. They don't make 'em tougher. Do you remember how he went after that Beastie? Fierce! Indomitable! Full of heart, like all great men. That's how men become great, Kermit. Hearts. *Broken* hearts."

"Yes, Father."

"What was I just saying?"

Kermit very nearly laughed then. He had come to heal a rupture, and now, thanks to the memory-erasing properties of fever, there was no rupture to heal.

"My!" The old man was fanning himself with his forearm. "It's warm in here. Must be the fire. Never mind. Makes it all the cozier, doesn't it? I was about to say something."

"Father. It's time for us to go."

"Go?"

"We must leave here. Go back to our friends." No light of recognition dawned in the old man's eyes. "Colonel Rondon is expecting us."

"Oh, yes! Work to do. Great and inspiring work. Can't be put off a moment longer." The old man paused. "We *have* lived up to our contract, haven't we, Kermit?"

"Of course."

"Never let it be said a Roosevelt cheated an Indian."

"No."

"We brought back a *Beastie,* I don't care what . . . do you know, I was talking with someone about something . . ."

While the old man plundered his memory, Thiago did two quite ordinary things. He tipped his head against the Colonel's knee. Then he stretched out his foot and touched it lightly against Kermit's boot.

The moment lasted no more than ten or fifteen seconds, but it seemed to seal off its own cordon of time. No word was exchanged. No word *could* have been exchanged. The rain continued to thrum, the air to swelter; the heat rose off the old man's skin like smoke from a griddle. They sat, that was all. And, for the first time, Kermit found himself wishing Belle were with him—*here,* yes, in this steamy, bug-ridden, fitfully illuminated hut.

"Aha!" The old man snapped his head forward. "I remember what I was thinking. Wouldn't Thiago be a . . . a *redoubtable* addition to our little band, Kermit? Our expedition?"

"Certainly."

"The problem as always is arranging it. Under the circumstances." The old man leaned forward, curled a finger under Thiago's chin. "Boy's lost a father, Kermit."

"Yes, he has."

"We must make it up to him."

The shout came over them in stages. It began as a long moan

from somewhere in the middle distance. With time, it grew more jagged and hopeless and then accelerated finally into a single unbroken shriek, nearly superhuman in its force. The old man clapped his hands over Thiago's ears, but nothing could have blocked that noise.

"There, there," the old man murmured. "It'll be done soon."

And it *was* done: as quickly as a spigot shutting off. From outside, a great silence welled up. Even the insects had subsided to a hush.

There was a rustling at the hut's entrance. A flash of brown, a flurry of droplets, and now Luz was standing before them, drenched from every side, her hair hanging like kelp over her face.

"Bokra is dead?" asked Kermit.

"Yes."

"They wasted no time."

"It had to be, Senhor."

"And why?"

"Bokra has killed," she said. "He must be killed. Even the Bible says this."

"The first part of the Bible, yes. Did Bokra actually confess to his crimes?"

She gave her wrist a soft flick. "He told all. How he joined with the demons who sent us the Beast. How he used their powers to destroy Anhanga."

"And did he explain why he would do such a thing?"

She gave her wrist another flick. "There was *evil* in him, Senhor. There has always been. He should have been killed with the rest of his village, but the chief took pity on him."

In the closeness of the hut, she sounded like a child mastering her catechism.

"Very well," said Kermit. "Bokra is dead. The Beast is dead. The time has come for my father and me to return to our friends."

She paused. Softly fingered the hair from her face. "That will happen, Senhor."

"Yes," he answered. "It will. When will that happen, Luz?"

"There is one more thing you must do."

"Yes?"

"You must be the ones to put Bokra in the earth."

He sat there, parsing her words.

"Very well," he said. "Have them dig a grave. We will gladly toss the body in."

"No, Senhor. The shamans have said it must be a . . . a great pit, nearly as high as a man. And . . ." Her teeth closed around a portion of lower lip. "Bokra must be buried in it tonight. Because the Beast is a creature of night, it must happen under the moon."

"Moon," he echoed, tipping himself out of his hammock to a standing position. *"Moon."*

"Please—"

"They mean to keep us here another day."

"Senhor—"

"This is an outrage. This is an *infamy*."

"When Bokra is in the pit, the village will be free of the Beast, and you will be free to go. They swear this."

"As they swore before. And to think you—you yourself!—told me these were men of honor. I tell you they are most emphatically not. They are the opposite of honorable. They are liars! Cowards!"

The old man looked up with a rubbery face. "What's the trouble?"

"Senhor, you must understand how these things go. Some of the men, they think you should not leave at all. They say—they say you did not kill the Beast, as you promised."

Kermit grimaced. It was an argument he himself had been making not half an hour ago.

"Were they *there*?" he cried. "Did they *see*?"

"Others say that you did kill the Beast, that you have a special gift, and for that reason you must stay to finish your work. This . . .

this arrangement, Senhor, it is—what is the—*compromisso*. It is the thing that makes both sides happy."

"Happy."

Kermit crooked his arm over his head. In a voice neither hot nor cold, he said:

"We will never leave here."

"You *will*." Luz took his hand in hers. "You will be free, Senhor. And Thiago, too."

"Thiago?" The Colonel staggered to his feet. "Some kind soul should really explain to me what's transpired."

But upon hearing the news, the old man's answer was a single shrugged shoulder.

"So they want us to bury that poor wretch? No great hardship."

"But, Father, it's another day lost. Worse, it's a . . . a violation of principle—"

"Oh, don't let's inflate it out of all proportion. It's a silly little grave."

Kermit threw up his arm, slumped back into his hammock. "Closer to a pit," he muttered. "If you must know."

"Pit, grave. No point quibbling. We're just the men to take it on."

"Take it *on*?"

"Think of it, Kermit! How many times do men of . . . of our degree of civilization have the chance to inculcate Western *knowledge*, yes, and *values* in savage minds? And what better means of effecting this goal than through an engineering project? Modest in scale, I grant you, but far-reaching in *import*."

"Father, we don't have to dig the—"

"Now, listen to me, Kermit, I'll need you to translate, because I have *exact* notions of how the thing shall go. It must be done by the book or it's not worth doing at all. I don't mind telling you, when Goethals and I were building the canal, we used to go at it something fierce. No detail too small: the number of steam shovels, the design of the flatcars. We'd chew it over for days on end. . . ."

Indeed, half an hour alone was spent transmitting the old man's specifications, which began in concept as a cube, ten by ten by ten, and became, through spasms of modification, a cylinder: ten feet in diameter and as deep as the natives could make it.

They chose a desolate, shaded spot just off the trash yard. The rain had left the ground as spongy and malleable as it would ever be, and as the Cinta Larga men bore down, scooping up bowlfuls of mud and flinging them over their shoulders, the village children made a show of throwing each clod back—until the chief himself, glowering like a bull, chased them away.

Lacking a sun helmet, the Colonel had wrapped a buriti palm leaf around his head and fastened it under his chin with a twig. Resting his hand on Thiago's shoulder, he began to circle the ever-widening pit, raining down encouragement as he passed.

"There's a brute for you! Give that root a nice hack, will you? Put your back into it, now!"

Events had somehow transformed the Colonel's fever into missionary zeal, and something of that mission must have vaulted the language barrier, for each digger would from time to time lift his head and stare in wonder at that hobbling, sun-dazzled figure before returning to his labors.

Certainly the old man would have been a more pleasing sight than Bokra's bent little figure, lying just outside their perimeter. Or Bokra's head, severed with no great delicacy, staring up at the bluing sky.

Before an hour passed, the pit had attained a depth of two feet. The achievement was inspirational enough that Kermit, who had until then been a spectator, grabbed the nearest implement—a sharpened length of bone—and joined in.

"That's my boy!" shouted the Colonel.

It was hard work. More than once Kermit found reason to curse the thin, famished Amazonian earth. But as he gouged through the humus, he found surprising reserves of color—ochers and tawny yellows—and shooting through the beds of clay were the white spindly threads of roots, gathering in capillary-like networks.

The sun hammered down. Mosquitoes attacked without mercy, and wasps danced across their eye sockets, up their noses. Yet each time Kermit brushed one of the bees away, he felt a lift in spirit, and as the sweat congealed and sickened against his skin and his muscles twanged and throbbed, he came to the gradual conclusion that he was, if not precisely happy, at ease.

Work had always been his best escape from himself. He remembered the day he had rushed to see Belle only an hour after grooming Wyoming. Some of the horse's lather had clung to his skin, and his hair was still sweaty at his temples, and Belle, striving to find some tone between censure and indifference, had said:

"Mother believes no man should ever sit down to dinner with dirt under his nails."

He had felt—hadn't he?—the tiniest contraction of his heart. A passing thing, forgotten a minute later, but looking back he could see it as the first breath of estrangement. Some echo of it carried down to the present, for his hand, rather than dancing to the packet of her letters, remained still. For some minutes he studied it, fascinated by its recalcitrance.

"Ha!" said the Colonel. "Taking a break, eh? I don't blame you one bit. Beastly hot. But look how far we've come!"

The pit was now chest-deep, wide enough for a giant, and, at the same time, delicately sloped according to the old man's specifications. In celebration, the village children came sallying out with bowls of water, one for each digger. One for the Colonel, too, but he took only a sip before passing it around.

"They may not be an *excavating* race," he said, mopping his face with the palm leaf, "but they do set themselves against it, don't they? Oh, but I wish I had some of my buffalo soldiers! A few days, they'd have the whole jungle dug up. Don't think some folks wouldn't thank us."

The old man's teeth shone like fire. A fine stream of saliva trickled down his chin.

"I'll be right back," said Kermit.

He went to his hut, intending to grab an hour or two of sleep before the interral of Bokra. But in the late-afternoon light, his hammock looked peculiarly uninhabitable. With a growl, he snatched up his rifle.

And just what exactly are you going to shoot?

He left the hut and, with the Winchester pressed to his flank, made a slow circuit of the village. Not a soul looked his way. White men and their thunder sticks had become, in the span of two days, part of the surrounding landscape. Without quite meaning to, Kermit drifted back to the swimming hole. He was alone now—except for a young mother who sat on the stream bottom, bathing her baby with water from a calabash shell.

"Senhor," said Luz.

He was no longer surprised at how silently she stole up behind him. He had come near to welcoming it.

"I have brought some cassava," she said.

The village women had lacked the time, perhaps, to roast the stuff, for it sat naked in the bowl, pale and greasy. He scooped his hands in and slapped it into his mouth, then, turning to one side, spat it softly out.

"The food doesn't suit you, Senhor?"

"Sorry, I'm not hungry. Just yet."

"Perhaps you would like to bathe?"

"No, thank you."

From behind them, the Colonel's voice came wafting, like the mating call of an unusually tenacious bird. *"Again! Again! Show your mettle, lads! No rest for the wicked!"*

"I am very sorry," said Luz.

"I know."

"I did all I could to convince them."

"It's all right, Luz."

He looked up at the sky, beetling with scarlet clouds. Then he gazed down the winding prospect of the black stream. As he stood there, he felt, like the probing of the most refined and exquisite needle, an infusion of cold air, reaching all the way to bone.

"Are you well, Senhor?"

"Fine."

"You look cold."

"No, I'm quite well."

How could he explain it to her? The Beast was still out there, and he—"alone among mortals," as his father had put it—grasped this most elemental of facts. He alone understood that throwing the remnants of an old man's body down a hole would change nothing, that as long as the Beast was still abroad, the Cinta Larga would never be safe, and Kermit and the Colonel would never be free.

And he would never see Belle. It was as if the very air throbbed with her now. Silently, he uttered the old litany—*I'm to be married in June*—but each word was an agony, because it was *only* a word.

He opened the chamber of his rifle. Three bullets.

"Back soon," he said.

"Where are you going, Senhor?"

"Bit of a job," he called back. "Needs finishing."

21

THE STREAM BOBBED AND DODGED, ACCORDING TO ITS OWN WHIM, and the margin of sand on each side shrank and then disappeared altogether beneath granite boulders. After a time, the only way to walk was to clamber over rocks or plash through shallows. Within seconds, the shreds of Kermit's boots were soaked through, no better than anchors. But he took some strange comfort in the fact that he was descending by slow degrees.

He remembered then the hope his father had raised the day before. That if they followed this stream out to its natural length, it might take them back to the river. The stream, though, betrayed no such intention. It bled outward, frothing and slapping, then fell back to an amble. A quarter mile on, it broadened without warning into a lagoon. Marbled blackish-green water, ringed in white sand, over which a brace of dragonflies hovered.

He dropped his rifle and stooped down, meaning only to take a handful or two of water, but a wave of tiredness took him and dropped him into the stream's shallows with a small dismal splash. The water bubbled around his ankles, coaxed some of the pain from his abscesses. The air curled around his neck, his ears. From far away came the caw of a parrot.

He looked down. The sinking sun had turned the black water into a mirror that captured his features with perfect fidelity. Or perfect infidelity, was that it? He couldn't even begin to recognize the man he saw there: pium scars, like flecks of shrapnel, and bat bites, and the welted outcroppings of a hundred mosquito bites. And that beard! Muddy, matted, as tangled as the jungle canopy itself. No wonder the Cinta Larga had mistaken him for a beast.

With a shudder, he jerked to his feet. In the water, his reflection quavered, then broke apart and eddied away.

Must shave, he thought. *Before Belle sees.*

From behind him came a tinny snap. Luz was walking toward him.

For once, she didn't have the advantage of surprise. For once, he could study her at length, consider her arms and thighs, waist and abdomen, all taut and coiled, ready for whatever might come. Except all he could see now was Luz as she'd looked yesterday— painted from head to foot in blood and guts.

The speculation wouldn't quit him. *What if . . . What if . . .*

Then, when she was roughly ten yards off, speculation was pushed aside by a bare, homely fact: Every time he'd felt the chill of the Beast's presence, Luz had been close by. When he was standing over the dead monkey . . . submerged in that cave . . . just now at the swimming hole! She'd been there the whole while. Standing just a few feet off.

Propinquity, that was all—nothing that would stand up in any court—but as he watched Luz come on, he thought of the jaguar, the peccary; he thought of the little girl in the cacao grove; he thought of Anhanga. Image piled upon image, until it seemed to him that Luz advanced on a train of death.

Never mind that her gait neither hurried nor slackened, that her eyes neither sought his nor avoided them. She looked for all the world like someone out for a stroll—except for the gleam of bamboo that flashed out from the scroll of her beads. A knife, freshly sharpened.

Numbly, Kermit picked up his rifle and reached into his pocket. He pulled out two cartridges and popped them into his gun's chamber.

Luz stopped, silently surveyed him.

"Boa tarde," he said.

"Boa tarde."

Silence.

"Perhaps you thought I was trying to escape," he said.

"I was worried, that is all. I did not wish you to be lost."

"I am not lost."

She looked at him awhile longer. Then she bent over and began to scull her hand through the water.

"When Thiago was young," she said, "we used to come here all the time. To watch the moon. Thiago always thought it was just a few steps away. No bigger than a campfire. He kept saying, 'Mamae, let's catch it.' He never understood why we couldn't."

The air was perceptibly thinner now, and the sun was beginning its crawl toward the tree line. He had an hour of light left.

"I'm glad you've come," he said. "You can answer a question for me."

"Of course."

"Why should Bokra wish to kill Anhanga?"

She paused. "Why must there be a reason?"

"No reason," he answered, with a half smile. "Except that people, in my experience, tend to do the things they want to do. When I think the matter over, the only one I can see who benefits from Anhanga's death is—I'm sorry—*you.*"

"How so?"

"You said yourself he was the only one standing in the way of Thiago leaving. With him gone, Thiago is free. So are you."

She stood now, wiped her hands lightly on her thighs. "Free? Is that what you think I am?"

"More free than you were last night."

"It is very strange, Senhor. I think you are accusing me. You believe I killed my husband."

"I've accused no one."

"You believe me strong enough to do such a thing?"

"Oh, I don't think Bokra was strong enough, either. Whoever did it would have needed some help."

"Where would this help come from?"

"The Beast."

Not a flinch anywhere—in her face, in her body.

"The Beast is dead," she said. "We saw it die. You and I."

"Oh, no, I say the Beast is alive, Luz. And living in someone else."

She smiled now for the first time. Only it was the most equivocal smile he had ever seen on her.

"In one of *us,* Senhor?"

"Perhaps."

"In me?"

He looked away. "I am only saying that whatever killed Anhanga appears to have your interests very much at heart." He glanced back at her. "*You* must have wished death on him many times. He killed your father. He took your innocence. He tossed you aside for another woman."

How brutal Kermit sounded, even to himself.

"If I were the Beast," she said, "it is not Anhanga who would be dead."

"Who, then?"

"The chief." She gave her hair a short, hard swipe. "He was the one who gave me to Anhanga. Tossed me to him like a stick to a dog. It was the chief who made sure I was *um pária* from the start. He made the others cruel to me—to Thiago. Anhanga did not do this; the chief did. And yet he lives, does he not?"

"The last time I saw, yes."

"Anhanga's death: This has nothing to do with Bokra or the Beast."

"Then who has avenged you, Luz?"

"God," she answered.

He nodded, rested his foot on a rock. "Your God has been slow about it, Luz. Many years."

"He can take his time. He has nothing but time." She raised her chin and took a step toward Kermit. "Trust me, Senhor. Nobody is safe from him."

It was a simple statement—a bromide—delivered with no particular menace, but it made every follicle on Kermit's arms tingle. He took a step back and swiveled his rifle toward her—even as Luz swung her bamboo blade toward him, stopping just a few inches shy of the rifle's muzzle.

And there they remained: the very definition of impasse. He knew, of course, he could squeeze off a round before she broke an inch of his skin. Surely it was his own mind holding him back. His *two* minds. One saying: *Save yourself.* The other (sounding very much like the Colonel himself): *Blackguard! To shoot a woman!*

With a convulsive sigh, he dropped his rifle to his side.

"Go," he said. "Please go."

He didn't watch her leave, but in some sanctuary of his brain he heard her receding into the distance, kicking up tiny spouts of water as she went.

He sat himself in the stream. He wrapped his head in his hands. He might have stayed there all night just like that, a study in despair, but he was roused finally by the faintest of phenomena: a stirring of molecules in the air.

Nothing like the cold of the Beast, but every bit as familiar. He could feel it on his skin, smell it, taste it. River air. The great black river, close at hand.

He wheeled his gaze in every direction, searching up and down the forest wall. At length his eyes fastened on something . . . the most fledgling of openings. Only when he drew nearer did he see it was an outright *trail,* clawed at some expense from the jungle interior.

Kermit hesitated, looked in both directions to see if anybody was watching. But he could only hesitate for so long, because the river air was streaming straight through him now. He was actually smiling as he stepped into the green shadows.

MORE THAN ONCE, HE wished for one of the *camaradas'* machetes. After the first flush of struggle, though, he and the path began to work toward the same end, and before he had gone even thirty feet, the forest was pulling away and he was standing in a corridor of air.

He took two steps forward. His foot slid into a cloud of dust, and the earth itself rushed up to meet him. For a second he hung there, all coordinates erased.

He was standing on a tiny bluff overlooking the Rio da Dúvida.

Even from this height, he recognized the river's tortuous shape, the rapids throwing up their whitecaps. Just one more step and he would have been enjoying a splendid bath indeed.

He scanned the vista from end to end, looking for a dugout or a tent and finding only . . . the sun, scuttling in and out of a cloud . . . the water, as black and opaque as ever . . . the vast green monotony of the forest . . . the *silence,* lying like deafness on everything. It was as if he'd never left.

He scanned the river up and down, looking for some trace of the Roosevelt-Rondon Expedition, but there was nothing. No way of taking latitude. His only compass was the sinking sun, which was fast taking all the light with it.

If he stayed much longer, he might never find his way back. Still, the prospect of being stranded here was preferable to returning—preferable, yes, to seeing that infernal pit and Bokra's butchered corpse and the chief's wizened scowl and the hollow, staring eyes of those Cinta Larga mothers, burning with hunger.

But *Father* was back there, too.

"God," mumbled Kermit. "If you're there. If you wouldn't mind . . . some clue . . ."

It came not half a minute later. His eye caught the downed trunk of a palm tree lying a third of the way across the river, its leafless branches rising up like . . .

Like the fingers on a hand.

He remembered this tree. He'd floated past it just two days before. To his addled, whimsical mind, it had looked like a hand waving good-bye.

And soon after—*very* soon after—Rondon called the boats to shore. And that was where they were now!

Assuming they hadn't broken camp, assuming they hadn't given up on their missing comrades, the men of the Roosevelt-Rondon Expedition were no more than a mile or two downriver. Why, the water could carry him there in a matter of minutes.

But how to get to it?

The drop was a good hundred feet down a sheer cliff face. There wasn't a path or rock trail to soften the descent; there was only gravity. Father would have taken one look at the situation and declared: *My kingdom for a damned rope!*

Then, realizing where he was, Kermit started to laugh. Because if there was one thing the Brazilian Amazon was pestilential with, it was rope.

Vine after vine, looping around every tree, vying for every last atom of sun and water. A vast *trampoline* of natural rope, capable of flinging a man to the nearest asteroid.

Yes, indeed. Kermit had only to peer over the ledge of the cliff to find a cataract of vines already draped along the rock face, each at a dozen feet in length and an inch in diameter. All he had to do now was connect them somehow, and he would have the most secure possible rope a jungle could devise.

And so he set to work.

The main challenge, he soon discovered, was creating the individual segments. He had to sever the vines from their attachment points, but, lacking any knife, he had to drag each vine like a saw across the nearest trunk. Even then it took him many minutes to break all the way through. His skin began to crack and bleed, but he consoled himself with visions of the Colonel and Thiago shouting with joy as they climbed to freedom.

In short order, he had yoked together four links and tied them to a vine-anchor. He was reaching for the fifth vine when, from the jungle interior, he heard a soft thrashing. He crouched on the rock, waited. Someone—some*thing*—was coming his way.

Kermit reached for his Winchester, stretched himself across the ground. The sound grew nearer, more *real*—like actual limbs contending against actual vegetation. He tapped his finger lightly against the trigger. He waited.

Indeed, so intensely was he following the sound from the interior that he quite ignored that *other* sound in the underbrush just to his right, never apprehended the point at which that sound acquired shape, then motion—a lightning-like trajectory that caught him squarely in the chest.

He gasped, rolled away. Now, too late, he saw it, half concealed in the mud, long and slender and sidewinding. A spade-shaped head and a pair of horizontal fangs and a pair of sooty eyes, regarding him with a curatorial interest. It seemed almost to be tracking his symptoms, one by one: the fire in the veins, the tingle in the skin, the thinning of the pulse.

Stay awake, Kermit ordered himself. But the world was swooning around him, and the feeling was stealing so quickly from his limbs that there was no way to bring it back. He saw, he *felt*, blackness. Then a new blaze of pain. His eyes trembled open.

Luz.

Luz was leaning over him. Looking as ravenous as any beast that had ever lived as she fastened her teeth onto his tender skin.

"Stop," he whispered. "No . . ."

But his mind was moving in the opposite direction. *Go ahead. Help yourself.*

The darkness pooled around him. He fell in without a splash.

22

"I DON'T BLAME YOU. . . ."

A voice, no more, but it had the exact effect of light.

"I don't *blame* you for wanting a good old-fashioned snooze."

Kermit pressed a thumb to his eyelid, peeled it open. A blurry moon of a face swam toward him. With great difficulty, Kermit picked out an ear, a nose, a confusion of teeth. With even greater difficulty, he connected these parts to the voice.

Father.

Father was there. Father was saying . . .

"It's not often a fellow gets nipped by a viper."

Nipped . . .

"Or a *Bothrops atrox,* if you prefer. Maybe Latin's a bit too much to ask right now. Let's just call it a fer-de-lance and be done with it, eh? Of course, I didn't see it for myself. Did it have a pointed head?"

"I don't . . ."

Kermit closed his eyes, tried to retrieve that last moment of consciousness. It was like crawling out on a ledge that kept shrinking beneath your weight.

Ledge. He was on a ledge. There was a *river*. He was lying flat on the ground, ready to shoot. . . .

Now the image of that snake flashed forth, and like its living embodiment, sent a wave of pain rolling in. So intense that it took him several seconds to identify the source: a scorched region just below his collarbone, raw and welted, recoiling at his touch.

"Oh, I know you can't see it," said the old man. "Take it from me, it's a beaut. Two of the prettiest little fang marks you'd ever want to see. And not a spot of blood to mar the view."

Kermit dropped his head back. He understood now that he was lying in his hammock. It was nighttime. He was . . . here. With Father in their hut. Among the Cinta Larga.

"How did I . . ."

"How did you *live*? Well, you have Miss Luz to thank for that. She's the one who found you. Got rid of that snake, for starters. Coiled it round some stick or other and threw it somewhere in the approximate direction of hell. Then she sucked a good part of the venom right out of you. And *then*—oh, what did she put on you? Some stone or other? Do you see what problems arise when I don't have you to interpret for me?"

Kermit's fingers inched down toward his chest. Something hard and thickened lay there. A plaster, smelling of fern and grass and mud.

"Whatever she did," said the old man, "it must have worked wonders, because you were still breathing when they found you. Which is more than I can say for *most* viper victims. One minute they're bleeding from the eyes, the next they're heading straight for that undiscovered country. You're a lucky young man, Kermit Roosevelt."

Lucky. Yes.

"One way or another," said the Colonel, "you seem bound and determined to get me in trouble with your mother. You get roughed up by *bats, snakes*—what's next, I wonder? No, I don't even want to wonder. Oh, but I almost forgot. In addition to thanking Miss Luz, you must give Belle an extra kiss the next time you see her."

The old man held up a square of oilskin. The perfect water-proof container for . . .

Letters. Belle's letters.

"What in—"

"It's the thing that got between you and your viper," said the old man. "Kept it from plunging its fangs any deeper. Otherwise, it really would have been lights out for you. Oh, don't worry, none of your precious missives was punctured. Nor did I *read* a single line. I'm not some gossipy old spinster, you know." Frowning, the old man weighed the packet in his hand, like a bag of rummy coins. "You'll want it back, I expect."

"Please."

"Well, we don't want it resting on the wound. Why don't I tuck it behind your neck? That works, doesn't it? I'll just tie the draw-strings . . . *et voilà!* Your little talisman, returned to its rightful home."

"Thank you."

"Don't mention it."

"What time is it?"

"Late. Late enough to *sleep*, if you get my drift."

"We can't." Kermit gritted his teeth. "Things to do . . ."

"If you're referring to Bokra's body, that's been taken care of. Don't look so shocked, I'm not completely decrepit, you know. I threw him right in—*both* parts. Each one light as a wren. We all had a grand time filling in the pit, the chief appeared to be most satisfied, and his various cabinet secretaries did me the great favor of spitting on our work. We've fulfilled our contract, my boy—to the letter. And tomorrow I expect a *formidable* royal escort back to camp."

With a soft wheeze, the old man lowered himself toward Kermit.

"So you see," he said, "there's nothing you need worry about."

"No. The Beast. It's—"

His father put a hand on his shoulder. "Easy, my boy. *Easy!* There's still a bit of poison floating around in you. Save your strength for tomorrow. And if you need an image to sleep on, think of the look on Rondon's face when he sees our two sorry carcasses staggering out of the jungle. That will be worth all the trouble."

The old man leaned closer, smoothed the hair from Kermit's brow.

"The sun will rise in just a few hours, you know. Let's be ready for it, shall we? *Sleep.*"

With that, he brushed Kermit's eyelids down. He couldn't do anything, though, about Kermit's brain, which churned away at full speed, plotting the next course of action. The only remaining course now was to wait—*wait*—until Father, the last remaining obstacle, was asleep.

It didn't take long, as it turned out. A matter of mere minutes before that ocean swell of snoring rose up from the other side of the hut. Kermit's eyes sprang open. He counted to five. Then, with a grim resolve, he swung his legs out of the hammock—too quickly, for they dissolved beneath him and left him in an inglorious heap on the ground. Silently cursing, he cast his eyes toward the other hammock. The Colonel still slumbered.

Kermit peppered his legs from ankle to hip with light slaps, until he could feel a modicum of blood flowing. Then, using one of the hut poles as an anchor, he hoisted himself to his feet—stood there swaying like a stalk of corn. His eyes, circling the hut's interior, locked on his own rifle propped against the wall. Just the walking stick he was looking for.

Kermit made three long steps toward the doorway. But as he ducked his head through the opening, his body once again spilled out from under him, and he was reduced to crawling. Never mind, he thought. It may not have been the most dignified position, but he had his rifle, he had some rudiments of his wits. He had a *purpose.*

He would kill the Beast. He would kill it once and for all. Because there was no one else who could.

With that in mind, it was no great hardship to crawl across the village clearing, peering around woodpiles and trash heaps for . . . he didn't yet know. But he would know it when he found it.

He crawled past the chief's hut, crawled over the freshly disturbed soil that covered the Colonel's pit. He crawled down trails of moon and starlight. At length, by a stack of fish cages, he found a campfire, darting and crackling in the dark. A small figure was hunched over it.

Thiago, his knees drawn to his chin.

Kermit held back, but the boy turned and found *him*. A smile scrawled across his face.

"Boa noite," said Thiago.

Grimacing, Kermit seated himself by the fire, rubbed his numb hands. *"Você não pode dormir?"* he asked. You can't sleep?

Thiago shrugged, gave the fire a pair of pokes. Then, with a crook of his mouth, he pointed to the plaster on Kermit's chest.

"Posso . . . posso tocar?" he asked. May I touch?

Kermit nodded. The boy's fingers landed as lightly as the legs of a fly.

"Uma cobra?" asked Thiago.

"Sim."

"Doi?" asked Thiago. Does it hurt?

"Um pouco."

With some hesitation, Thiago pointed at his own chest. *"Um pouco,"* he said.

Kermit's brain was too foggy to catch the meaning at first. Then it hit him: *The boy has lost his father.*

"Seu pai," he said. *"Lamento."*

The boy shrugged again, stared into the fire.

"Minha mãe é viva," he said. My mother lives.

If he'd been any good at consolation, Kermit would have said . . . well, what, exactly? *Your mother is a fine woman. No boy could ask for better.* But he found himself incapable now of saying anything on the subject of Luz. He knew only that he owed her a debt. The greatest of debts.

So, in the absence of words, he and Thiago sat in companionable silence. From time to time, Kermit would point to a chain of stars and recite its mythological name: Ursa Major, Orion, Cassiopeia. Thiago would supply his own name, some animal it reminded him of—*jaguar, tamanduá, anta*—and Kermit came to see that the boy wasn't connecting the stars at all but finding the shapes in the spaces between, and it didn't matter; it was enough just to see that finger of his and hear that softly abraded voice.

Even this was more speech than they could sustain after a while, so they contented themselves with listening to the forest's sounds. It was a fact that no matter how many days Kermit spent in the jungle, he heard a new sound every evening—something he'd never heard before. Tonight it was a long melancholy whistle, descending on a diatonic scale and then modulating upward. Within a minute it was gone, and the night air was filled with other noises: the humming of bees and sand flies, the sawing of crickets, bats flitting in the trees. The goatsuckers with their peculiar call: *Wac-o-row, wac-o-row.*

And, from a nearby hut, sounds of a more intimate nature. *Conjoined* sounds: male and female. Celebrating their deliverance from the Beast perhaps. Kermit cast a look at Thiago, but the boy didn't seem to hear anything. For a minute or two, his head lolled on the stem of his neck and then landed noiselessly on Kermit's knee.

Wouldn't it be extraordinary? thought Kermit, resting his hand on the boy's head. To bring Thiago back to the expedition. To see him claiming pride of place in Colonel Rondon's canoe. To see him fall back in wonder before steamships, automobiles, ice cream . . . gaze in terror at the Atlantic Ocean. Such was Kermit's fancy he could even imagine leading the boy by the hand through the Madrid railway station, wrapped in a thin cotton blanket that had been filched from one of the ship's cabins. Oh, he could just see him, staring up at that lovely yellow-haired lady with the parasol.

Belle, Kermit would whisper. *I've brought a little guest.*

Smiling, he reached around the back of his neck for that familiar pouch. The letters were still there. He closed his eyes, imagined her voice sailing toward him across the ocean, joining with the symphony of night sounds—

Just like that, the symphony stopped.

Kermit shook himself back to alertness. The campfire had flared in a great parabola, as if someone were fanning it with a bellows. But, on closer inspection, it wasn't oxygen that made the flames billow—it was the creatures of the Amazon jungle. Insect after insect, rushing to its destruction.

Never in his days had Kermit beheld such a sight. A cavalry of moths and wasps and hornets and gnats and piums, flying straight into the fire. And, on the ground below, a swarm of ants and beetles, mites and millipedes, scorpions and spiders, filing one by one into their crematorium. With each sacrifice, the flames grew higher and the surrounding air buckled and bubbled. The heat was so intense that Kermit had to drag himself away, and even as he moved, his eye snagged on the one element that didn't fit with the others.

A single snowflake tumbling from the sky. Settling on the fire's peak and resting there.

How long he sat! Watching that absurd snowflake. Waiting for it to melt, *willing* it to melt. But it only hung there, uncharred, in the fire's embrace. So transfixing a sight that he never noticed the change that had grown about him until, like a man bursting through water, he leaped to his feet.

He caught his breath, looked down. Thiago was gone. He swung his head around. The village, too, was gone—vanished into air.

He snatched up a branch, plunged it into the fire until it became a torch. Then he swung the torch in wild arcs, waiting for something to blaze into view—a hut, an ash heap, a bone. Nothing. It was as if the whole village had been carried away in the night. Or had never been.

"Thiago," he whispered. "Thiago . . ."

In a spasm of terror, he grabbed his rifle. Some part of him would have loved to fire off a round—ten rounds—for the whole jungle had lost its voice. No toads, no crickets, no monkeys. Not a single mosquito chittering in his ear. And rising up on every side, the forest's cobalt ramparts, fixed and cold.

For some time, Kermit stood listening. With an air of expectation, as if someone had arranged to meet him there.

From the undergrowth came a rustling. As he turned toward the sound, he could feel all his senses squeezing down to a point. Something was out there—just bleeding into his sight line.

"Show yourself," he whispered.

The campfire surged up once more, and, in the shock of light, the figure shone forth. Against the backdrop of the jungle stood Elliott.

UNCLE ELLIOTT.

In his top hat and riding coat, leaning against a white porcelain café table.

"Good evening!" he drawled.

For the first time, Kermit was able to get a fix on the accent: rigid Locust Valley vowels, softened by a hint of Grandma Mittie's Georgia cadences.

"Care for a snort?" he asked, holding out a tumbler of amber liquor, clouded with mint leaves and orange peels. "Brandy smash. I mixed it myself; just the thing for tropical climes. Oh, but what are you waiting for, my lad? Down the hatch!"

The brandy passed through Kermit so quickly, there was nothing to hang on to.

"Thank you," he managed to say.

"You're quite welcome." (His smile a less explosive version of the Colonel's.) "Come along, now."

The tails of his coat fluttered behind him as he strolled toward the jungle. When Kermit declined to follow, Elliott wheeled back and, in a tone of friendly exasperation, added:

"We don't have all night."

"But where are we going?"

"You'll see."

"Are we going to kill the Beast?"

"I shouldn't wonder."

With a long guttering wheeze, the jungle parted before them: vines and trunks and branches feathering apart into a combed furrow, as dry and white as a scalp.

"Time to get a move on," said Elliott.

A swarm of fireflies materialized before them. Tiny blue and yellow orbs flicking on and off at random.

"Keep up," said Elliott. He walked with an easy stride, swinging a riding crop. "My," he added, "how cold it's grown."

Kermit was just beginning to decode the information of his senses: the chapped nose, the water vapor condensing around his head. The jungle's great soaring palms had turned arid and brittle, as though a slow cold fire had been smoldering inside. The vines were dry as paper. The leaves shattered into fragments beneath his feet.

"Any minute now," said Elliott.

But they kept on walking, the minutes piling atop one another. It was Kermit who began to falter. His feet ached. His skin chafed with old bites. His stomach had become a cobblestone. Yet every time he opened his mouth to protest, the same thought rushed in: *Father wouldn't like it.* And so he held his tongue and watched Elliott's slender, elegant figure grow smaller and smaller in the distance.

At length, after climbing to the crest of a steep rise, Elliott came to a stop.

"Here we are!" he cried.

Kermit looked up. Looked all around. Nothing.

With a polite clearing of throat, Elliott pointed *down*. There, welling from the forest floor, was a hole, no more than three feet wide.

"It's here?" asked Kermit.

"Yes, of course."

"Down *there,* you mean?"

"Naturally." Elliott giggled. "As if you didn't know."

With numbed hands, Kermit swung his rifle toward the hole.

"Oh, come, now," said his uncle, catching him by the wrist. "A hunter *looks* before he shoots."

"But it's dark."

"Ah! So it is." Softly abashed, Elliott reached into his vest pocket and drew out an old-fashioned phosphorus match, some nine inches in length. He swiped it on the sole of his boot, and an eye of blue flame blossomed forth.

"Go on."

Taking the match, Kermit knelt and bent toward the hole until his head had disappeared inside it. The darkness flooded around him, but the light drove it back. He realized that he was staring down a tunnel, eight or nine feet deep. Nothing there. Not a moth, not a bat, not even a pool of water. The only thing that seemed alive was the air itself, clammy and cold, sharp with sulfur.

"Dear boy," he heard Elliott say. "We haven't got all night."

Irked, Kermit swung the match toward his uncle's voice—and then stopped as a counter-pulse of light surged from the rock. From that light there resolved a face, inches from his own, conjured up from the granite and studying him with an inscrutable intent.

Kermit jerked back, but the face followed him, sliding up the rock wall. What a sight it was! Bestial and gnarled, livid and cruel. White worms crawled out of its craggy brow. Beetles swarmed from its matted hair. Maggots spilled from its nostrils.

Kermit couldn't bear to look—or to look away. He waited—for what he couldn't have said—until, with a leering smile, the thing screwed its mouth into a kiss.

Kiss wasn't adequate to describing the oily motion of the tongue, the skeletal retraction of the surrounding skin. Those *lips*—greasy with life—pushing so hard against the rock's membrane that the saliva bled through to the other side and ran down the tunnel walls in long viscous stripes.

"*No!*"

Panting and groaning, Kermit drew his head from the hole. Rolled onto his back.

Elliott was looking down at him.

"Well, Kermit. What did you find?"

"Nothing," he said.

Such an obvious lie, he almost felt the need to apologize. He saw a seraphic smile spread across his uncle's face.

"Exactly." Bending down on one knee, Elliott lowered his face toward his nephew's. "We're alike, aren't we? You and I. Brothers under the skin."

"Brothers . . ."

"Oh, that reminds me! If you see your old man, tell him from me: I never minded about the sanatorium."

"Sanatorium . . ."

"The one in Purkersdorf. He was right to do it. I'd have done the same."

Before Kermit could even guess what this meant, he felt himself sliding away—down the very hole he had just escaped. Through the cloud of dirt and rubble that billowed up after him, one thing shone clear: Elliott's smiling face.

23

KERMIT'S EYES TREMBLED OPEN TO A LEMON SKY.

It was morning: sudden, unexplainable. A shaft of light had broken through a canopy of trees and was sparking against everything it touched—a spray of golden allamanda, a cluster of scarlet tacsonia. A light breeze was blowing at his back; mosquitoes were warming up like violinists. It was morning.

But it might have been the end of the longest day ever, so sore were his muscles, so sluggish his breathing. Something thick and greasy lay over his pores. Where was he? How had he gotten here?

Groggily, he assembled his coordinates. Water. He was standing in water. On either side of him stretched a blackish-green pond, necklaced with foam. Yes. Yes, he knew this place. It was the lagoon he'd first seen yesterday—where Luz used to take Thiago to watch the moon.

But why was he here?

He just needed to orient himself, that was all. And having done that, he would return to the village and reassure Father and pay his last respects to the Cinta Larga, and within hours he would be standing before Cherrie and Rondon and the other expeditioners. In a few short weeks, he would be holding Belle in his arms.

The rest of his days were awaiting. He had only to move.

But no matter how hard he tried to drive his leg forward, the water caught hold. He looked down, thinking he had entangled himself in kelp or wedged himself under a rock. It was some other barrier, though: as solid as rock, nearly granitic in the dawn light, but with the contours of a human being. Drawing up his right leg with all the power he had left, Kermit watched the object rise and swell and then, shockingly, flip over.

He was staring at the remnants of a face.

A face that had once belonged to the chief of the Cinta Larga. A body, too. Torn apart, hollowed out.

No. Kermit gave his head a shake. *There's some mistake.*

The chief wasn't really dead. Any second now he would rise up and, with a scornful flick of his wrist, stride back to the village, to his rightful throne.

But he didn't rise up. Death, lacking any respect for the great leader's station, had subjected him to the greatest possible indignity— and revealed him for what he was: a small thing, barely five feet, with vein-stitched skin and a corded neck, floating in the water like a swath of bark.

How appallingly silent it was! Even the mosquitoes had gone mum. The only sound left was a strange hollow jeering: a fly, buzzing for all it was worth. On and on went the sound, neither tuning nor falling out of tune. Kermit covered his ears, closed his eyes, tried to find the one part of his mind that the buzzing couldn't reach.

Speak, he commanded himself. *Say what you know.*

"My name is Kermit Roosevelt. I am twenty-four years of age. I am a graduate of Groton and Harvard. My father is Theodore Roosevelt, formerly president. My mother is Edith Roosevelt, née Carow. My fiancée is Belle Wyatt Willard, soon to be . . ."

He drew his hands away. The buzzing had gone. A new sound, though, had welled up in its place. Feet—human feet—plashing through water and sand. A single spare figure was approaching him.

Luz. Coming not as she had yesterday, with an air of assumed casualness, but on a mission.

Like crackles of thunder, the words echoed back to him now. *Her* words. "If I were the Beast, it is not Anhanga who would be dead. . . . The chief . . . was the one who gave me to Anhanga . . . like a stick to a dog."

Dear God, he thought. She had all but announced her intentions. She had wrought her revenge against the chief—with joy in her heart—and she was coming back to the very scene of her crime. . . .

For what purpose? Once again he felt himself enlisted in a conspiracy that remained hidden even to him. He groped half blindly for his gun—it was nowhere to be found. *You're as good as dead,* he thought. But Luz's face, as she approached, betrayed no sign of what her mission was. She was merely eliminating the distance between them.

"Senhor," she said, with the barest hint of wariness.

Say something. Anything.

He watched her eyes swerve toward the freshly devoured carcass at his feet. He saw the breath catch in her throat. It was so credible an imitation of surprise that it had the perverse effect of magnifying her crimes.

"How could you?" he whispered.

Her eyes, cutting back to his, showed no remorse, no rage. All she said was:

"You must not blame yourself."

Oh, he thought. *This is a deep game.*

"And why?" he asked, hearing the note of petulance in his voice. "Why should I blame myself?"

"You did not mean to do it, Senhor. This is not what is in your heart."

"In my *heart*? You must be mad! You must be . . . trying to *shield* yourself, that's what you're doing!"

"From what?"

"From the . . . the shame—the *ignominy*—that is rightfully yours!" He leaned forward, his lips frothing with outrage. "It was *your* revenge that has been carried out, Luz! Anhanga. The chief. You wished them dead, and they are dead. Gaze on your handiwork!"

She studied him for a long time. Then, with a voice of ineffable sweetness, she said:

"It was not I who killed them, Senhor."

Unexpectedly, she reached for his face, turned his head so softly he might have been excused for thinking it was his idea, his idea *alone,* to stare into that black, seething water—to find, once more, his image reflected with all the definition of a daguerreotype.

Blood.

Blood everywhere. On his arms, on his shoulders. On his naked torso. Blood soaking from his hair, dripping from his beard, coursing down his face.

In a series of abbreviated motions, he raised his hands until they were level with his eyes. His hands! They were the bloodiest part of him. As red as garnets.

"No," he whispered. "It can't . . ."

He fell to his knees. He plunged his hands into the black stream and dragged up flume after flume of water. Somewhere inside, a voice hissed:

That's right. Wash yourself clean.

Only it wouldn't wash clean. Nothing would wash clean. The blood. The bodies. The *faces*—the faces of Anhanga and the chief—flashing back to him now in fragments of martyrdom.

Overriding everything else, the image of that wretched howler, locking him in its death grip. How lucky he had counted himself to emerge without a scratch! But the Beast needed nothing so plebeian as broken skin to ease its passage. It traveled soul to soul. Now Kermit understood—too late—the look of boundless sorrow in the howler's eyes. The creature was awash in pity for *him*. It understood that *he* would be carrying the Beast to its next round of victims—and bearing the burden for all its sins.

Poor you, the howler was saying. *Poor you.*

"No!" he cried, half-gagging. "No!"

From the firmament above, he heard Luz's voice.

"You are not a bad man."

"Not bad."

He began to laugh in hard diaphragmatic pulses.

"Senhor," she entreated. "You must listen to me. This is not your doing. Some evil spirit has gone into you, that is all. It isn't . . . This is not *you*."

With a long, winding moan, he flung himself in the water, let it rise up over his head, caress his joints, wash off the last residue of blood and human tissue. *Carry me away*, he thought. But Luz had already wrapped her arms around his chest, and she was hauling him to the surface—her will crowning his. Before he could even lodge a protest, they were back on dry land, his head resting in her lap.

"*Não faz mal*," she cooed. "*Não faz mal*."

No, he thought. *It does matter. It won't be all right.*

But the sky was staring down at him as if nothing had happened. The jungle was as green as he had ever seen it.

"I didn't . . ."

"Yes?"

"I didn't know."

"Of course."

"I don't remember. I don't remember any of it."

She stroked his face. "I know, Senhor."

"The doing—the *wanting* to do it . . ."

"I know."

Her voice was like an unguent pouring over his temples. Oh, he had no illusions. Judgment was *out* there—dangling even now by the slenderest of hairs. But for now there was only this sky, whitening with sun, and this fresh-scrubbed air, and a pair of flecked hazel eyes.

"Luz," he said. "Forgive me."

She hadn't the time to answer. For in the very next instant, something erupted from the plane of her forehead.

A speck or a blot, that was his initial impression. Then the blot took on color and depth. It burrowed *down,* as if an awl were being driven through the skin, straight to the bone.

Luz shrank back, pressed her palm against the wound, but the blood came on.

"No," croaked Kermit, gaping into her face. "Stop . . ."

But it was only starting. Within seconds, a new hole had been driven just beneath her clavicle. Another sprang up above her left breast. A jagged line crawled across her sternum. Sector by sector, she crumbled before him, blood pouring in jagged rivers.

"Stop!" he shouted. "I do not wish this to happen!"

He tried to stanch the flow, but the blood kept surging; it spilled through his fingers and down his forearms, it spattered his face, it stained the ground. *Easier to stop the sea,* he thought. With a glottal cry, Luz toppled into the sand. Her eyes sought the farthest region of sky as her skin passed by degrees into translucency. Beneath the skin, everything crowded forward. Veins, arteries. Sinews, tendons. Every muscle and bone, clamoring to be known.

"No," he groaned.

He understood now. This was the Beast's final gift to him. To be conscious of what he was doing, to be *sentient* each step of the way. All he could do now was watch. *Watch* as exquisitely deep lines engraved themselves across the canvas of Luz's body. *Watch* as the vivisectionist demonstrated its art on a still-living patient.

"No!" cried Kermit, but the harvesting went on unabated. Flesh and muscle *peeled* off her breasts, her stomach, her legs, in long serrated strips, tissue vanishing as soon as it was torn and the skeleton itself climbing inch by inch to the light.

Never once did she lose consciousness or even the capacity for speech. When virtually every organ had been gouged out of her and her jaw was no more than a hinge, a germ of consciousness yet remained and sound still bodied forth—fragments that, if he pressed his ear to her mouth, he could still hear.

"Thiago . . . não se esqueça . . . de Thiago. . . ."

Don't forget Thiago.

Looking back days, months, years later, *this* would be the greatest astonishment, the most extravagant miracle: that, after seeing all he was capable of, she would still entrust him with her richest jewel. But in the moment itself, all he could grasp, all he could *feel,* was her dissolution.

The Beast, it turned out, had no need for tooth and claw; it could devour merely by looking, and its host would be as helpless as any other bystander to stop it. So when at last he reached for her, there was nothing left to save.

"Luz . . ."

Her eyes were staring now with such quiet fixity that he waited in all sincerity for one last instruction. None came. With the most exacting of care, he fingered down her eyelids. Silently, he composed her epitaph.

So passes Luz. Daughter to a missionary. Wife to a Cinta Larga brave. Mother to . . .

"Kermit!"

How peculiarly horrible the Colonel looked now, laboring downstream, shining with cheer and resolve.

"There you are, my boy! Luz told us you might be here. We'd have come sooner, but I went back for my rifle—just in case some critters showed themselves—and then you *know* how slowly I gad about these days. My, but aren't these rocks treacherous? If not for my personal escort, I'd have tumbled more than once into the drink, isn't that so, Thiago?"

In the next second, the boy himself stepped out from the old man's shadow, stood grinning in the sun.

No . . .

"He's got the most amazing tracking ability, Kermit. We should hire him out on safari; he'd give those little Kenyan boys a run for their money, eh? Do you hear that, Thiago? It's Africa for you."

"Send him away," muttered Kermit.

"What was that?"

"Send him away!"

"Not exactly neighborly, he's just—"

"Father, please! Tell him he's *wanted.* Back at the village."

"I can't tell him that, I don't speak his damned language. Either one."

With a cry of suppressed rage, Kermit ran to the boy. A frightening-enough specter he must have made, soaked in blood, eyes asmolder. But Thiago didn't shrink. He only said:

"Mamãe."

"Sua mãe . . . quer que você volte." She wants you to go back. *"Esperar por ela."* Wait for her.

Thiago only cocked his head.

"Deixe!" shouted Kermit. *"Agora!"*

Leave now! But how could a child respond to such an injunction? When a bloodstained adult yells at you for no clear reason, you must learn *why,* and that's just what Thiago was prepared to do. His jaw was taut; his lips were cinched. He would stay as long as it took.

It was the Colonel who came to the rescue, putting a gentle hand around the boy's neck and bending his head down and whispering . . . who could say? But some note of reassurance must have passed between them, because the boy turned and walked away without a word.

"There's a good lad," the Colonel called after him. "We'll be along in a spell, all right?"

Smiling and waving, he watched the boy the whole way, waiting until his lean figure had disappeared around the stream's bend. In that instant, the smile dissolved. He set down his rifle, and his face composed itself for the worst.

"What in God's name has happened?" he asked.

24

Rather than compose a reply, Kermit seated himself in the thin margin of sand at the lagoon's rim and watched his father inspect the scene. The old man looked as stony as a god of war, bending over the two bodies, scowling, squinting, muttering to himself.

"It seems," he said, "I owe you an apology."

Like a child pushing through layers of gauze, Kermit raised his head. "Apology for what?"

"You maintained all along that the Beast was still among the living. I refused to believe you. I was wrong, and I'm man enough to admit it."

Kermit stood now. "I was wrong, too, Father."

"How so?"

"I thought the Beast had infected one of you."

"One of—"

"Our hunting party. I thought it might be Thiago, perhaps. Or even *you*. Or *Luz*, can you believe it? Seems ludicrous in retrospect." He cast an indulgent smile at her corpse. "The Beast was in *me*, Father."

The old man's Adam's apple swelled froglike from his throat.

"I consider your joke to be in poor taste, Kermit."

"It's not a—"

"Under the circumstances, this brand of *levity*—"

"I'm not joking, Father! I wish I were."

"Do you honestly expect me to believe that this savagery is *your* doing?" He gave his head a violent shake. "I can't think of anything more preposterous, more brazenly offensive. More *convoluted*—"

"No, Father, it was the easiest thing in the world. I didn't even need to know it was happening. For most of the time, I didn't."

"Ohh! Come, now!" The old stump speaker's voice came roaring up. "I must regretfully inform you, Kermit, that if you persist in this line of insanity, I must write you off as a lost cause. To suggest that you have somehow been *devouring* human beings? Nothing could be further from the young man I raised. If you ask me, Kermit, the heat has rotted your brain! Or else lack of sleep or—or stress—*hunger*—"

"Father." Kermit pressed the old man's hands together. "An hour ago, I wouldn't have believed it, either. But it's the truth."

"No."

"I killed Luz."

"No."

"I killed the chief. I killed *Anhanga,* Father. It wasn't that poor old wretch's doing, it was mine."

"This is beyond laughable."

"Don't you see? That's why I was . . . why I was privy to the Beast's consciousness. That's how it was able to know my thoughts, my history."

"No! No! I was *with* you."

"You weren't. Not when the attacks were actually happening. Ha! Even *I* wasn't with me."

With a throttled groan, the Colonel pulled his hands free. "I will not listen to another word. *Not another word!*"

"You must."

"*I won't!* I don't care if you're my flesh and blood; if we were back in civilization, I'd . . . I'd—"

"What, Father?"

"God help me, I'd have you committed on the spot."

"As you did Elliott."

The old man fell back as if somebody had swung a hammer at his chest.

"Elliott," he whispered. "Why? Why must you keep speaking of him?"

"Because he came to me."

"No! No! You must stop!"

"*Last night,* Father. He spoke to me. He said to tell you . . . no hard feelings about the sanatorium. The one in Purkersdorf. He said he'd have done the same in your place."

For the first time, Kermit saw his father struggle for words.

"I never . . . *told* . . . not a word . . . ever. . . ."

"You didn't need to. *He* did. He said something else, too. He said he and I were brothers under the skin. What did he mean by that?"

The old man's eyes squeezed shut.

"You know why he killed himself, Father."

"No."

"Because he couldn't bear what was inside him—what *wasn't* inside him. He had the same hole as I do, didn't he? Only he filled it with liquor."

"Please."

Kermit let his head drop back until he was staring at the very crowns of the palm trees. "I don't know how it should be, Father, but this Beast, it looks for *holes*—empty spaces it can fill. That's why it sent Elliott. It's been *marking* me, waiting this whole time."

"No, this is . . . the absolute height of senselessness. . . ."

"You're right, Father, it's senseless. It makes no sense, it makes no *thing*. That's what the Beast is, it's *nothing*. It takes the nothing inside us and uses it to . . . empty the world—and it won't rest, Father, until the whole world is empty. As null and void as the Beast itself." He paused. "As me."

Never before had he seen quite such a look on his father's face. Fear and tenderness and who knew what else, washed together in the most unstable of compounds.

"My dear boy," he murmured.

For long moments they stood, watching each other. Then, with a bitter smile, Kermit placed his hands on the old man's shoulders.

"We made a bargain, Father. With the Cinta Larga."

"What of it?"

"We said we would kill their Beast for them. And we are men of honor, are we not?"

A tremble began to rise up the old man's frame. "Of course . . . naturally . . ."

"Well, then." Kermit spread his arms. "What are we waiting for?"

And when he saw the Colonel's eyes shrink to slots, he added, "I am sorry this should be my final gift to you, Father. My legacy. I know you wished for more."

With infinite gentleness, he picked up the Springfield rifle, set it in the old man's hands. He took three steps back and, in a voice of utmost steadiness, said:

"Your *medicine*, Father. Just as you always called it. I should like it to cure me."

The old man stared at the rifle as though they'd never been introduced.

"Begone," he whispered.

"It's the only way."

"Begone!" With a despairing cry, the old man flung the gun to the ground. "You cannot. You *may not* ask such a thing."

"If you don't, someone else will die. *Many* will die."

"And if I do it, what's to keep that . . . that thing from escaping? Inhabiting someone else?"

"I don't know, Father. I just—I don't want it in me. Not one second longer."

Still the old man refused to take up the rifle. Suddenly, there stretched before Kermit's fancy a stalemate for the eons: one man pleading, one resisting, until time itself stopped.

"Please!" he cried. *"I want you to!"*

A long silence. Then, from the Colonel's eyes, a new look gleamed forth.

"Listen to me, Kermit. We will get you away from here."

"It won't do any good."

"We will heal you. You'll *recover*, Kermit. You'll forget all this madness. You'll have a wife and a family, and we need never again—"

"It will still be part of me! I will still be this! Dead bodies and dead souls on my conscience. Forever."

It was as loud as Kermit had ever allowed himself to be in his father's hearing.

But far from flinching, the old man gritted his teeth and muttered, "You will forgive me—I hope—if I decline to take orders from *beasts*." With a jut of jaw, he brought his face forward. "You are not what you believe yourself to be. You are not—God preserve you—empty, you are *full*. You are . . . you are *me*, Kermit. You are your mother. You are your brothers and sisters and . . . and Belle and . . . and everyone—*everyone*—who has ever loved you." His voice caught. "And there are so many who have and *do,* and you are *not* Elliott, you are—the beautiful white-haired boy we brought into this world, and you will always be that boy, and I will *not* abandon you, I will not *cede* you to any beast—to any creature that has ever lived. Do. You. *Hear?*"

They were both weeping freely. But it was the old man who recovered himself enough to give Kermit's chest a mighty thump.

"I am here! Inside you." He pounded once more. "And I will not abandon you. And that is—my—last—*word*."

In that same instant, the first strip of flesh peeled off the old man's face. Stunned, he clapped his hand to the wound. Felt the blood leak through his fingers.

"Do you see?" cried Kermit, backing away. *"Do you see?"*

The old man stared at the pink wash on his skin. "Oh," he said. "I see."

And then he came straight on, advancing on his son in long tigerish strides.

"Stay away," begged Kermit.

"I will not."

"Hold off."

"Make . . . me."

Two more strips of skin sloughed off the old man's face—as quickly and silently as if a barber had swung at him with a razor. The blood was no longer flowing but seething, *roiling.* And somehow, from out of that cauldron, the Colonel's voice came through undimmed.

"You are my son. Whoever wants you will have to come through me."

A ribbon of skin and tissue sliced away from his neck. Lesions sprouted across his hands and forearms, burrowed deeper and deeper until the first traces of bone smiled through the jaw.

"Shoot me!" implored Kermit. "Now!"

The old man only shook his head and drove on. And in those next few seconds, it was as if he were walking through a wind storm of knives. They scourged him from corner to corner. His clothes crumbled to dust. The skin around his thighs unraveled in long linen bandages. That pale flaccid torso bubbled into an incarnadine sea, heaving with severed veins and fringes of muscle. Even the old man's spectacles flew off for want of anything to hold them and went pinwheeling through the air, spraying droplets of blood in every direction before landing at Kermit's feet.

"Father! Stay away!"

But like some mortally wounded bear, the old man staggered on. Blinded by blood. Pelted on every side by the strands and coils of his own body. By the time he reached Kermit, there was just enough left of his arms to wrap round his son and draw him close.

In that final moment of fusing, Kermit could no longer be sure which of them was disintegrating. He felt himself part of one skin. One bone. One blood. Disappearing into blackness.

25

HE WOULD NEVER KNOW FOR SURE WHEN THE DARKNESS BEGAN TO fray. Or how it was that, from nothing, shadows and outlines should shimmer back into view. Fronds and trunks and vines. Then a turbid half-light washing into his eyes' chamber.

He understood that he was upright—standing exactly where he had been before—and that something or someone was wrapped around him.

"Father . . ."

With a tremor, Kermit pried himself free, already bracing himself for what he would find—and completely unequipped to fathom what was *there*. The old man himself. In all his entirety. Breathing and whole and unbloodied.

"Father!"

Like a man fitted with new limbs, Kermit fell on him. Gripped him around his neck. This time, when they embraced, it was with the awareness of their very ordinariness—the magic of their intact skins, their *intact* bones. They were, as the psalmist said, fearfully and wonderfully made.

They had done it.

"That was . . ." Chuckling, the old man reached for the spectacles by Kermit's foot. "That was a near thing. . . ."

There, in the heart of the Amazonian jungle, with no one to listen to them but parrots and mosquitoes and midges and toads, they laughed until their bellies screamed for mercy. When one stopped laughing, the other started up again. They might have gone on like that for hours, *days*, but at some point the laughter died away and a new sound emerged. Not a toad or a mosquito or a parrot. Something human, stirring behind them.

Thiago.

HE HADN'T FOLLOWED ORDERS after all. He had crept back to see what these adults were concealing from him—and now concealment was impossible. For there they lay: the bodies of Luz and the chief of the Cinta Larga. And there stood Kermit and his father, both awash in blood.

Thiago saw it all and reached his conclusion and became something Kermit hadn't seen before. A body *consumed* by rage, by bafflement and fear, all coursing like tributaries into a single torrent of feeling.

"*Mamãe . . .*"

What must he have thought? Seeing those two men coming toward him, their voices soft and propitiating, as if their only wish was to ease his mind. But there was no easing. There was no feeling at all, only this *conclusion* sweeping everything before it. Thiago's muscles trembled almost to their bursting point, and from his throat there poured a sound such as he himself had never heard. A howl that seemed to frighten away the sun and call back the moon.

All his lightness and agility were gone. As he ran back toward the village, he thrashed through the water and tripped on stones and kicked up mud and sand, but that sound carried him over every obstacle. Even when he had disappeared from the white men's view, the howl was still traveling back to them.

So this is how it will go, thought Kermit.

Thiago would sound the alarm. In seconds, the villagers would mass. They would grab their spears, their arrows. They would come for the white men and would carry out the vengeance that Thiago had been unable to exact on his own.

Would it go slowly or quickly? It hardly mattered now. The only remaining consideration was how Kermit would present himself for that final ordeal. Kneeling, standing, lying—none of the outcomes held any particular horror for him. No, the only thing that could disturb his perfect equanimity was this.

The sight of his father.

That hobbled, cussed, half-blind old man whom he had pledged to preserve and protect and defend. How could he think of leaving him to the justice of the Cinta Larga? On what ledger in heaven could such an offense ever be blotted out?

No, he thought. *They can't have him.*

In a nearly disembodied voice, he heard himself say:

"We must go."

"Go?"

"Before they get here."

"Nothing would please me better, Kermit, but I hardly see how we—"

His son was already sprinting toward a small aperture in the jungle front. Nothing more than a chink when you first looked at it, but Kermit was charging as if he expected the forest to part before him.

"Come!" he cried.

When the old man hesitated, Kermit had to bellow just one word.

"Now!"

* * *

THE PATH WAS EXACTLY as he remembered: barely existent in its earliest stages, then broadening with each step, gaining confidence. The sound of water thickened into a rush, the sky came dropping down, and, sooner than they could have expected, they were standing on that shelf of rock.

"Awfully far down," offered the Colonel.

"Yes."

"Don't suppose you mean us to jump the whole way."

"No."

Crouching, Kermit reached for the rope of vines he'd cobbled together—still hanging from the cliff's edge. Clumsily knotted, irrepressibly jerry-built, it earned a look of rawest skepticism from the Colonel.

"How far does it reach?" he asked.

"No idea."

"All the way to the water?"

"No."

"Do you think it will hold?"

"Not sure."

The old man nodded, turned his head back toward the jungle, where the sounds of the oncoming Cinta Larga were swelling into acclamation. A grin exploded across his face.

"Then this should be quite the adventure, Kermit! Only do let me go first, will you? If the thing snaps, I think I'll prove a tad more buoyant than you. And *here*." He tossed over his Springfield. "You may need this on the way down. No need to check, it's loaded. Are we ready then? Very *well* . . ."

The old man drew up a length of vine, wrapped it twice around his waist, tested his weight against it. He took two quick sharp breaths. "Nearer my God to thee," he murmured.

The first part was the hardest: a backward step straight off the cliff, with only faith and a vine to keep him from free-falling. For a second or two the old man dangled there in utmost helplessness, but his boots found a purchase against the rock face, and he was able to lower himself another few feet.

"Why, it's no worse than . . . than Rock Creek. . . ."

Even this spasm of effort was costing him. He grunted and huffed and cursed, and blotches of coral splotched his skin as he took the next leap down, sending up a shower of dirt and pebbles.

"Come *on*, Kermit! We haven't got all day."

The vine was stretched too taut to make a belt. If he were to descend, Kermit would have to depend on his hands alone—and whatever docking points the cliff face provided on the way down. Already he could see how the swings from his father's descent were sawing the vine against the rock's edge. *Three minutes,* he thought. *Perhaps four.*

Through every quadrant of jungle now, the pursuers were coming hard on. Kermit crouched at the precipice, uttered a wordless prayer, then flung himself over.

He felt the earth flying away, his bare chest scraping against the rock. Flailing, gasping, he pushed out still wider, the vine scalding his hands as he slid down. Blood bubbled from his palms, but in the next instant his feet found a cranny. Emboldened, he flung himself out again, spilling out another freshet of blood, thicker than the last, spidering down his forearms.

From below, he could hear the old man calling his name, but his eyes were fixed on that tiny promontory just above. The little shelf of rock where, any second, the Cinta Larga would be converging.

How would they first show themselves? A hand? A head?

But what appeared finally wasn't human at all but an arrow, of supernal sleekness, tipping downward like a dowsing rod in search of water, locking him in its sights.

By now Kermit was no longer rappelling, he was *sliding* down the rock, and the vine was whipsawing in and out of his grip, and his hands were boiling with blood, but all he could see was that pitiless shaft, silently tracking him, preparing to fire.

"Stop," he hissed. "Stay off."

In the same breath, though, he knew there was only one retort. The steel barrel he'd jammed into his belt loops before descending. Father's rifle.

If he could just fire off a shot—a single warning shot—he might buy the time he needed to get to the water. But how to manage it?

Wincing, he gripped the vine more tightly, swiveled his legs in every direction, seeking a ledge, an outcropping—anything— but all he got were more contusions . . . until, with a joggle of surprise, he found himself standing on a lip barely wide enough to support his weight.

He gazed up the side of the cliff. The arrow was still in plain view, still aiming straight down at him. Using the vine as a brace, Kermit planted his feet, drew out the rifle, centered the arrow in his sights. *No need to hit it,* he reminded himself. *Just make some noise.*

And yet his finger hesitated in the act of pulling the trigger, and it seemed to him that the arrow, too, was hesitating, trembling with cross-purpose. Time shrank down to a small, still point, infinite in its possibilities, so that afterward it was impossible to say who fired first, because everything played out in the same endlessly unfolding instant: the arrow singing down and the bullet screaming up and his own body flinging itself outward.

And a face . . . a *face,* pushing out from the promontory's edge and then disappearing in a cloud of smoke.

Thiago's face.

Untethered from rock and vine, Kermit dropped straight and true, his body curled as softly as a sleeper's, and his eyes . . . his *eyes* open the whole way down . . . taking in *everything.* The arrow, sticking from the ledge he had just occupied. Directly above it, the miasma of smoke from his rifle blast, blanketing the rock like the most porous of cotton.

And there . . . through the smoke . . . a single arm. Small, still. Draped over the cliff's edge.

* * *

HE FELL INTO DARKNESS. The old familiar.

Then a *new* darkness—cool, tannic, beaded—bearing him along.

And for an escort, look! Fire-hardened bamboo arrows, nearly six feet long, piercing the membrane just above his head and brushing his skin and raking his hair. *Longing* for him, but brought up short again and again by the strange dark medium that carried everything along.

Water. He was swimming in water.

With a convulsive movement, his head broke toward the sky. The air came shrieking into his lungs and pinned him to the river's surface. Roused to a nearly erotic thirst, the arrows redoubled their whistling and crooning. With a martyr's patience, he waited for that first blow . . . and listened, with something very close to disappointment, as the sound faltered and sickened and died away.

Sorry . . . so sorry . . .

He gulped down more air, squinted into the morning dazzle. On either side, the jungle was a sheer shadowless front of green. Ahead of him, a large rock was bobbing in the water.

How curious. The rock was Father.

Kermit opened his mouth to call out, but no words came. It didn't matter. All things considered, this was quite a pleasant way to pass the morning, riding the river's shoulders toward some unknown destination. It felt almost like home.

If he felt his legs straining to keep him above water, if he felt the air dribbling from his lungs, if he felt the last of his reserves burning down to a tiny pyre . . . well, that felt like home, too.

Voices were raining down.

"Senhor Coronel! Senhor Coronel!"

On the bank to his left, people had gathered. They were watching him with great interest.

"Senhor Kermit!"

Wrong man, he thought, with a suppressed giggle. The jungle was slipping past with mysterious swiftness, and the water ahead was beginning to wrinkle and roil, and from a distant veil of mist a dull roar went up. Why, he thought, it was just like the day he and Simplício went over the falls. Nothing to be done, was there? You let the water take you wheresoever it listeth. And if for some reason a branch should come along . . .

IN THE END, THE branch came for him.

Not a branch, after all, but a hand, hooking around his shoulder. His eyes swam back into focus, and he saw that the hand belonged to the Colonel—*Hello, Father!*—and that the old man was at the tail end of a human chain extending all the way to shore, and that this chain comprised the tiny adamantine figure of Colonel Rondon and the bent-sycamore profile of good old Cherrie, and there were Lieutenant Lyra and Dr. Cajazeira and João and Juan and all the rest of the *camaradas,* all braided together, *reaching* for him, coaxing him out of the water, and stretching him across the white warm sands.

He lay there for some time, coughing up water. His ears were ablaze with sound. Rondon's woodpecker cadences:

"Il ne faut pas entrer dans la jungle sans escorte."

His own father's mollifying reply:

"Ah oui, je m'excuse. Je l'ai oublié."

And the sound of his *own* words, still unspoken, clogging in his brain. It wasn't until he was sitting up, spewing out the last draft of the Rio da Dúvida, that the words found a way out.

"We must . . . leave . . . now. . . ."

Then, because nobody seemed to be listening, he started to bellow. As loud as he could, in every language he knew.

"If you value the lives of this expedition, you will leave at once!"

26

Say this much for Rondon. The gear was packed, and the canoes were ready to go. It was as if he had been planning for just such an eventuality. They had only to climb in and be off.

Yet, to a mind as beset as Kermit's, how slowly that process unfurled. Never before had the *camaradas* moved with such deliberation. Never before had the canoes been quite so balky or the paddles so clumsy, the breezes so contrary. Five minutes passed—ten, fifteen—and still they were lolling in the black water, as stymied as rabbits in a cage. And the whole while, the same injunction played itself out in Kermit's brain.

Don't look back. . . . Don't look back. . . .

For he knew they would be there. He knew, too, that if he kept his eyes trained forward, in the direction of the current, he needn't hear the whistling of their arrows, he needn't see Thiago's arm hanging off the cliff's edge, he needn't see the look in Luz's eyes as she crumbled before him. . . .

At last Rondon gave the command, and the men let out a ragged cheer as the river took hold and the canoes gathered speed. Only Kermit was silent.

AFTER ALL THESE WEEKS of deprivation, God was finally smiling on them. How else to explain why they made three kilometers before noon and another four that afternoon? The rain held off, and the sun hid itself behind every passing cloud, and whatever rapids they met were child's play to what they had come across in the days and weeks before. One could almost imagine a chant rising from each paddle in turn. *Out . . . of the jungle . . . out . . . of the jungle . . .*

They brought in the boats with half an hour of daylight left. Kermit dragged his canoe to shore, then wandered down the shoreline for fifty or sixty yards, ostensibly looking for game, but really looking at nothing. Nothing at all.

"Roosevelt!" Cherrie had followed him from a discreet distance. "I've brought you one of my shirts if you'd like to . . ."

Kermit's gaze tilted downward. What a shock to see his own torso! No longer soaked in blood, it was true, but bare as a beggar's. Bruised and abraded and seared with a full day's worth of Amazonian sun. Only now was the pain breaking through.

"Thank you," he murmured. "That's very kind of you."

"You don't mind my saying, you look done in."

"A bit, yes."

"We had quite despaired of you both."

"I don't doubt."

"You'll need another rifle, I expect."

Kermit stared down at his hands. "Yes. That would be just the thing."

"Dear God, what happened out there, Roosevelt?"

What happened . . .

If Kermit had ever possessed a tongue, now was the time to use it. Now was the time to speak of an orphan named Luz and an orphan named Thiago. A warrior named Anhanga and an old wretch named Bokra. A little girl who went to fetch cacao for her mother. A chief who looked like a bookmaker. A howler monkey with the saddest eyes you ever saw.

A beast.

The whole tale lay there, queued up on his tongue, ready for a confessor. And still he balked, for he could see what the end point would be. He would speak his piece, and Cherrie would nod and think all the thoughts that a resident of *his* world would think and would say nothing, nothing at all, and that silence would be the greatest rebuke of all.

"Sorry," said Kermit. "I can't . . . I can't quite . . ."

Cherrie, with his natural tact, rushed right in.

"Let's have a nip of whiskey, shall we? Just the thing."

SUPPER THAT EVENING WAS the usual paucity. One of the men had snagged a pair of catfish. Kermit had caught a side-necked turtle. The rest was crackers and palmito, plus a handful of Brazil nuts, painstakingly divided. They were done in less than five minutes. Nothing daunted, the Colonel reared up like the laird at a manorial feast.

"Fills the old gullet!" he declared as he tossed down his plate and gave his belly a hard squeeze. "Couldn't ask for better!"

In a trance of horror, Kermit watched as the *camaradas* began to gather around the fire. He knew what was happening. This was, by common consent, the Colonel's hour, the time for him to speak of old adventures. To most of the men, of course, the words were unintelligible, but the *flavor* of the words, that had become as hard for the *camaradas* to give up as their morning coffee. It didn't matter that the Colonel had disappeared for two days under mysterious circumstances, that he had come back drenched in blood and even worse for wear. He was *back* now, and the words could once more flow.

"Father," said Kermit. "Perhaps tonight we might dispense with . . ."

But the sight of all those shy smiling faces brought out all the old man's volubility.

"Well, don't just stand there! Sit ye down! Now, it so happens I've been meaning to tell you boys about the first grizzly bear I ever shot. Has anyone ever seen a grizzly? No? Well, take it from *me*, you won't want to meet one in a back alley. The claws *alone,* my friends! Shred you before you blink an eye, no lie. . . ."

Just like that, the Colonel fell back into the old rhythms—as if everything that had happened in the jungle held no more sway over him than a dream.

But it wasn't a dream, Kermit wanted to say. *It can't be sloughed off. It can't be talked away.*

"Picture it, now. He's lying on a bed of spruces. Just waking up when we stumble across him. Well, I know as sure as I'm sitting here now, this is my God-given chance, so I take a bead right between the eyes—small, evil eyes they were—and I pull the trigger. Bam! Ball goes straight into his brain. Lord, but he jumped. Monstrous thing, too! Twelve hundred pounds if he was an ounce, I do not exaggerate. . . ."

Kermit listened as long as he could. Then, without a word, he rose. He walked toward the river's edge and watched the moon shimmering in the black water. He was still there an hour later when the Colonel came limping out.

"There you are! I was hoping you'd be so good as to join us."

"Us?"

"We won't keep you more than a few minutes, I promise."

He found Cherrie and Colonel Rondon frowning by the campfire. He started to sit, then stood again, then lowered himself to a half crouch. One by one, his offenses scrolled out before him. Should he beg pardon now? Angle for clemency? Perhaps they would just leave him here in the jungle. That would be the height of mercy in the grand scheme of things.

"Kermit," said the old man, folding his hands behind his back. "I've called you here . . ."

"Yes?"

"Because my French is not up to the occasion."

"Your French . . ."

"I mean for the purpose of speaking to Colonel Rondon. I must therefore entreat that you translate into Portuguese. Oh, no, Cherrie, don't leave. You'll need to hear this, too."

Knitting his hands behind his back, the old man squared his shoulders.

"Gentlemen, regarding the events of the past two days— beginning, I mean, with the disappearance of Kermit and myself and concluding with our return—I would like to say that it is the fondest wish of both my son and me to put these events entirely behind us. If you take my meaning."

No, thought Kermit in the midst of translating. *They don't take your meaning.*

"I am puzzled," said Rondon with a scowl. "Why must we overlook what has happened?"

"My dear Colonel, I hope that, in reflecting upon our personal history, you will credit me with being as frank with you as any man could be. In this one instance, I fear I cannot be frank. Except to say that speaking of what has happened will bring no credit to anyone. Least of all . . ." He paused. "Least of all *me.* I should further add that any publicity accruing to these events might also bring unwanted exposure . . ." He paused once more. ". . . As I said, unwanted exposure to a tribe of savages who desire no part of our civilization. No, not even your telegraph wires, Rondon."

Kermit hesitated to translate that last part, but the Brazilian, true to his character, neither bridled nor smiled.

"I recognize," the old man went on, "that my request is contingent upon our making it out of this jungle. I tender the request, anyway, because it is my firm belief we *will* make it out. And with that in mind, I ask you both now, as a great personal favor to me, to remain ever silent on these recent events. Never to speak of them, never to write of them."

He turned his gaze back from the fire.

"The log books, I hope, may be rewritten to elide or conceal our untimely disappearance. In this and in every other regard, I implore you to consign this unfortunate episode to oblivion." As if to underscore his point, the Colonel kicked a shard of kindling into the fire, watched it flame up. "If you could give me your word as gentlemen, I should be your eternal servant."

Both Cherrie and Rondon were silent for a time. Then the Brazilian looked up.

"You are asking us to lie, Colonel?"

"I am asking you to omit. Surely, amidst the . . . the infinite gradations of human venality, that particular sin ranks low." The old man kneaded the folds of his throat. "What happened out there *belongs* out there. The jungle has it; let the jungle keep it. And let us get about *our* business with all due haste." He looked at each one in turn. "We still have history to make, gentlemen."

THE NEXT MORNING, A fit of shivering swept over Colonel Roosevelt as he climbed into the boat. By mid-afternoon, his temperature had climbed to 103 degrees, a new high. Dr. Cajazeira wrapped him in a poncho, injected quinine straight into his belly, but the fever held on. Too weak even to lift his head, the old man lay in his dim tent, quivering and sweating, slipping in and out of delirium.

That night, the officers took turns watching him. Cherrie was there when the old man began reciting a line from Coleridge, over and over: *"In Xanadu did Kubla Khan a stately pleasure-dome decree . . ."* But Kermit was the one keeping watch when the old man startled awake as though a visitor had entered the room.

"You can't have him," he hissed. "You can't have him. . . ."

God was no longer smiling on the Roosevelt-Rondon Expedition. The rapids returned, the insects feasted, the sun beat down, the rain beat down, the food dwindled to nothing. One of the oarsmen was murdered by another *camarada*.

Hour by hour, Theodore Roosevelt slipped closer to death.

Malaria raged inside him; the poison spread from his abscessed leg. He hadn't enough strength now to stand, let alone walk. In the canoe, all he could do was lie across a row of food tins, with a pith helmet across his face. More than once, when the expedition had to halt to let him rest, the Colonel whispered (to no one in particular):

"Go. Leave me here."

Until Kermit, reeling from his own malaria, growled, "You'll leave with us, or I'll carry you the whole way back."

When they reached Saõ João, they looked so much like savages themselves that the rubber tapper who spotted them feared for his life and turned his canoe to shore. It took Rondon jumping up and waving his cap and shouting assurances in immaculate Portuguese for the tapper to paddle out again.

The Colonel was so enfeebled by now he could barely lift the helmet from his face. A dying king, that was the rubber tapper's first guess, babbling in a strange tongue.

"Pleased . . . to . . ."

ON THE AFTERNOON OF April 27, they reached their long-awaited destination: the confluence of the Rio da Dúvida with the Aripuanã. At the sight of Rondon's relief party, the men in the boats flung their oars and stamped their feet and gave out terrible shouts of joy. Kermit tweezed open his sweat-caked eyelids and saw an American flag, fluttering like a dream.

* * *

BY THE TIME THE Colonel was carried off the steamer at Manaus and bundled into a waiting ambulance, he had lost a quarter of his body weight.

In the hospital, he ate sparsely, read nothing, never spoke above a whisper. He had ample leisure, however, to ponder the magnitude of his achievement. Over the course of two months, the Roosevelt-Rondon Expedition had traveled more than one hundred eighty miles through the heart of the Brazilian wilderness. They had charted a river as long as the Ohio. They had put a lie to all existing maps. These were claims so bald, so exorbitant, the Colonel would later have to defend them before the National Geographic Society, but as he was carried onto the steamer to Pará, he could see no cloud on his horizon.

"By God, Kermit . . . into the gazetteer we go. . . ."

FATHER AND SON PARTED on May 7. The Colonel was bound for New York, where he would be met by a cresting tide of well-wishers: newsboys, office workers, subway conductors, dockworkers, residents of every borough and station swarming around him, clamoring for a look, a word (some already whispering at his frailty, his shrunken body).

Kermit, by contrast, would be leaving for Lisbon. He would travel alone. There would be no delegation to meet him.

"Ah, well," said the old man. "I hate good-byes, but no sense getting all womanish. I'll see you in just a few weeks."

"Belle and I will look forward to it."

"Ha! Of all the countries for a Roosevelt to be married in. Spain! I hope they have no hard feelings about San Juan Hill."

"I'm sure they're past it."

The old man met his eyes for a moment, then turned away a fraction.

"I'm sorry Mother can't make it. Some feminine ailment or other, I didn't want to inquire too closely."

"That's all right."

"But you know you can count on me, my boy."

"Of course."

They stood for some time on the gangway, watching the Colonel's trunks pass in parade.

"Kermit."

"Yes?"

"You understand, of course—I mean, without *you,* we'd have . . ." He screwed his lips together. "I suppose I just wanted to thank you. For everything you did."

An hour later, the words were still reverberating in Kermit's ear. *Everything you did.*

It was the smoothest Atlantic crossing he had ever known. Like skating across a pond, said all the first-class passengers. He dined every night at the captain's table (going lightly on the wine). He played skat with a Rochester industrialist and his pinched, unhappy wife. He read Camões. Late at night he paced the upper decks, imagining that every step was bringing him closer to Belle.

He reached Lisbon on the afternoon of May 20. He was offered accommodations at the YMCA, but he refused to stay another minute, and because none of the direct lines to Madrid were running, he caught a local train to Entroncamento. After a five-hour wait, he caught another to Cáceres. Evening melted into morning into afternoon. He slept ten or fifteen minutes at a time. He read as best he could—Lorca, Spanish phrase books—but his eyes stung from the dust and cigar smoke and the smell of raw milk.

Late in the evening of May 21, his train pulled into the Atocha station in Madrid. The other passengers quickly dispersed, and he was left to wander with his porter through the wrought-iron plaza: an oddly tropical space dominated by gardens of towering ferns and palms. For a second or two, he thought he was back in the jungle. Then he stopped.

By the departure board, next to a large woman in a black mantilla, stood a willowy figure—so tiny!—so poignantly American in her moiré coat and Billie Burke cap.

Nearly two years had passed since last he'd seen her. It was natural, wasn't it, perfectly natural, to take a moment? To reconcile the living face with the one he'd held in memory all this time? Only he couldn't manage it, not at first. It was as if he had fallen in love with two women.

"I have arrived," he said. "As you see."

"But how brown you are!" she cried.

He was glad he'd shaved.

He could smell the powder on her face. He could see the feathering of rouge on her lips and ears.

"Darling," she said.

With her gloved hands, she reached for him. They brushed lips, then drew apart. And as Belle looked him up and down, the blaze of her teeth subsided.

"Are you all right, Kermit?"

He was going to ask her the same question. For he was gazing right into the flawless china of her face—and a flaw had, against all odds, emerged. A tiny dark lesion in her brow, no greater in diameter than a mosquito bite. Within seconds, though, it began to deepen and metastasize, sweeping with bewildering speed across her forehead, down her face. He watched in helpless terror as the skin and tissue peeled away from her skull, leaving the barest of bones, snapping and flapping.

"No," he whispered.

He buried his face in his hands, and as the destruction carried on out of view, he uttered a silent prayer. *Take me. Don't take her. Take me.*

Dimly, in the near distance, he could hear the tinkling of her voice.

"Kermit . . . Kermit, look at me! Darling, *look* at me!"

She had to pull his fingers from his face and pry open his lids before he would consent to look.

And there she was! Just as she had been a minute earlier. Pristine, porcelain, intact.

He fell into her arms, and in the middle of that cavernous train station, they held each other.

"It's all right," she kept saying. "You just had a bad dream, darling. A bad dream, that's all."

But her litany was already being drowned out by two declarative sentences, repeating themselves endlessly in his head.

We didn't kill it. . . . It's still alive. . . .

From deep inside came that unspeakably familiar chill, crawling out of his bones, coiling around every nerve and fiber, grasping at his heart.

"Why, Kermit! You're shivering."

27

THEY WERE MARRIED IN JUNE.

THE WEDDING TOOK PLACE in a little chapel on the grounds of the English embassy and was followed by a formal breakfast and a Virginia reel, which the Colonel regretfully sat out. "Even an old bull moose needs to convalesce from time to time. Isn't that so?"

Kermit and Belle honeymooned in Toledo, but whenever they looked back on their time in Spain, every day had the aura of a honeymoon. They sat, holding hands, in El Greco's garden. They went to church with the Infanta Beatriz. They ate with peasants; they lunched with the king and queen. They automobiled across the Sierra de Guadarrama. They attended teas, dress balls, a bullfight. They sniffed out the bookstores that time had forgot. They quizzed each other in Spanish inflections. They dozed, still holding hands, on stone benches.

Every night, Kermit lay down beside the prettiest girl who had ever lived. Every morning, he awoke to her. If ever he had occasion to remember that troubling vision from the Madrid train station, he had only to recall its immediate aftermath: Belle, whole and unimpeached, folding him into her arms.

How could he not rejoice in his great good fortune? Twice—twice!—he had been rescued from the Beast's clutches. And what had saved him each time? *Love.* The love of a father, the love of a wife. As long as he held fast to them, what had he to fear?

The future came rushing toward him. He and Belle, with the blessing of their families, moved to Buenos Aires. He became an assistant manager for National City Bank. It was a gentleman's job, the kind that his brother Ted might have gravitated to, which may have explained why Kermit—even at the height of his blessings—grew so quickly to hate it, why every minute he spent in the company of functionaries and accountants became a canker on his soul, why he found himself at odd moments longing for the days of collapsing bridges in the Xingu Valley. Once, in an unguarded moment, he confessed as much to Belle.

"Kermit." She took his hands in hers. "That was young man's work. You're to be a father soon."

It was true. In short order, they had a boy. Another boy followed and then a girl and, later on, still another boy. Piece by piece, they were building the family he had always dreamed of, the life he had wanted. Who could want anything else? Yet he did, he passionately did.

Salvation came in the form of war. A *European* war, to be sure—President Wilson would never rise to the Huns' bait—but when had such a thing stopped a Roosevelt? The Colonel pulled some strings, and Kermit snagged a berth as staff officer to the British general in Mesopotamia. Within months, he had mastered Arabic. He rode through blinding heat across biblical landscapes in an armored LAM Rolls-Royce. Superiors marveled at his courage, which bordered on recklessness. Once, during the battle for Baghdad, Kermit kicked open the door of a house and found a heavily armed Turkish platoon on the other side—and himself with no revolver. In a stroke of improvisation, he pointed his swagger stick at the commander and secured total surrender. *Well played!* he could hear the old man saying. *Well played, indeed!*

And when at last America entered the war, Kermit relinquished his British commission and joined the American Expeditionary Force in France. Ted was there, too. As were Archie and Quentin. All four of the Roosevelt boys, proudly positioned in harm's way— exactly where the old man would have wished them.

The only thing he wished more was to join them. But his health had never completely recovered from the Brazilian adventure, and when President Wilson turned down his request to organize a private regiment, the old man retreated to the sidelines with the least possible grace. He raged against the Germans, the Russians, the Wilson war cabinet. He raged against doves and mollycoddlers and thumbleriggers and puzzlewits and honeyfuglers.

He raged against his own body. The malaria always came growling back; rheumatism flamed up in every joint; his heart failed him in ways he could no longer ignore. Even the simplest tasks were beyond him now, and in moments of pure prostration, when the delirium took hold, he would conjure up the ghosts from his past. Dead Alice, dead Elliott. And to their ranks he could now add dead Quentin—dear Quentin!—shot down in a field near Chamery.

One afternoon, as his wife was plumping his pillows, the old man muttered another name. A name she'd never heard.

"Thee-AW-go."

She lowered her face to his. "Who's Thiago?"

The old man fell silent, and his wife was about to leave the room when she heard him say: "We should have taken him . . . with us. . . ."

Then, to his wife's surprise, he added:

"Tell Kermit he's not to blame. . . . It wasn't his fault. . . . Tell him that."

Years later, recounting the incident to her son, Edith would ask, "Do you have the foggiest notion what he was talking about?"

"Not a clue," said Kermit.

IN NOVEMBER, THE OLD man took to his bed for good.

On January 6, 1919, a telegram came for Kermit in Coblenz, where he was stationed with the occupying forces. It was from Archie.

THE OLD LION IS DEAD.

Two sensations. First a peculiarly intense cold—unrelated to the weather—pouring straight from his marrow. Then the bottom dropping out of everything.

ONE OF THE TROUBLES with losing a famous father was that the world never stopped offering its condolences. Shoe shiners, barbers, nursemaids, shopkeepers, stevedores, ministers of every denomination—they never hesitated to stop Kermit in the street and tell him how sorry they were. The words rattled inside him like coins in a can. Indeed, the more distinguished the consoler, the more jarring the sound. Mayor Hylan was a trial; Governor Smith, an ordeal.

Then there was Senator Lodge, who, just prior to addressing the Washington Naval Conference, put a hand on Kermit's shoulder and said, "He knew how to live, your father. And he knew how to die."

It was just possible Kermit might have stammered a reply, but he couldn't take his eyes away from the senator's forehead, where a long serrated band of white skin was even now lifting to expose the raw tissue beneath. Before Kermit could intervene, another band of skin peeled off the senator's aristocratic cheekbone. Then another and another—insult upon insult—until it seemed as if the senator's entire head were dissolving, down to the last reddish-white hairs of his beard.

It was the Madrid train station all over again. Like Belle, the senator never once grasped what was happening. On and on he talked, a perfect font of policy—obsolescent warships, disarmament, the restraining of Japanese capacity—and all Kermit could see were the bared bones of his jaw, flapping in the cavity of his head.

"Are you quite all right?" the senator asked.

Kermit closed his eyes, opened them again. In a trice, the senator's face had reassembled itself. And yet the memory of what he had just seen hit Kermit with the force of a pathogen. His heart thrummed; his chest swelled.

"Very sorry, Senator. . . . Feeling a bit . . ."

He staggered outside, stood amidst the press of Constitution Avenue. The pounding of feet and the rumble of coupes and trolleys and milk wagons and the shrieks of children reverberated in his ear as the most dismal form of laughter.

He was prepared to write off the whole episode as an isolated incident, but the same thing happened again a month later, and a week after that, and the day after that. There was no way of predicting it or preparing for it. At any moment he might be talking to a mechanic or the Romanian ambassador, remonstrating with the cook or the nanny or the secretary of defense, quizzing a Sherpa on the best route through the Vale of Kashmir, discussing linguistics with a professor of Aramaic. Whoever he was speaking to—young, old, male, female—would decompose in exactly the same way: strips of shredded flesh flying off in a great gale of decay, until the buried skull shone forth.

And not a single one of them felt it happening! How extraordinary, how horrifying to see them talking—talking talking talking—as if nothing were taking place. All he could do after a while was wait for their faces to reassemble and then, with mumbled apologies, steal away.

*   *   *

ON THE RECOMMENDATION OF a stockbroker friend, he went to a doctor—an alienist (though they were calling themselves something else now). The midtown Manhattan lodgings, with their neo-Georgian exterior and wood accents, were not too removed in appearance from the Harvard Club, where Kermit had told his wife he was dining. The doctor himself was a Galician Jew with full cheeks and rather kindly eyes that retreated for safety behind wire-rim spectacles.

"Tell me something of your history," he said.

"Surely we don't need to go into all that. You know who my father was."

"Your *father*, yes."

Kermit waved his hand. "It's the same thing. We've been in all the papers. We're public domain, I tell you."

A smile peeped from under the doctor's well-tended mustache. "The true components of human personality are rarely the stuff of newspapers or magazines."

"Perhaps that's a good thing."

From somewhere in the adjoining room, a clock was coughing and rattling.

"I see things," said Kermit. "Certain things. If you must know."

After all these years, confessing was easier than he expected. He had only to imagine himself back in France, an artillery captain once more, getting drunk in some shell-cratered café with dirty marble tabletops and oak benches—bending the ears of any enlisted man in view. They would have to listen, wouldn't they? Rank had its privileges.

"Excellent, Mr. Roosevelt! I am decidedly intrigued! Now, then, I propose treating these 'visions' of yours as part of some larger tale—a *mythos*, if you like. Shall we begin the work of untangling?"

So their sessions became, against all expectations, literary seminars—preceptorials on the subject of Kermit, with attention lavished on every act and utterance. Not even Dante, he thought, had received so thorough an exegesis. And when he was moved at last to speak of the jungle—of Luz and Thiago and the Beast—the good doctor fairly shook with glee.

"But this is fascinating!" he cried. "Do go on."

So they did: week after week, sifting through a great sandpit of clues. And the more they dug, the more Kermit felt himself floating free of the whole operation. One afternoon in October, he leaned forward in his leather armchair and said, "See here, Doctor. What if we were to stop thinking of all this as a story?"

"How else are we to think of it?"

Kermit stubbed out the end of his cigarette. "Suppose the things I see aren't delusions at all. Or metaphors. Suppose they're real."

"And if they are real, Mr. Roosevelt, what are we to conclude?"

"We don't have to conclude anything. We need only recognize them. Accept them."

"As what?"

He was silent for a time. "If you must know, I used to think them a curse. Now they seem to me a kind of gift."

"Who has bestowed this gift upon you?"

"The Beast," he answered, surprised by the calmness in his voice. "Living there inside me, it's able to . . . to *show* me how matters stand. I can see straight into the heart of things."

"And what do you see there?"

"Nothing. There's nothing there, Doctor. Nothing. Nothing to pin a life on, anyway. Or a legacy. We're all just . . ." He could feel the glitter of tears in his eyes. "We're built over a *pit*, Doctor, and I'm one of those rare, rare, blessed mortals who *knows* it, who is permitted to *see* it, every minute of the day. *That's* my gift, Doctor."

"If I were you, I should return this gift to the giver."

"There's no returning it."

The doctor sat for a while, tapping a fountain pen against his wrist.

"Let's say, Mr. Roosevelt, that I comply with your wishes. Let's say I believe everything that you tell me has actually happened. Men and women were devoured, yes, simply by your looking at them. Faces *vanish* before your eyes—on a weekly, sometimes a daily, basis. A beast, an actual beast, uses you as its vessel. Suppose I were to grant you all this. Would it free you?"

Kermit sat in his armchair, nearly as familiar to him now as the one in his own study. He could see where his hands had left soft stains in the leather. In the next room, the doctor's clock was still shuddering.

"No," he said.

IT WAS, AFTER ALL, a terrible thing to stake all your hopes on love and find even love insufficient. Fathers died. Wives became . . . something other. Or else their husbands did. He still had heartful moments, it was true, when the memory of Belle (sitting next to him in his father's car on a summer night) would flush through his veins or one of his own children (running into a room, falling asleep on top of the family Labrador) would tap some lode of joy. But these were the very moments when the Beast gripped the hardest—when the company of others became an unearthly torment.

"We have the most charming, accomplished friends in the world," Belle once said. "Why must you always steer clear of them?"

"Because that's the kindest thing I can think to do."

It was startling then to see the rage well up in those still-beautiful eyes. "The kindest thing you could do would be to stop drinking."

She didn't understand; how could she? Drink was the one thing that stilled the Beast . . . kept faces from dissolving . . . preserved a sprout of hope in life's humus. And so he drank. He drank at breakfast, at lunch, at dinner—every hour in between. He drank with a quite childish gratitude. Once, at a party for Admiral Byrd, he blacked out and woke the next morning in a corner of the club, under somebody's raccoon coat. Pinned to his dinner jacket was a five-dollar bill for cab fare.

Belle's doing. She could never quite give up on him, and for this, she could never be forgiven.

ARCHIE WAS THE ONE who sent him to the sanatorium. A lovely place in Hartford.

"You're right to do it," said Kermit. "I'd do the same."

He had to laugh at how neatly Elliott's words fit in his own mouth. It was almost a source of sadness that his uncle never came to visit anymore. They now had so much to talk about!

"I *know*," Kermit would have said. "I *understand*."

IT WAS IN HARTFORD, during a particularly grueling episode of withdrawal, that Luz unexpectedly walked into the room.

"Please," he said to her.

(The orderly swerved around.)

"You have to see," he said. "There was no way to bring him with us. He wouldn't have come."

(The orderly beckoned to someone in the hallway.)

"I would never have fired if I'd known he was there."

She left without saying a word.

THE MOMENT HE WAS sprung from confinement, he called an old mistress.

"Let's get lost," he said.

IN THE END, THEY found him. (Cousin Franklin had the FBI at his disposal.) They sent him to Anchorage, the one place on earth where he couldn't embarrass anyone. "Best to separate him," said Archie, "from all those bad influences."

But you've got it all wrong, he wanted to say. *I* am *the influence. Wherever I go . . . I go. . . .*

And so he did, all the way to the rim of the world.

June 3, 1943
Anchorage, Alaska

Every last trace of skin and muscle has peeled away from Major Marston's face, and still he stands there in the slow-stealing twilight, flapping his jaw, his skull shining like a moon.

"I'm here to tell you," he says. "There's four thousand miles of coastline along the Bering Sea and the Arctic. Four thousand miles. How can we possibly patrol it? But the Eskimos, they know the terrain. Just one Eskimo guardsman is worth more than a dozen of our sentries. If you were to ask me which soldiers I'd walk into enemy gunfire with, I wouldn't have to think about it, I'd say right out—"

"Please," gasps Kermit.

He can feel the scrutiny from those barren eye sockets.

"You don't look well," says Marston.

"I'm not—I don't—I'm not sure what's . . ." Kermit's hand forms a quivering lattice across his face. "I really must go."

His limbs, without warning, jig into life and send the rest of him tottering up the hill. Toward the barracks.

"You don't need any help?" calls Marston.

"No, thank you."

"And you think you might speak to someone on my behalf?"

Someone . . . someone. He wants me to speak to . . . Cousin Eleanor? Cousin Franklin? One or the other. Both . . .

"Of course," he calls back, with a reassuring wave.

"Good night, then."

"Good night."

He is no more than ten yards up the hill when the contents of the evening's dinner spill out in a black sludge.

Panting, he rests his hands on his knees. Watches the last strands of vomit detach from his chin. Then he wipes his face and keeps walking.

HIS QUARTERS ARE, BY his own choosing, sparse. A bare lightbulb on the ceiling. Venetian blinds. A cot that sags and creaks even when he's not in it. A plain wooden desk and a single bookshelf that holds a dictionary, a compendium of Portuguese sonnets, and a couple of signed Kipling volumes—all furry with dust, for even reading has lost its savor.

He goes to the washstand, pours some cold water on his face, then stands before the mirror. Normally he can only stand to look at himself in the morning. Now, with the sun finally bleeding into the horizon, he looks, if anything, paler and more bloated than before. How Father would cringe at the sight of him.

And for a moment he could actually be the old man, for he seems to be regarding himself from a great distance. Then, as if it were happening to somebody else, he watches a face slide into the gap over his right shoulder.

Luz.

It nearly stops his heart to see her standing there in plain view. Looking as she did when they first met. Her dark hair parted down the middle. Her eyes a flecked hazel. A necklace of vegetable beads against her dusky skin.

She is untouched by age—and such a rebuke to his own decay that he has to close his eyes. And then she speaks. For the first time since he left her by that lagoon.

You have carried it long enough.

He opens his eyes.

It is time, she says.

And now the tears are flowing, fat and warm, down his face. This is the sweetest thing anyone has ever said to him.

"Yes," he says.

Somewhere, in some buried recess of him, a voice of officialdom is registering its opposition.

What about your commission? Your estate? The disposition of your effects? What about your note? *You can't go running off without a note! There are considerations. . . .*

That's when the full beauty of his situation washes over him. He has nothing left to consider. One way or another, without even meaning to, he has cleared his life's field of every last encumbrance.

Now, with that emptied prospect lying on every side of him, how soft, how frangible, is the line that tethers him to it. One snip of the scissors, that's all he needs.

It is time, says Luz once more.

But still he hesitates. Living is a hard habit to break, after all. What pitches him forward at last is a voice.

Not Luz's, not his own. Indeed, he spends some time identifying it, ruling out Father and Mother . . . Belle . . . the children . . . brothers, sisters . . . arriving finally, by process of elimination, at the most surprising speaker of all.

The Beast. Calling out in the weakest imaginable voice.

I want you to.

And with that, the final barrier falls. He is very nearly laughing as he sits on the edge of his cot and reaches into the drawer of his side table and draws out the Colt .45 service revolver.

How heavy it feels in his hands. Yet how nimbly his fingers

push out the cylinder. (He can't help smiling at those five bullets, snugly placed. *Always loaded, always ready.*) He positions the empty chamber at twelve o'clock. He pushes the cylinder back into place, listens for the click of the latch. He checks the chamber position one last time.

He casts his eyes toward the washstand and finds Luz still there. Smiling.

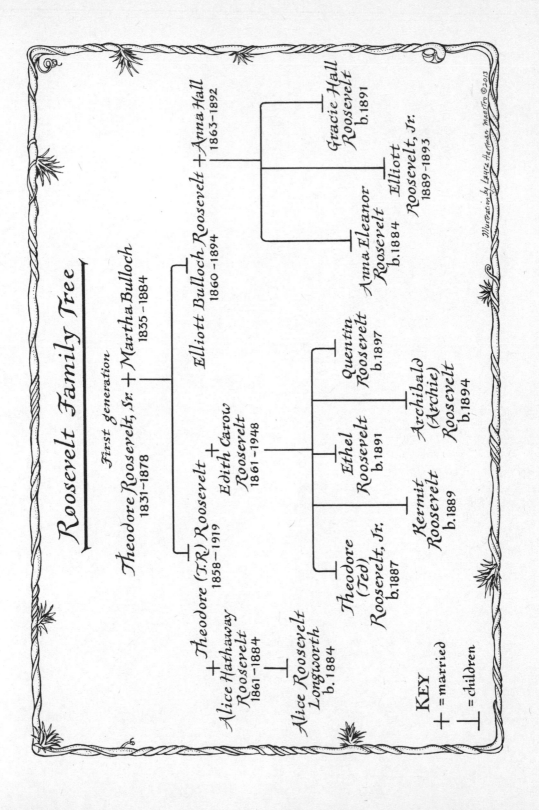

Roosevelt Family Tree

First generation

Theodore Roosevelt, Sr. + Martha Bulloch
1831–1878   1835–1884

Theodore (T.R.) Roosevelt
1858–1919
+
Edith Carow Roosevelt
1861–1948

Alice Hathaway Roosevelt
1861–1884

Alice Roosevelt Longworth
b.1884

Theodore (Ted) Roosevelt, Jr.
b.1887

Kermit Roosevelt
b.1889

Ethel Roosevelt
b.1891

Archibald (Archie) Roosevelt
b.1894

Quentin Roosevelt
b.1897

Elliott Bulloch Roosevelt + Anna Hall
1860–1894   1863–1892

Anna Eleanor Roosevelt
b.1884

Elliott Roosevelt, Jr.
1889–1893

Gracie Hall Roosevelt
b.1891

KEY
+ = married
⊥ = children

Illustration by Laura Hartman Maestro ©2013

ACKNOWLEDGMENTS

This book is, by design, a psychological fantasy built out of historical events and should not be confused with actual history. For the true story of the Roosevelt-Rondon Expedition, the place to go is Candice Millard's gripping and authoritative *The River of Doubt*.

Thanks as always to my research angel, Abby Yochelson. Thanks to my agent, Christopher Schelling, and my wonderful tag-team of editors, Marjorie Braman and Sarah Bowlin. Thanks to Marcio and Luisa Duffles for backstopping my Portuguese. I'm grateful for the ongoing counsel and company of other writers, including (but certainly not limited to) Dennis Drabelle, Adam Goodheart, Jennifer Howard, Tim Krepp, Gary Krist, Thomas Mallon, Thomas Mullen, Bethanne Patrick, Robert Pohl, James Reese, Frederick Reuss, Daniel Stashower, Hank Stuever, and Mark Trainer. Grateful, too, for the kindness and encouragement of Kim Roosevelt, who will excuse (I hope) the liberties I've taken with his ancestors.

And thanks to Don.

About the Author

LOUIS BAYARD is the author of the critically acclaimed *The School of Night* and *The Black Tower*, the national bestseller *The Pale Blue Eye*, and *Mr. Timothy*, a *New York Times* Notable Book. He has written for *Salon*, the *New York Times*, the *Washington Post*, and the *Los Angeles Times*, among others. He lives in Washington, D.C.